OCCUPIED
SEATTLE

OCCUPIED SEATTLE, BOOK TWO
(2ND EDITION)

Chris Kennedy

Chris Kennedy Publishing
Virginia Beach, Virginia

Publisher's Note: This is a work of fiction. Names, characters, places, and incidents are a product of the author's imagination. Locales and public names are sometimes used for atmospheric purposes. Any resemblance to actual people, living or dead, or to businesses, companies, events, institutions, or locales is completely coincidental.

Ordering Information:
Quantity sales. Special discounts are available on quantity purchases by corporations, associations, and others. For details, contact Chris Kennedy Publishing at: Chris@ChrisKennedyPublishing.com

Occupied Seattle/Chris Kennedy. – 2nd ed.
ISBN 978-1942936060

As always, this book is for my wife and children. I would like to thank Linda, Jennie and Jimmy, who took the time to critically read the work and make it better. I would like to thank my mother, without whose steadfast belief in me, I would not be where I am today. Thank you.

Note: All times in *Occupied Seattle* are given in military time, using the 24-hour clock. To find a time that occurs after noon (12:00 p.m.), simply subtract 12 from the first two digits of the number. For example, 1400 becomes 2:00 p.m. Of note, most countries use this as their standard method for keeping time, with the notable exceptions of the United States and Canada.

* * * * *

"In the event that...possibilities for a peaceful reunification should be completely exhausted, the state shall employ non-peaceful means and other necessary measures to protect China's sovereignty and territorial integrity."

— Anti-Secession Law, Article 8

Seattle Area

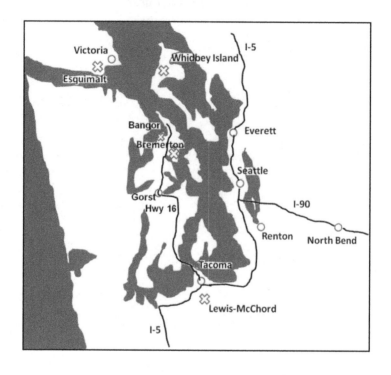

CHAPTER ONE

Morning, August 20

Snoqualmie National Forest, Washington State, 0630 PDT

Ryan attached the note to his door and stepped back, wondering if he would ever see the cabin again. This wasn't the first time he had left home; Ryan, formerly 'Senior Chief Petty Officer Ryan O'Leary,' had gone away more times than he could count during his 24 years as an elite Navy SEAL. In fact, there had been a time in his life when he had been called away from home on a nearly continuous basis to take care of situations his country needed fixing. That period of his life had ended several years previously when he was forcibly retired, a victim of navy budget cutting due to the sequestration process.

Sighing, he straightened his six feet, two inch frame and turned to leave. "All right," he said. "Let's go." Dark-haired, Ryan had a lean, well-muscled look acquired through years of strenuous physical activity as a SEAL and then living in a cabin he built by hand in the mountains.

"Okay," his companion, U.S. Navy Lieutenant Shawn 'Calvin' Hobbs, said. "You're the boss." Calvin was a couple of inches shorter than Ryan and blond. He was also a lot softer around the edges from a lifestyle that included less physical training and more time at the bars.

The day before, the Chinese had finally made the long-predicted attack to retake the island of Taiwan and reunify their country. Part of China's plan had involved an invasion of Seattle and Tacoma, Washington, and the capture of nearly four million American hostages living in the Seattle metropolitan area. The Chinese believed taking the hostages would keep the United States out of the war in Taiwan, allowing them to bring it back into the fold.

The Chinese plan also involved the capture of American nuclear weapons from a base in the area and the threat of one of those weapons exploding 'accidentally' if the American military tried to recapture the area. With the threat of nuclear blackmail paralyzing the U.S. government into inaction, it appeared the Chinese bid to take over Taiwan might actually succeed. The only question was whether the Chinese would leave Washington peacefully at some point, or if they intended to stay long term.

Letting the Chinese stay was unacceptable to the two men.

Word that something strange was going on in the Seattle area had reached Fallon, Nevada, where Carrier Air Wing Two was training prior to going on cruise, and the air wing commander had sent a flight of aircraft to determine what was happening. All of the aircraft were shot down, and Calvin was the flight's sole survivor. As luck would have it, he parachuted into the wilderness of the

Snoqualmie National Forest, 35 miles east of Seattle, in the vicinity of Ryan's cabin. Ryan had found him and taken him in for the night.

While Calvin had been airborne, Ryan had attacked the Chinese forces nearby, resulting in the destruction of a Chinese anti-aircraft gun, as well as Ryan's jeep, so both men were well aware that there were Chinese soldiers with hostile intent in the area. They did not, however, know their long-term intentions. By going into Seattle, they hoped to get some additional information to pass up through Calvin's chain of command.

"Who is the note for?" Calvin asked.

"Well, if things are as bad as we think they are in Seattle and Tacoma," Ryan explained, "then the bases there have probably been overrun. There's no way the Chinese could ever hope to hold the cities without securing the bases. And if *that's* the case, I imagine some of my Ranger and SOAR friends will come by the house. If nothing else, this is a good place to plan and organize for whatever we end up deciding to do. And I *do* have some weapons, which we'll probably end up needing."

Although he lived out in the wilderness, Ryan had a well-stocked arsenal in his basement. Along the lines of the military truism, 'If it's dumb but it works, then it isn't dumb,' Ryan had fortified his house along the lines of 'If it's paranoid but it's needed, it's not paranoid.' As it turned out, he wasn't paranoid. All of the weapons he had in his basement might be needed in the coming days.

A member of the close-knit special forces community, Ryan had many friends in both the Rangers and the Army's 160th Special Operations Aviation Regiment (SOAR). Although they had higher headquarters based in the eastern United States, both organizations had detachments at Joint Base Lewis-McChord in Tacoma, Washington. The 2nd Battalion of the Army's 75th Ranger Regiment was there, as well as the 4th Battalion of the 160th SOAR. While Ryan had a few friends in the Ranger community, including a Rifle Company's first sergeant, he had a lot of friends in the 160th SOAR. The 160th was the helicopter squadron that provided support not only for the Army's special operations forces, but also for the special operations troops of the other services when needed. The pilots of the unit had taken him into and out of enemy territory on more occasions than he could remember...or wanted to remember. He owed his life to many of them.

As the two men walked away from the cabin, Ryan's phone vibrated, interrupting the conversation. He took it out and activated it. "Hello?" he asked.

He listened for a while and said, "I don't think so." He hung up.

Within a couple of seconds, the phone rang again. Ryan answered it, listened for a few seconds then said, "I already told you 'no,' and that's what I meant." He hung up again.

Within a few seconds, the phone rang a third time. Ryan answered it, said, "I've given you my answer, now stop bothering me!" and hung up again. This time, he turned his phone off.

"There!" he said.

"That sounds like a wife or ex-wife," Calvin said. "Are you married?"

"No," Ryan answered, shaking his head. "I tried it a couple of times, but it didn't stick. I have a thing about authority and being told what to do."

"You have a thing with authority?" Calvin asked, his brows knitting. "But you're a SEAL. You took orders all the time, didn't you? How could you be a SEAL and not take orders?"

"You've got it wrong," Ryan said. "I *was* a SEAL, and *when* I was a SEAL, I took orders all the time. It was part of the job and part of being in the military. Doesn't mean I liked it; it was just something I had to do. As you may have noticed, I'm not in the military anymore, and I don't have to take orders, despite what those idiots seem to think." He indicated his phone.

Calvin had a bad feeling. "What idiots are those?" he asked.

"Those idiots would be the folks in Washington, D.C., who keep trying to task me. I have a good friend serving as the Command Master Chief for the Chief of Naval Operations. He apparently told his boss I was in the area, had some skills and might be useful in helping them determine what's going on out here." Ryan paused. "He's going to owe me *big* time for volunteering me."

"So, the Chief of Naval Operations, the most senior four-star officer in the navy, just called you?" Calvin asked. "What did he want?"

"Nothing," Ryan said. "Don't worry about it. I don't need tasking from an organization that screwed me over."

Calvin looked confused. "He's the most senior person in the navy, an organization you gave a large part of your life to," he said. "Your country needs you. You aren't going to do what he asked?"

Suddenly angry, Ryan stopped and glared at Calvin. "I have a problem with authority, okay?"

Calvin stopped, too, and waited patiently. Saying nothing seemed like the prudent thing to do, rather than further antagonize a man who could kill him in more ways than he could count. After a couple of seconds, Ryan sighed and said, "Apparently, the Chinese have taken possession of some of our nukes and are using them to hold Seattle hostage. If we attack anywhere in the Seattle area, one of the nukes might 'accidentally' go off, killing tens of thousands of Americans and irradiating thousands more."

"As much as I hate the navy brass," he continued after a couple of seconds, "I hate allowing the Chinese to hold my country hostage with nuclear weapons even more. So yes, I'm going to do something about it. I'm just not doing it so much to help the navy as I am to fix things for my own purposes. Both missions are just kind of aligned at the moment."

Calvin shuddered. "Nukes, huh? I can't wait to get out of here, then."

"You're not leaving that easily," Ryan said with a wry laugh. "I can't do this alone. I'm going to need your help. Your trip to Fallon is going to have to wait. This supersedes anything else."

"Wha...what?" Calvin stuttered. "I'm no ground soldier. What the hell do you think I can do to help?"

"I don't know yet," Ryan replied. "One thing I *do* know is that any mission I've ever been on has required a team; you can't do everything yourself. There are going to be times where I need support, and right now you're it. As you so eloquently mentioned, your country needs you. Are *you* going to step up to the plate?"

That stung. Calvin didn't like the way his words had been used against him, but he was a military officer who had sworn an oath to protect his country against all enemies, foreign and domestic. Even though it was outside his element and training, he knew there was only one answer. Ryan was confident in his own abilities and apparently believed Calvin could do it. He squared his shoulders and said, "Yeah, I'm with you. I might not have your training, but I'll do whatever I can to help."

"Good," Ryan replied. "We've wasted too much fucking time already. The nukes could be anywhere…and we've got to find them. If we can locate them and somehow take them out of play, then the rest of the military can come in and do their part. Our task is easy—we don't have to beat the entire Chinese army, we just need to take care of one little task and then step back and let the combined military might of our great nation do the rest."

Calvin wasn't sure how two people securing an unknown number of nuclear weapons was supposed to be considered 'easy,' but didn't see the need to argue the point. It must be part of the whole SEAL 'can-do' thing, he guessed. Before he could say anything else, a female's voice in the near distance began calling Ryan's name, violating the early morning stillness of the forest.

"You're a popular guy," Calvin said. "Sounds like someone's looking for you."

"I can't imagine why anyone would be looking for me," Ryan said. He shrugged. "But then again, I doubt there are many other Ryans running around out here, either." Ryan paused, judging the distance to the voice and the amount of additional time they would lose. He sighed. "All right," he added. "Let's go find out what she wants."

"Okay," Calvin agreed, in no particular hurry to go looking for nuclear weapons. "Lead on."

The woman was moving slowly through the forest, and they caught up with her in no time. She continued calling periodically and did not hear the men stalking her, nor see them coming up behind her. Seeing the woman was alone, Ryan asked, "Can I help you?"

The girl jumped in surprise as she heard Ryan's voice. The former SEAL noted to himself that Calvin had some decent outdoor skills, as they had been able to move quietly enough through the forest to sneak up on the woman. Calvin might not be too big of a drag, after all, he thought. Seeing the woman's face, he said, "Wait, you look familiar. I know you from..."

"I met you last spring while my friend and I were hiking near here," the woman confirmed. "My name is Sara Sommers."

Ryan thought for a second. "I remember. I spoke to you up at the 'Infinite Bliss' outcropping. She was a little shorter than you and blond, right?" Ryan's SEAL training had enhanced his recognition skills, as well as his ability to remember and report things later.

"That's right," Sara agreed. "Her name is Erika." She realized Ryan wasn't alone as another man stepped around from behind him. While a little older than she, the second man was much closer to her age of 20 than Ryan's 45, and he was tall, blond and very good looking. He was wearing a green flight suit, which seemed out of place as there weren't any airports in the vicinity. She was surprised to see both of the men appeared to be heavily armed, with rifles slung over their shoulders, pistols in holsters and bulging packs on their backs.

Looking back at Ryan, Sara continued, "I was looking for you because I need your help."

"I'm sorry, but I can't help you right now," Ryan replied, looking at Calvin. "We already have some pretty high-level tasking we are working on."

That was not what Sara had hoped to hear, and tears began to well up in her eyes. She looked to Calvin, hoping to enlist his aid. Their eyes met, and they both experienced a psychic shock as they connected at some level neither of them had experienced before.

Calvin didn't know what sort of help she needed, but he knew that if it was within his ability to do it, he would.

Ryan saw the looks passing between them and knew he was close to losing Calvin. "Why don't you tell us about it as we walk out?" he asked. "By the way, this is Calvin. Calvin, this is Sara."

"Calvin?" Sara asked. "That isn't a name you hear very often. Is it a family name?"

"No," Calvin replied, "it's a name my friends gave me. My real name is Shawn Hobbs; my call sign is Calvin."

"I see," Sara said, not sounding like she did. "Did you come up to see Ryan, too?"

"No," Calvin answered; "he found me after I got shot down by the Chinese."

"They're Chinese?" Sara asked. "I didn't know what they were. They just parachuted into the University of Washington, shot some people and took a bunch of students hostage." She looked at Ryan. "My friend Erika was one of the people they took. I came up here today to try to get your help in setting her free."

Ryan smiled. "I'm honored you think that highly of me, having only met me once, but we're on a mission from the president."

"The PRESIDENT?" Calvin asked, shocked. "That was who you hung up on? The president? Of the United States?"

"Yeah, well, what can I say?" Ryan replied. "I've got a problem with authority." He paused, looking annoyed. "I'm still going to do what he wanted. He's just got to learn that he's not my Commander-in-Chief anymore, and he can't boss me around. Besides, I didn't vote for him, and he was being a pain in the ass with his whole, 'Do this, do that' spiel. I was done talking with him."

"Still," Calvin replied with a touch of exasperation, "he's the president! You can't just hang up on him!"

Ryan shook his head. "I'm sorry, Sara," he said, "but the bottom line is we're on an important mission at the moment. I'd be happy to do what I can for you afterwards, but we've got some other things to do first."

"I understand you need to do what the president asked you to do," she said, a tear running down her left cheek, "but I've got nowhere else to go. I pinned all my hopes on you being able to help get her back. I don't have any other options. Can I ask how long you think it'll take to complete the president's mission?"

"Yeah," Calvin added, "can I ask what you plan to do, too, since you haven't told me yet?"

"It's classified," Ryan told Sara, "and trust me, you *really* don't want to know." He looked at Calvin and said, "He needs us to find what was lost in Bangor; we'll start looking in that area."

Sara thought back to the day before, when she had seen the Chinese bringing in a group of big, heavy boxes onto the campus of the University of Washington. "Some *thing?*" she asked. "Or some *things?*"

"It probably is some things," Ryan admitted, "although we really don't know for sure. Recapturing them would be very important to our ability to take back Seattle."

"They wouldn't happen to be in boxes about six or seven feet long, would they?" Sara inquired.

Ryan thought for a few seconds. "Yes, that would probably be about right, I think."

"And how many would you be looking for?" Sara asked.

"Well, I don't know, actually," Ryan answered, looking frustrated. "Nobody is really sure, and the information we have was intentionally incomplete."

Calvin could see there had to be a reason for her questions. "Why are you asking? Did you see something?"

Sara nodded, starting to smile. "After the Chinese captured Erika, I followed them to the gym where they were herding all of the students they captured. While I was watching, a group of helicopters flew in. While four smaller helicopters circled overhead, two big helicopters came in and landed on one of the intramural fields. A large group of men came out of the building with flatbed carts, and they unloaded six large boxes with the help of the men in the helicopters. The boxes each appeared to be about six feet long and must have weighed several hundred pounds, judging by how many men it took to move each of them. The Chinese took the boxes into the building, and then the helicopters flew off." She hoped these were the 'missing things,' as the men might be able to rescue Erika while doing whatever it was they needed to do with the boxes.

Ryan looked at Calvin. "You know what? She might have just made our jobs a whole lot easier."

"I can do even more to help," Sara added. "I've got a car not too far down the road and can give you a ride wherever you need to go." She paused. "As long as we make it back past the Chinese, anyway."

Ryan looked thoughtful. "Did the Chinese put a checkpoint up on the road?" he asked. When Sara nodded, he continued, "Let me guess. It's at the turnoff for Granite Creek Road, right?"

"Yes, and it looks like they've already caught and destroyed a jeep and a black van. How did you know?" Sara asked.

"I know that because it was *my* jeep, damn it," Ryan replied. "They were following me and probably set up the checkpoint there because they didn't know which way I went. Obviously, they don't want me to come back."

"He blew up an anti-aircraft gun," Calvin interjected, happy to be part of the conversation again.

"The one at the Travel Centers of America?" Sara asked. "You did that? It burned for a long time. They seemed pretty mad when I went by there last night. They sent me back home because of the curfew they imposed from midnight to 6:00 a.m."

"Did they let you through the checkpoint this morning?" Ryan asked, trying to formulate his plan for getting into Seattle.

"No, they didn't," Sara replied. "No one gets into or out of occupied Seattle. However, they don't seem to know about the back way up over the mountains, so I came up via NF-9010, across Bessemer Rd. and then down NF-5600 to get here. All very Chinese-free. I can take you back that way in my car if you would like."

"I would like that a lot," the former SEAL said, "I had been dreading the time we were going to lose walking all the way to town."

Calvin smiled. "I'd like a ride, too!"

White House Situation Room, Washington, D.C., 0945 EDT (0645 PDT)

"So, this is your good idea?" the President of the United States, Bill Jacobs, asked. "This SEAL is going to find our missing nukes for us? He seems like an asshole to me."

"Well, sir," the Chief of Naval Operations, Admiral James Wright, explained, "you have to understand that Senior Chief O'Leary is a little bitter about how he was dismissed from the navy. He doesn't have a lot of positive feelings for politicians in general and your party in particular. Add in the fact he's always been a little twitchy about authority, and that's what you get. Still...he's never once failed to accomplish a mission, so if there is someone you'd want working on this, it's him. He may be a bit abrasive, but he is the best operator we have...uh...well, that we *had*, when he was forced out."

"*Abrasive*! He hung up on me for God's sake! *Three times!* Hanging up on the president is more than just 'abrasive!'" the president said, his voice rising. The president was a big man, who had learned to project his voice when he needed...or when he wanted to make a point.

"That's certainly true," Admiral Wright acknowledged; "however, if there's any way at all for him to find those nukes, you can count on him to do it."

The president growled, "I hope so, for your sake. This house of cards you're building rests on him!"

I hope so, too, thought the admiral. He had suggested using Ryan based on the recommendation of his Command Master Chief, who had served with Ryan 'back in the day.' An aviator by trade, the admiral was an excellent planner, and his staff had spent most of the night putting together options for what they would do once the weapons were found, assembling and disassembling various strike packages to try to form some contingency plans. They had put together a variety of recovery options; unfortunately, there was no way to know where the nuclear warheads were, or how well they were guarded. For all the effort that had been put into it, they were mostly just pissing in the wind until they had some better intelligence.

That went the same for Carrier Air Wing Two, which was training at the air base in Fallon, Nevada. Admiral Wright had told them to be "ready at a moment's notice" to carry out missions against the Chinese in the Seattle area, but without any sort of intelligence there was no way for them to adequately prepare. Even worse, the aviators hadn't flown much in the preceding two years and had flunked their first air wing practice strike on the test range the day before. While being held to the 'moment's notice' time frame, it was impossible for them to gain any further practice or better prepare their jets. This whole thing could well and truly suck, he thought.

Changing the subject, the president looked to his Secretary of State, Isabel Maggiano. "Where do we stand with NATO?" The evening before, the president had invoked Article 5 of the North Atlantic Charter, the pledge of mutual defense. In Article 5, the parties agreed that, 'an armed attack against one or more shall be considered an attack on them all.'

"The ambassador to NATO has invoked Article 5 with the North Atlantic Council, NATO's decision-making body," Isabel replied, "and it seems that nearly all of the nations are in favor of a unified response. I don't see why they wouldn't be; the Chinese announced their invasion on TV, for goodness sake. I've also held offline discussions with the Prime Minister of Canada, and he assured me we have their complete military support. They have already begun moving forces to the Vancouver area to support us in whatever we decide to do. I also spoke with the Prime Minister of Estonia, who contacted the NATO Cyber Defense Center in Tallinn, Estonia. They have already begun work on defensive and preventative measures against any further cyber attacks."

"Who can we count on for military support?" the president asked.

"In general, most of the nations are around the globe are supportive, but only a few have pledged military support," the Secretary of State replied. "Britain, Canada and Germany have been the most supportive in NATO and are working on providing forces to us. Outside of NATO, Japan, South Korea and Chile have all pledged their support and their forces. Just like they did after the September 11th attacks, Nigeria has also pledged its support, although I don't think they have any forces that will be able to assist us. I also just got off the phone with the president of India. They will back us in whatever we decide and have started moving some of their troops to their borders with China. Hopefully, this will draw off a little of the pressure on us.

"*Outstanding!*" the president exclaimed. "It's good to have friends you can count on. Please make sure they know I will remember who stood with us in our hour of need."

The Secretary of State nodded. "I will, sir."

Mentally changing topics, the president turned to the Chairman of the Joint Chiefs of Staff. "What are we doing to increase our intelligence on the Seattle area without risking a nuclear incident?"

Dozer 37, **Overhead Fairchild Air Force Base, Spokane, WA, 0645 PDT**

"I'm not sure what we're supposed to be doing out here," Major Jim 'Pokey' Bryant said from the back of the aircraft. Based on the venerable C-135 Stratolifter airframe, the 45th Reconnaissance Squadron 'Rivet Joint' aircraft was a large reconnaissance aircraft used by the U.S. Air Force to collect theater and national-level intelligence.

"We're supposed to be trying to figure out what the Chinese are doing in Seattle," Lieutenant Colonel Steve 'Taco' Byers, the pilot of *Dozer 37*, replied. "You know, where they are, what equipment they brought, and so forth."

"I understand that," Pokey said; "I *am* the evaluator after all. No, what I'm talking about is that we're not going to collect *anything* worthwhile from this far out." He looked out the window and could see Fairchild AFB in Spokane, Washington, below them. "We're 217 miles away from Seattle. We can't pick up *shit* this far out, and then trying to accurately geo-locate what signals we *do* get is going to be next to impossible."

"I heard there were nukes in play in Seattle, and we aren't allowed to get any closer until they get secured," Taco said. "Honestly, I think the only reason we're up here is because the senior leadership in D.C. felt that they needed to be doing something, even if there isn't anything that can really be done."

"I saw the head Chinese guy in Seattle on the news," the copilot, Captain George 'Pasta' Macari added. "He said there was a 200 mile exclusion zone, and they would shoot down any aircraft that comes within the area. Personally, I'd rather not start the day by getting shot down."

"Roger that," Taco concurred. "I heard they already bagged some Navy aircraft that tried to fly into the exclusion zone. I'm making sure we stay at least 200 miles from Seattle, plus a couple of extra miles for mom and the kids."

Sommers' House, North Bend, WA, 0730 PDT

"I knew it!" Calvin exclaimed, looking out a crack in the drapes covering the back window of the Sommers' house. "That's one of the missile transporters for a S-400 system. It may even be the one that shot down the guys from my air wing last night! We've got to do something about it!" His distress was obvious, and Sara put a hand on his shoulder in sympathy.

Not believing Calvin's situation report when he called back to Fallon after getting shot down, his carrier air wing commander had sent a second flight of aircraft into the Seattle area to look for the other pilots who had been shot down with Calvin. Only one of the three aircraft in the second group had returned to Fallon.

Located on 6th Street, the Sommers' three-bedroom ranch backed up against E.J. Roberts Park, where the system was located. He could see two of the missile launchers from the window and was careful not to move the drapes; he could also see several Chinese soldiers walking around, providing security for the big missiles.

"What's so bad about it?" Sara asked.

"It's just a da...darn good missile system," Calvin replied. "If it's not the best one in the world, it's in the top two or three. The system was a joint venture between Russia and China, and it brought together the best scientists from both of those countries. The engagement radar is cutting edge and better than anything we have. It can track 100 airborne targets and engage up to a dozen of them at a time, out to a range of 250 miles."

He pointed to the missile transporter out the window. "That transporter can hold three different types of missiles, which can be used to shoot down anything from low-level aircraft to low-orbit satellites, depending on which missiles are in its tubes. All three types of missiles fit into the canisters on that truck, so it's impossible to tell which missiles are loaded. Each of them are about the size of a telephone pole and travel at 12 times the speed of sound, which just boggles my mind." He shook his head. "Even worse, they all have high-explosive warheads weighing 53 pounds, which is about double the weight of our Patriot missile warhead."

"The system has a better radar than ours, a missile that has twice the range of our best missile and a warhead that's twice the size of ours." Calvin let the drapes fall and looked back at Sara. "It's just darn good," he summarized.

Sara's father called her, and she left the room. Calvin turned to Ryan. "I don't care what else we do," Calvin said, "we've *got* to do something about that missile system or more aviators are going to die."

"I agree," Ryan said. He sent the text he had been working on and turned off his phone. "In fact, I'm trying to set up a little party for the Chinese out there. If they're going to hang out in our park, we ought to have a little fun with them, eh?" He smiled at Calvin, then sobered. "Before we do anything, though, we have to find the nukes. I just got a text from the CNO, and those have to be taken out of play before anything else can happen. That's straight from the president, who has threatened to reinstate me to active duty if I 'give him any more lip.'"

"Is that a good thing or a bad thing?" Calvin asked, knowing Ryan had been forcibly retired from the Navy due to budget cuts.

"I'm not sure," Ryan said. "I'm still trying to make up my mind." Both men turned as Sara and her father walked into the room carrying a bundle of clothes.

"My dad's the right height for you, Calvin, but I think he's going to be a little bigger in the waist."

Calvin looked at her dad and thought, 'No kidding, he's at least 30 pounds heavier than I am.' Looking at himself in the mirror, he had to revise his estimate down to 25 pounds or maybe even 20 (but no less than that!) Too much time at the bars and not enough exercise, he thought. He mentally shrugged and said, "Well, he's pretty close, and if you have a belt, I'll make it work. Especially if you have something dark so that I'm harder to see at night."

"These should work," Mr. Sommers replied, handing him a pair of dark jeans; "my wife shrank them in the washer, so they're too small for me."

"Unlikely," Sara said with a laugh. "What's more likely is too many desserts and not enough hiking."

Mr. Sommers shrugged, smiling. "That's possible, too, I guess."

As Calvin went to change, the doorbell rang. Sara and her father jumped, worried the Chinese had come to their door. "Don't worry," Ryan said, "I was just about to tell you I had invited some friends to come by."

"How well do you know them?" Mr. Sommers asked, worry tinging his voice.

"Don't worry," Ryan said. "I've known the head of the group that's coming for almost 20 years since we collaborated on a mission in Kosovo. He's good people." Ryan paused and then added, "Don't worry, we'll be leaving soon; I don't want to bring any more attention to your house than I have to."

"Okay," Mr. Sommers said with a nod. Ryan ducked out of sight, and Mr. Sommers answered the door. Five men and a woman waited outside, looking around nervously. Although two of the men were Asian, the other three were definitely not, nor was the woman. Mr. Sommers let them in.

"Thanks for coming," Ryan said in welcome as he came around the corner. "I'm glad you were able to make it. Did you have any trouble getting here?"

"No problems," the first man through the door said. He turned and shook Mr. Sommers' hand. "Hi," he said; "I'm First Sergeant Aaron Smith, the senior non-commissioned officer of Alpha Rifle Company, 2nd Battalion of the 75th Ranger Regiment. Please, call me 'Top;' everyone else does." He turned back to Ryan. "Everything is pretty calm at the moment," he added. "The Chinese apparently meant it when they said everyone should go about their normal business. We saw one checkpoint, but it was on the other side of the road. No one can get onto any of the bases, but that's about it."

Calvin walked into the room as Top introduced the rest of the newcomers. "This is Sergeant Jim 'Shuteye' Chang," he said. "His family emigrated from the Guangzhou region of southern China when he was a child; he can speak Cantonese like a local as well as a little Mandarin."

"That will be helpful," Ryan said, nodding.

"I also have Private First Class Steve 'Tiny' Johnson, our sniper," Top said, "as well as his spotter, Private First Class Mike 'BTO' Bachmann, and Private John 'Jet' Li. Private Li's family also emigrated from China, but his family was from Beijing. He can speak Mandarin and read a little of it, too."

Ryan nodded again.

"The last person is Corporal Suzi 'Deadeye' Taylor, who just joined the company from Ranger School yesterday. She was formerly in the intel community, so she may be able to help on a variety of fronts."

"I'm glad you guys could make it after all," Ryan said with a smile as they gathered around the kitchen table where some maps had been spread out.

"What do you mean?" Calvin asked.

"My commanding officer (CO) was a little put out when I told him I was taking the unit to conduct some operations with a SEAL, rather than working on the CO's own little guerilla war," Top said. "He forbid me to come."

"How'd that work out for him?" Ryan asked.

"Well, at first he was mad at me, but that only lasted until the Chief of Staff of the Army called," Top said. "He gave my CO a reaming the likes of which I've never heard an officer get. I wish I had a recording of it, Ryan; you'd have loved it. He ended by promising to have my CO reassigned to muck out horse stalls at Fort Sill if he in any way interfered with our mission again. I think my CO was crying by the end." He laughed. "In any event, here we are, as requested."

"Too bad I missed it," Ryan said. "Serves him right for not letting you come to my housewarming. However, unless my math is bad, he shorted us quite a few people. I asked for 20, and I only see five."

"No worries," Top said. "You've actually got 21. In addition to the six of us here, we've got a rifle squad and a couple of M240 machine gun crews," Top said. "We couldn't get onto base to get our weapons, so I sent the other men to go by your armory and pick some up. I hope that's all right. We'll meet them at the university. Shuteye and Jet are here in case you need to plan any undercover operations, and Tiny and BTO are here because they're the sniper team. They need the big picture so they know who to target. Deadeye just checked into the company from Ranger School, but like I said, she is a former intelligence specialist, so we thought she might come in handy for any planning we needed to do."

"Smart thinking to send them to my place," Ryan said; "however, we'll need to give them directions to get past the checkpoint on the way there. I'm glad they'll be at the university ahead of time, too, so they can start reconnoitering the area. Do we have any of their cell phone numbers so we can call them?"

"We can call them now, but we won't be able to once they're at the university," Sergeant Chang said. "My girlfriend lives close to the campus, and cell phones aren't working in the vicinity. They must have a cell phone jammer or jammers in the area. Anywhere within about 10 miles of the downtown area is a no-cell zone."

"Oh my god!" Corporal Taylor exclaimed from the window. "Did you know there is a missile transporter in your backyard?" At six feet, two inches tall, anything that worried Deadeye should have been a cause for concern; however, Calvin found himself distracted by her voice. It was way too high for her. Or really for any normal human.

"Yeah, we know about the S-400," said Ryan. "It's currently on the top of Calvin's list of things that must be blown up."

"I agree we need to do something about it," Deadeye said, "but it's a HQ-19. It's Chinese."

"Yeah, we know it's Chinese," Calvin said. "Does that matter?"

"Well, yes sir, it sort of does. The Chinese have been working on some sort of exo-atmospheric kinetic kill vehicle for their version. Not only does that system give them an outstanding anti-aircraft capability, but it also can probably perform ballistic missile defense and anti-satellite operations as well."

"Well, hopefully the U.S. isn't going to start lobbing missiles at us," Ryan said. "Although the anti-satellite capability is something that will move it higher on the targeting list. Our pilots may need the GPS capability for their bombs, so we probably don't want the Chinese shooting them all down."

"Exactly," Deadeye said with a smile.

"We'll get to that later," Ryan said. "Right now, we've got other things that are more important, like how we're going to find our wayward bombs. We'll just have to plan around the no-cell zone Sergeant Chang was talking about. We can work out a couple of contingency plans and finalize things once we get there. How are we set for transport?"

"We're good," Top replied. "I had a couple of the guys drive their own cars here. I thought it would look a little funny to have six or eight guys who look like soldiers all driving around together."

"Yeah, it probably would, at that," Ryan agreed. "What intel do we have on the area?"

"You told me earlier that Miss Sommers saw a big group of students being taken into the Intramural Activities Building (IAB) at the University of Washington," Top said. "As near as I can tell, that's one of three groups of hostages the Chinese captured yesterday; they also took prisoners at the convention center and at Safeco Field. They released the hostages from the convention center and Safeco

Field last night after the announcement was made, but they never released the students from the IAB. Why do you suppose that is?"

"They obviously had different purposes in holding each of the groups," Calvin answered, happy to be contributing something to the discussion. "They wanted to be able to threaten the big groups of hostages in the event we tried some sort of military attack on them. If they could threaten to kill a big group, they could probably make us back down. When they met all of their invasion goals for the first day, though, the Chinese must have decided they didn't need them anymore."

"That's what I think, too," Top replied, to a chorus of nodding heads. "However, that doesn't tell us why they're still holding the students in the IAB. There's got to be a different reason."

"Well, that brings us to why I need you, and why the head of the Army is willing to place you at our disposal," Ryan said. "We think there is a different reason. We believe the Chinese also have six nuclear weapons in the building. Wouldn't that be a good reason for them to hold onto the students? To use them as a shield so that we don't attack the building? As long as they have the hostages, we won't go near the building for fear they will kill them."

"What is everyone here for, if you aren't going to do anything to rescue the hostages?" Sara asked from behind Ryan.

"Oh, we can and will do something about the situation at the IAB," Ryan said. "I was just emphasizing what the Chinese would like us to believe. By the way, I didn't know you were standing behind me. You didn't hear me say 'nuclear weapons.' Please forget you ever heard those two words."

"I figured the boxes I saw had to be something like that," Sara said. "Why else would you delay everything else that needs to be done until you completed this task? It just didn't make sense any other way."

"Smart girl," Ryan said. Noticing a sick look on Calvin's face, Ryan asked, "Is something wrong, sir?"

Calvin noticed Ryan's use of the word 'sir,' as it was about the first time Ryan had called him that. As the planning had gone on, Ryan had lapsed into his former role of SEAL Senior Chief. Gone was the blustering bravado of the 'backwoods hermit;' he was now 100% the consummate, confident professional. Calvin approved. The navy had lost a tremendous asset when Ryan had been forced into retirement. However, the realization did nothing to help Calvin's own state of mind.

"Yeah, Senior Chief," Calvin said, willing to play the 'professional' game with him. "I don't see what my role is in this anymore now that you have experienced special forces backup. I'm thinking that maybe I should be trying to get back to Fallon and my air wing."

Now that he had said it, Calvin realized he *was* out of his league. Although he had initially wanted no part of being a ground troop, he had been looking forward to the challenge, the opportunity to make a difference and, if he were honest with himself, the danger of doing it. Now that the professionals had arrived, he was nothing more than a fifth wheel, at best, which was far more disappointing than he would have ever thought it would be. Sara's presence only added to his distress. He didn't know why, but he really wanted to impress her.

Ryan smiled and said, "You've got the most important role of all, sir; you're our platoon leader! Every military organization has to have an officer to take the blame when things go wrong and give us enlisted men and women the credit when things go right. You're the one responsible for looking at big picture things and making sure we don't desecrate dead bodies or burn holy books or anything else that looks bad on the nightly news."

"That's great and all," Calvin replied, "but I don't know anything about special forces stuff. How am I supposed to plan what we're doing?"

"Well, sir, that's the best part about being you. You've got Top and I here to do all the work for you. We've got over 50 years of experience between us. Your part is to look at the operational and strategic level and make sure that what we're doing is in accordance with the United States' goals and objectives in pursuing this war. We're good at killing people and breaking things. You just handle the rest." He paused and then said with a grin, "Besides, I voted for you!"

"What is that supposed to mean?" Calvin asked.

"It means that, when the CNO asked who was in charge of this mixed platoon, I, of course, said you were. I told him how you were taking charge of all of the planning out here, how you were giving us great direction and inspiration for getting back the nukes *his* navy lost and what a great job you were doing, blah, blah, blah. He now thinks you are the '*absolute best*' man for the job here and wants you to stay and watch over all of us so we don't get into trouble. I think he also told the Army Chief of Staff the same thing."

"*You told the CNO I had taken charge?*" Calvin sounded shocked. He thought about it a second and then said, "Thanks, I guess...but wouldn't it be better to have Top's CO in charge? Doesn't he have a lot more experience in this sort of thing?"

"Well, sure, he's more tactically qualified," Ryan answered, "but he's an ass." The Rangers all nodded in agreement. "Besides, all my issues with authority aside, military operations need to have responsible leadership, and I think you'll do just fine. You're the big picture guy. You just give us the objectives and let us handle the details." Ryan's phone rang. Looking at it, he smiled as he handed it to Calvin. "Oh yeah, I almost forgot," said the former SEAL. "You also get to deal with higher authority." He chuckled and then winked at Top. "By the way, the CNO's on the phone for you," he added.

The other shoe dropped for Calvin, as he saw how he had been neatly maneuvered into doing the thing Ryan hated most, dealing with senior leadership. Still, someone had to do it and, while he never thought he'd be personally talking to the CNO, this was something he *could* do. Taking the phone, he said, "Okay, I'm in. You guys work out the plan, and I'll go talk to the brass." Switching the phone on and walking away from the table so he could hear, he continued, "Lieutenant Hobbs, may I help you, sir?"

PLAN LHD *Long*, Pier D, Naval Base Kitsap, WA, 0830 PDT

Admiral Zhao Na looked around at the small group of officers assembled in his conference room onboard the PLAN *Long* to ensure he had their attention. "I just spoke with one of the vice premiers," he said, "and we are to send the American nuclear warheads back to the People's Republic of China (PRC), where they can be disassembled and studied. It is my intention to leave one of them at the university in case we need it; however, we shall send the other five back to the PRC as soon as we can arrange it." A large man, both tall and stout, the admiral didn't need to raise his voice to be heard; everyone was *very* attentive, as befit a discussion on handling nuclear weapons. He looked at Lieutenant

Commander Lin Gang, the Air Operations Officer of the *Long*. "What craft do we have to get them back?"

Lieutenant Commander Lin, a tall and studious-looking man, looked at his notes and said, "We have a variety of options, sir, as we can fly them out of Whidbey Island Naval Air Station, Seattle-Tacoma Airport or McChord Air Base. We have six Y-20 Kunpeng aircraft standing by at the military bases, as well as several Air China 747s available at the civilian airport." The Y-20 was a heavy-lift aircraft similar to the U.S. Air Force's C-17.

"Here's what I want," the admiral said. "In order to maximize the chances for getting at least one back, I want you to send two Z-8 helicopters, along with four Z-10 attack helicopters for support. Each of the Z-8s will carry two of the weapons; one will go to Whidbey, the other to Seattle-Tacoma. Load them onto two Y-20 aircraft at Whidbey Island and two Air China 747s at Seattle-Tacoma. When all are ready, I want them to launch at the same time, although I want their routes of flight to be different. All of them should avoid American bases or known American positions and ships to the greatest extent possible."

"That accounts for four, admiral," said Lieutenant Commander Lin. "What do you wish us to do with the other one?"

The admiral looked at Captain Chan Ming, the Commanding Officer of the *Long*. "You will send one of our landing craft to bring it back to this ship by sea. We will take it home with us, ourselves."

Captain Chan bowed. "It will be done as you order."

Sommers' House, North Bend, WA, 0835 PDT

"**O**kay," Ryan said; "that's it, then. Are there any last minute questions or anything that I missed?" He looked around the room but didn't see any questions.

"I've got one," Calvin said, coming back into the room. "What did I miss?"

"Here's what we've got, sir," Ryan said. "First off, we'd normally do something like this under the cover of darkness, but it's not possible because we need to recover the weapons before the Chinese can disperse them and further complicate things for us. Also, the rest of the military can't do anything until they're recovered, so we have to get it done ASAP."

"We've come up with two broad plans that accomplish the mission," Top said. "The first of these relies on trickery. If we can get a couple of Chinese army uniforms, Sergeant Chang and Private Li will put them on and infiltrate the building where the students, and presumably the nuclear weapons, are being held. Once inside, they will take care of any forces watching the building's entrance, so the rest of the platoon can enter the building."

"If there aren't any uniforms to be had," Top continued, "then we will have to go with the 'smash and grab' approach, where we overcome any Chinese resistance by hitting them hard and fast. Hopefully, we get away with the weapons before any major forces can respond."

"Hopefully?" Calvin asked. "I'm no special forces guy, but that doesn't fill me with a whole lot of confidence."

"Well, we don't have any intel on the targets yet," Ryan said, "so it's really hard to say exactly what we're going to do. In all likelihood, we're going to have to make it up as we go."

"Once again," Calvin stated, "it doesn't sound like even you have confidence in that plan. Hopefully, we'll find some uniforms so it doesn't come to that...crap, now you've got me saying 'hopefully' too." He sighed. "Okay, what else have you got?"

"Both options involve eight soldiers with SUVs driving up to the building to remove the weapons," Top replied. "This leaves us with only 13 Rangers, a SEAL and a pilot as the assault force...which I didn't think would be enough, so I called and asked for another squad of soldiers. We've got another nine people coming; most of them are riflemen, but I also wanted a couple people to man the Ranger Anti-tank Weapons System (RAWS) Ryan had in his armory."

"Any problem getting them?" Calvin asked.

"Nope," Top said. "When I called my CO, he was *very* agreeable."

"Apparently, he hadn't gotten over his reaming yet," Ryan added.

"So we're all set?" Calvin asked.

"Yes, sir," Ryan said. He smiled and asked, "How'd your call go?"

"My call was...interesting," Calvin said. "I'm not used to dealing with senior admirals, but I did my part as platoon commander and briefed the CNO on our plans to recover the weapons, as well as our intentions to take out the HQ-19 battery as our next target. He liked our plans, as it will give our forces the ability to operate on this side of town."

"So we're ready to go?" Ryan asked.

"Well, not quite," Calvin replied. "Before everyone goes, I need to take care of one administrative thing as your new CO."

"Look at that," Ryan said. "He's only been in charge 15 minutes, and he's already trying to get us to do paperwork. Maybe he *is* a typical officer, after all."

"No," Calvin said, "this is important." Seeing he had everyone's attention, he looked at Ryan and said, "Hold up your right hand and repeat after me, 'I, Ryan O'Leary, do solemnly swear that I will support and defend the Constitution of the United States against all enemies, foreign and domestic; that I will bear true faith and allegiance to the same; and that I will obey the orders of the President of the United States and the orders of the officers appointed over me, according to regulations and the Uniform Code of Military Justice. So help me God."

"Umm, yeah, all that stuff. So help me God," Senior Chief Petty Officer Ryan O'Leary said, recognizing the oath of office for an enlisted man, having said it many times previously. "Are you authorized to do that?"

Calvin nodded. "By the power vested in me by the Chief of Naval Operations, I am so authorized. Face it, I couldn't have you running around in a military operation as a civilian, so it was a decision that had to be made, whether you wanted it or not. Congratulations, Master Chief Petty Officer O'Leary."

"Thanks, but that's *Senior* Chief," Ryan corrected.

"Actually, no, it's Master Chief," Calvin said with a smile. "I had them reinstate you from when you were retired in 2013, which includes your promotion in the 2016 or 2017 time frame, which we'll have to argue about with the Navy's Personnel Department at a later date. The most important thing to know is that you now have about five years of back pay coming, so, if we survive this, the drinks are most definitely on you!"

"Damn, sir, I don't know what to say," the newly minted Master Chief said humbly. "I guess a pretty big thank you would be in order."

"Hell, don't thank me," Calvin said. "As the senior enlisted, though, you need to get the troops moving, so they can get into their positions for the—" He was interrupted by a 'woooosh' and a window-shaking roar as a missile roared out of the tubes of the HQ-19 missile transporter closest to the house, followed closely by a second missile, then a third. Running to the window, Calvin could see all four tube doors on it were open; either the fourth missile failed to fire or was aborted for some reason.

"We've got to get the nukes back, so we can take care of that missile system," Calvin said. "It's *killing* us. I told them not to fly around here until we could get rid of the missiles, but obviously, they didn't listen to me. Let's go get those nukes."

"Aye aye, sir," Master Chief O'Leary said. "Move 'em out, men! And Suzi!" he added as an afterthought.

Dozer 37, Overhead Fairchild Air Force Base, Spokane, WA, 0845 PDT

"**D**amn," Lieutenant Colonel Steve 'Taco' Byers said, looking out the window, "they're getting awfully close to the exclusion zone." The Rivet Joint aircraft had flown up from Nebraska and immediately commenced its collection mission; after several hours on station, they were short on gas and had joined on the KC-135 tanker aircraft to refuel.

Although the crew of *Dozer 37* had been careful to stay outside the 200-mile exclusion zone, the KC-135 tanker pilot was not. Once *Dozer 37* had plugged in and the fuel started flowing, the tanker began following a straight line to make the refueling process easier.

"No kidding," the copilot, Captain George 'Pasta' Macari, responded. "We haven't been this far west since we got here. Do you suppose the tanker guys know about the exclusion zone? Should we call them and say something?"

"I don't want to transmit while we're refueling," Taco replied, "and we're almost full. As soon as we are, we'll unplug and go back to where we're supposed to be orbiting."

"Hey, umm, do you guys realize we're within the exclusion zone?" the evaluator, Major Jim 'Pokey' Bryant, asked from the back of the aircraft. "I show us at 198 miles."

"Yeah," Taco answered, "we were just talking about that. We're getting a little uncomfortable up here. We're almost full. As soon as we are, we're going to detach and head straight east away from the exclusion zone. Really, do you think the Chinese can see the difference between 200 and 198 miles? We haven't done anything aggressive or provocative all morning. I doubt they'll be worried about us..."

HQ-19 Battery, North Bend, WA, 0845 PDT

"Got them!" Captain Chao Ming, the HQ-19 battery commander, cried from his seat in the missile command vehicle. He had been waiting all morning for the reconnaissance aircraft to stray far enough into the exclusion zone that he could prove the violation. The Americans had finally done it, and he was cleared to fire. "It's a long-range shot," he added, "so I want you to fire two missiles at each aircraft."

"I have a firing solution," the tech replied. "Two missiles are aimed at each aircraft."

"Fire!" he commanded.

One missile failed to launch, but the other three roared from their canisters and streaked across the sky in the direction of the refueling aircraft.

Dozer 37, Overhead Fairchild Air Force Base, Spokane, WA, 0847 PDT

"I've got missile engagement! Emergency breakaway! Emergency breakaway! Dive! Dive! Dive!" Pokey screamed from the back of the aircraft.

"Emergency breakaway! Emergency breakaway," Taco yelled over the radio as he broke contact with the refueling aircraft and started a turn to the right to get clear. "Kanza 22, Dozer 37, *we have active missile engagement! Dive! Dive!"*

Taco rolled the 225,000 pound aircraft away from Seattle and into a steep dive.

"Roger, 37, understand missile engagement."

"We need to get down, and we need to get down *now!"* Pokey called. "Those missiles are coming at 12 times the speed of sound. They will be here in another minute!"

"How low do we have to get to be below their radar horizon?" Taco asked.

"The radars won't see us below 25,000 feet, due to the curvature of the Earth," Pokey replied, "but we need to get the *fuck* out of here. Those missiles have their own active radar seekers; we need to be *gone* from where they're going to be looking!"

Taco pushed further forward on the yoke and looked outside the cockpit window. All he could see was ground; it was the steepest dive he had ever put the aircraft into. "Pasta, I'm going to need your help to pull this out," he said as the airspeed continued to build.

"*Now!*" Taco cried as the altimeter unwound through 10,000 feet, and both men pulled back on the yokes with all of their strength. Taco could see the aircraft start to come out of the dive, but it was full of fuel, and he could tell they weren't going to pull out in time.

"Hold on!" Taco called. He let go of the yoke, unstrapped and braced both of his feet on the dash. With the extra leverage, he was able to pull harder and the aircraft's rate of descent slowed, but the radar altimeter continued to unwind...

5000'...

3000'...

1500'...

900'...

600'...

Before the massive aircraft finally leveled off at 400 feet on their altimeter.

"Fuck," Taco said, taking a hand off the yoke to wipe away the sweat dripping into his eyes. "We almost flew into the ground and did their work for them." He took a breath and let it out slowly, savoring being alive. "Give the tanker a call and find out where they went so we don't run into them."

"Don't bother," Pokey said. "I could look up and see them from back here. They didn't dive fast enough, and two missiles hit them. They're gone."

Canadian Forces Base Esquimalt, Victoria, Canada, 1000 PDT

In 2014, Canada ranked 133rd in the world in military spending as a percentage of Gross Domestic Product (GDP), behind such notable military powers as the country of Lesotho and the island nation of Togo. The average for the world was 2.2%; that Canada felt it only needed to spend a miniscule 1.0% of its GDP on defense was an indication it felt very secure about its position in the world, and especially its position in North America. Why spend more? Its closest neighbor and ally, the United States, was spending over $581 billion a year on defense, almost 40% of the world's total. With the United States spending so much, there was no need for Canada to do so; it could focus its budget on social programs, secure in the knowledge the United States would keep it safe.

This plan worked well for many years, until China invaded the United States and took up residency a mere 100 miles from one of Canada's largest cities. Overnight, Canada was forced to evaluate its ability to repel an invasion or assist the United States with the one it had.

Having spent so little for so long, Canada's military was not up to either task.

Canada didn't have any significant combat power close by, so it was unable to provide much in the way of immediate assistance. Its armed forces were tiny, with an active duty military of only 92,000. This ranked Canada 52nd in the world, behind world powers like Nepal and Bangladesh. That isn't to say Canada shirked its duties as a world leader; in fact, it was very active in a number of United Nations and NATO peacekeeping missions, and it spent more of its citizens' life's blood around the world than most other nations. Canada just didn't have the ability to bring large amounts of combat power to bear on the situation.

Canada did, however, have a submarine.

Launched in November of 1989, the HMCS *Victoria* (SSK 876) was the first ship in the British *Upholder* class. A long-range hunter-killer submarine, the submarine had a very brief career with the Royal Navy as the HMS *Unseen* (S41); however, the United Kingdom decided to do away with the nation's fleet of diesel-electric boats shortly after her launch and decommissioned her in 1994. Looking to recoup some of its investment, the British government offered to sell *Unseen* and her sister submarines to Canada, but it wasn't until 1998 that Canada accepted.

Unseen was the first of the submarines to be reactivated, and it was handed over to the Canadian Navy in 2000. By that point, the *Unseen* was in poor condition and suffered from a number of problems, and the submarine spent most of the next 12 years in and out of dry dock for repairs. Finally, in 2012, the *Victoria* was declared operational, becoming the first Canadian submarine in the Pacific since the 1974 decommissioning of HMCS *Rainbow*.

"After almost 30 years of waiting, the *Victoria* finally gets its chance," the commanding officer of the *Victoria*, Commander Rodney Jewell, said. He scanned the harbor at Canadian Forces Base Esquimalt from the conning tower of the submarine. Located on the southern tip of Vancouver Island, he could almost feel the Chinese presence just over the horizon to the south, and he was itching to take the fight to the enemy. "Is everything ready to go?"

"Yes sir, we're ready to get underway," his XO, Lieutenant Commander John Gray, said. "Did we get permission to enter the Seattle exclusion zone?"

"Yes we did," Commander Jewell replied. "The government promised to do everything it could to honor its NATO obligation to the United States, and right now we're it. Seattle's only 75 miles away, though; we can be there by dinner."

The CO scanned the harbor again. Nothing obstructed their passage to the sea. "This ship has been a laughing stock for two decades, ever since Prime Minister Chretien authorized her purchase," he said. "It's time we showed the country what she's got. *Cast off fore and aft!*"

Conibear Shellhouse, University of Washington, Seattle, WA, 1030 PDT

"Sara was right," Calvin said to Master Chief O'Leary as he looked around the docks of Conibear Shellhouse. "This is a great place to meet up." As planned, the mixed special forces platoon had reassembled at Conibear Shellhouse on the University of Washington's campus. Located next to the Intramural Activities Building (IAB), the boathouse for the school's rowing team made a great place to rendezvous as the docks were on the opposite side of the building from the IAB, and the platoon couldn't be seen from it.

"Yes sir, it is," Master Chief replied. "Most of the Rangers are young enough that they wouldn't look out of place on campus if they ran into a squad of Chinese; even you could probably get by. And if any of them looked nervous, it could surely be attributed to the presence of so many armed soldiers. I guess if the Chinese had looked closely at them, they might have noticed our guys had shorter hair and more tattoos than normal, but that was pretty unlikely."

"Yeah," Calvin agreed. "The only thing that would have given them away would have been if they'd been carrying guns."

They had been over this several times, and Master Chief knew the only reason Calvin kept talking about it was he was nervous about going into his first ground combat. That was normal; Master Chief would just have to watch how the young officer handled it. Some people used the extra energy to hyper-focus, and they became better soldiers once the adrenaline started flowing. Others completely freaked out. He hoped Calvin wouldn't fall into the latter group, but there was nothing he could do about it now. He shrugged internally; he'd worry about the things he *could* affect.

He kept talking to the younger officer to distract him. "Yeah, I feel naked without a weapon," Master Chief said, "but we couldn't risk getting caught with them."

"Private Li's solution was a good one," Calvin observed as a small boat came into view from around the corner, "and it looks like they're here." While they were planning the mission, the private had noticed they were meeting at a boathouse and suggested bringing the weapons in by boat. That way, they could walk through campus without having to worry about being spotted by the Chinese.

"Yep, that's them," Master Chief said, looking at the Boston Whaler coming their way. "I can see Top behind the wheel, and it looks like Sergeant Chang is up on the bow. Private Li must be down below with the weapons."

The boat eased into the dock and was quickly tied up.

"Any problems?" Master Chief asked.

"None," Top replied. "We didn't see any Chinese. They must not have enough manpower to patrol the water as well as the land."

Master Chief posted lookouts on the corners of the building to watch for Chinese soldiers while they tied up the boat. The weapons were quickly unloaded and distributed.

"Okay," Master Chief said to the group; "there's no deniability from here on out. If we're seen with weapons, they're going to raise the alarm, and the Chinese will rapidly respond to the threat. Use overwhelming firepower and move as quickly as possible."

"Did you have any luck finding uniforms?" Top asked.

"No," Master Chief answered. "We didn't see any soldiers that we could easily grab. The only soldiers we saw were the two guarding the doors at the front of the IAB." He sighed. "I think we're going to have to go with the smash and grab option."

"Shit," Calvin said, "I was hoping to do it the easy way." He no longer seemed nervous, Master Chief saw. If anything, he was beginning to look confident.

Calvin was just about to give the order to begin the assault when a new sound was heard. Although low at first, it rapidly grew louder. "What the hell's that?" Jet wondered as he stepped off the boat. The noise sounded like several jet engines operating in concert, but was somehow different. Additionally, it seemed to be coming from out to sea, not from the air.

As the noise continued to build, Calvin finally recognized what it was. "That's an LCAC!" he cried, recognizing the noise from one of his summer ROTC cruises during college. "This may be the opportunity we've been looking for. Quick! Master Chief, get everyone hidden. Sergeant Chang, get in its way, talk to the crew and get it to shut down!"

Everyone threw themselves behind whatever cover they could find as the Chinese *Yuyi*-class LCAC came around the breakwater from the south. The Landing Craft, Air Cushioned (LCAC) vehicle was a large hovercraft used to move vehicles, material and men from a ship at sea to the shore. Hearing became impossible as the hovercraft approached; it used two jet engines for propulsion and another four to power the four enormous fans underneath it that provided its lift. Calvin estimated the vessel was at least 100 feet long, big enough to carry a fully-loaded tank.

The LCAC slowed as it approached the dock area and started to climb up the shallow bank in the direction of the IAB. Its forward progress slowed and then stopped, as Sergeant Chang ran out in front of it waving his arms. His lips moved, but he couldn't be heard over the roar of six jet engines.

Faced with an obviously agitated Chinese man, the four crewmembers of the hovercraft were unsure what to do. Sergeant Chang acted like he had every right to command them, indicating they should land the craft and turn off its engines. They were unsure, however, because he wasn't in uniform. Finally, they decided to stop the LCAC, and the boat touched down. Obviously worried that something was wrong, though, three crewmembers ran out of the port pilothouse to man the three 14.5mm machine guns the LCAC mounted, while the ship's craftmaster shut down its engines and came out to talk to Sergeant Chang. Two of the machine guns pointed in the general direction of Sergeant Chang, while the other maintained a lookout behind the hovercraft.

Calvin stood up where the crew of the LCAC could see him. "Tell the crew to come out of the boat," he said to Sergeant Chang, who translated his order into Chinese. The answer he received was obviously a negative, and the two machine guns that had been focused on Shuteye reoriented to point at Calvin. Sergeant Chang translated, "They want to know why they should."

"Tell them that they are greatly outnumbered," Calvin said, who didn't appear scared anymore, "and if they don't, they will all be killed."

Correctly interpreting the response from the Chinese sailors as another negative, Calvin said in a loud voice, "On the count of three, everyone stand up, with your weapons pointed at the crew. One...two...three!" Suddenly, the four crewmen had 31 rifles pointing at them.

Calvin watched as the machine gunners' eyes scanned the group of Americans, trying to calculate their chances. While they could probably kill a number of the Americans, they also had to realize they would probably lose their own lives in the attempt. The un-armed craftmaster gave up first, putting his hands in the air. One of the machine gunners quickly followed his example, followed by the other two crewmen. They put down the boarding ramp and were swiftly taken into custody.

"I believe you were looking for some Chinese uniforms?" Calvin asked Master Chief. "Here you go."

"That'll work," Master Chief said. "All right, take 'em into the boathouse and get their uniforms, then zip-tie their hands and ankles." He directed several of the troops to watch the perimeter while Shuteye and Jet put on the two uniforms closest in size to them.

"Hang on a second," Top said. He ran out to the Chinese LCAC and into the port cabin. After a few seconds, he came out holding two QBZ-95 rifles by their carrying handles. "Found 'em," he said. "I knew they'd have some rifles around somewhere; this completes the uniform." He handed the two rifles to Shuteye and Jet.

Suitably armed and dressed, the two Chinese-Americans approached the six people who had been chosen to play the part of 'prisoners.' Waiting in two lines of three were Master Chief O'Leary and Top, with two Rangers behind each of them. Each of the soldiers was chosen for his hand-to-hand and small arms combat skills. Calvin had decided to stay behind to watch the 'big picture' things, leaving the combat assault duties to the people trained for it.

"Does everyone know what they're doing?" Calvin asked.

"Yes, sir, we're all set," Master Chief said, looking at the men lined up behind him. "All right, Shuteye, lead us out."

With Sergeant Chang in the lead and Private Li following the group, the two Chinese 'sailors' marched their 'prisoners' into the open space between the buildings. No outcry was heard or alarm raised; no Chinese soldiers were even in sight. The marching men signaled and the rest of the platoon began advancing stealthily, clinging to the shadows and other cover. Calvin rounded the corner of the building, his senses almost on overload, but didn't see any Chinese along the back of the IAB.

Shuteye continued marching the group past the tennis courts and around to the front of the IAB, where two Chinese soldiers guarded the main entrance. Calvin peeked around the corner and got his first look at the building. Over half of it was made of glass, probably so the students exercising could look outside. At the moment, it also allowed the Americans to see the platoon of Chinese soldiers on the inside. Calvin quickly ducked back around the corner out of sight.

The group marched up to the front doors as if they had every right to do so. As they approached, they could see the Chinese soldiers inside were doing nothing more than relaxing in the fitness center. The foreigners had pushed the machines into the center of the room to give them a clear field of fire out of the building and now appeared to be using the room as a barracks. Master Chief knew the rest of the platoon would not be able to approach any further without being seen; the group would have to go the rest of the way alone.

"Damn, that's a lot of 'em," Private First Class Christian Woodard said in a low voice from the back of Master Chief's line.

"Steady!" Master Chief growled under his breath.

Shuteye was a little more optimistic. Looking at the guards, he saw they were wearing army uniforms, while he was dressed in a navy one. The Chinese soldiers wouldn't know the navy personnel, exponentially raising their chances of success. Buoyed by this thought, he reached the two soldiers at the front door and reported, "We're from the crew of the assault craft. It just broke down behind the building. While we were working to fix it, we found these people standing around and thought you'd like some more hostages. They're all yours!"

"It's about time you got here," one of them said in an annoyed tone of voice. "Our lieutenant has been waiting for you. You'll have to take the prisoners to where they're being kept yourselves; we have to stay here at the door."

"Bah," said Chang. "Try to do a good deed and get screwed over for it." He sighed. "Where do the hostages go?"

White House Situation Room, Washington, D.C., 1345 EDT (1045 PDT)

"So," the president said as they waited anxiously to find out about the recovery of the nuclear weapons, "once we recover the stolen weapons, how do we keep the Chinese from going back to the storage facility and taking more?"

"I've got every person in the 7th Infantry Division who can find and hold a rifle headed toward the Bangor Trident facility, as well as any of the Reservists they can find," the Army Chief of Staff said. "They may not have all of their normal equipment, but they will, by God, hold that facility until they can be properly relieved. I don't know if you've ever been to the northwest, sir, but most of the people there have their own weapons. Those that don't will have to beg, borrow or steal their neighbors' weapons, their friends' weapons or whatever they can find on the shelves of their local department stores. With the Chinese allowing free movement throughout the area, they can get close to the base and then infiltrate overland. They'll be there to prevent a reoccurrence. Either that, or they'll die trying."

The CNO nodded, happy they had resolved that problem earlier. He was pleased the Army was taking care of it; he had enough problems of his own.

Outside the IAB, University of Washington, Seattle, WA, 1050 PDT

Calvin decided one of the first things Master Chief needed to do with his new money was stock his armory with some of those radios and ear buds you always see the SEALs using in the movies. He felt completely out of touch while he stood waiting on the side of the IAB. The group appeared to have made it inside the building without any problems, but now they had been out of contact for five minutes. Every minute he didn't hear rifle fire was another minute the team inside got closer to the nukes...unless they'd already been captured. How would he know if they had?

Still no word from the group on the inside. This should have been better planned, Calvin thought, starting to get a little frantic. At what point should he give up on the group inside and try the smash and grab option? Too many questions, not enough training, he thought. He was definitely *not* the right person for this job. As he came to this conclusion, he began to hear a thumping in the distance. It grew in volume, and he got a sick feeling in his stomach as he recognized what it was.

Helicopters were coming.

"Shit," he said under his breath. "Shit, shit, *shit!*" Both of his senior enlisted leaders were inside the building, leaving him alone. Without them, he realized it was up to him to do something. "Everyone come here!" he ordered in a stage whisper.

When Calvin had first seen the armory under Master Chief's house, he had been amazed at all of the war-making material Master Chief had assembled there. Impressive as it seemed at first glance, being faced with a live enemy had quickly revealed its inadequacies. First, the lack of radios kept them from coordinating their actions, and now he had found a second problem. As the beating of the incoming helicopters' rotor blades got louder, he hoped there wouldn't be more than two of them; his makeshift platoon only had two Stinger surface-to-air missiles.

"We've got helos coming in," he said. "If this is a mixed group of helos, go for the attack helos with the guns on the front first. They'll be tough because they're probably not going to land, but circle around the field. Try to take them when they're headed away from you so they don't see you shooting. We've only got a couple of missiles, and we've got to make them count. When the first helo touches down, shoot!" He watched as the 23 soldiers spread out to take their positions.

Inside the IAB, University of Washington, Seattle, WA, 1052 PDT

So far, so good, thought Master Chief as they continued into the building. In addition to the guards outside the front door, there had been another two soldiers on the inside who were hidden. If the Americans had tried the smash and grab, it would have failed miserably, as the alarm would have been given, and they would have had to fight their way past several squads of soldiers aware of their presence.

Walking into the enormous room that housed the gym's basketball courts, they found the hostages. Several hundred students were huddled in the middle of the central basketball court, looking miserable. As Master Chief stopped to take it in, Private Li prodded him in the back with the butt of the rifle, saying something in Chinese that was probably "move!" He continued walking. There were five soldiers in the room armed with rifles. Two were at the entrance, and the other three were scattered throughout the gym. All appeared observant, although a little bored, as they held their rifles cradled in their arms and not at a ready position. While Shuteye stopped to talk to the two guards at the door, Private Li continued to shepherd the rest of the group toward the students.

As they reached the hostages, Private Li had an idea. In broken English he commanded, "You no stay in group. Move out! Go to all sides!" The six prisoners spread out with two going in the direction of each of the guards, hands in their pockets.

"Where did you find them?" one of the guards asked Sergeant Chang. "I thought we already had enough prisoners." He grinned. "Are they to be punished?"

"We found them on our way in," said Shuteye. "They were hanging around outside and looked suspicious so we thought we'd bring them in."

As Private Li walked up to rejoin him, Sergeant Chang's eyes widened in surprise as he looked over the shoulders of the two guards. Both guards involuntarily looked behind them to see what Chang had seen. When they did so, Chang yelled, "Now!" and he leveled his rifle at the two guards. Private Li did the same, and the two guards looked back to see two rifles pointed in their direction.

The other six Americans drew silenced pistols from their pockets, with two Americans pointing at each of the other three guards. The soldier in front of Master Chief tried to bring his rifle up, and Master Chief shot him twice in the chest, his pistol coughing quietly. The Ranger standing next to him, Private First Class Woodard, also got off a shot, but he fired too quickly; the round missed the soldier and buried itself in the concrete wall of the gym. Looking around, Master Chief saw the other two guards had put their hands in the air and were being relieved of their rifles. He was starting to feel pretty good about their chances.

And then a hostage screamed.

Her neighbor clamped a hand over her mouth, and the scream was cut off as suddenly as it began, but it echoed in the gym and trailed off down the hall.

"Cover the door!" Master Chief ordered, stationing his two Chinese imposters to watch the hallway in case anyone came looking for the source of the scream. "Top, take care of the prisoners."

Master Chief checked the soldier he had shot. The soldier didn't need to be zip-tied; one of Master Chief's shots had struck him in the heart, and he was already dead. Master Chief hadn't wanted to kill the soldier, especially dressed as a civilian, but it was either that or let the soldier shoot *him*; he hadn't had a choice.

Surveying the gym, Master Chief saw a door that led to the outside. Addressing the group of students still sitting in the middle of the gym like sheep, he said, "When I say to, I want you to walk, not run, to the door over there." He pointed at the one he meant, which led west toward the tennis courts. "Walk, *do not run*, away from the building. Most things are back to normal outside, but if you run, you will draw attention to yourselves and to us. Remember, *walk*, don't run. Ready, move!" he commanded.

The students began moving toward the door. One of them, a short blond, said, "Thanks!" as she walked past. Master Chief recognized Sara's friend Erika; he was happy he had found her.

As one of the students opened the door, Master Chief heard the distinctive sounds of approaching helicopters.

"Aw shit," he muttered. Changing his mind, he yelled, "On second thought, *run!*" He hoped Erika would make it to safety, but right now he had other problems.

Outside the IAB, University of Washington, Seattle, WA, 1050 PDT

"Shit, shit, *shit!*" Calvin swore as the side door to the gym opened just after they passed by it, and the students emerged at a walk that quickly turned into a run. They couldn't have come out at a worse time. After a subjective eternity waiting for information on what was going on inside the IAB, the team had to send all of the hostages out right *now*, with Chinese helicopters flying into the area.

Calvin had a second thought. With the helicopters inbound, the Chinese soldiers inside the IAB would be on full alert; Master Chief would need more people. He grabbed the five soldiers closest to him and sent them to join Master Chief. That left him with 18 troops; hopefully, there wouldn't be more than a couple of helicopters.

"Shit!" he swore again as they came into sight. Unless the Rangers really knew what they were doing, they were screwed. He counted at least five helicopters inbound...no, wait, six, as another attack helo came into sight from behind the tree line. Six helicopters, and they only had two Stinger surface-to-air missiles. The odds weren't good.

Calvin watched from the IAB as the helicopters came in to land. At least the hostages were escaping from the opposite end of the building; hopefully, they wouldn't be seen and targeted by the helicopters. As the helicopters came closer, he could see two of the big Chinese heavy-lift helicopters, accompanied by four attack helos. Four attack helos and two Stinger missiles...he did the math and didn't like the answer.

The two heavies came into the empty field at a fast rate of speed, flaring to land in a combat approach. They couldn't have seen his men, or they wouldn't have landed; they must be doing the combat landing just to be safe. As the two big helicopters set down on the soccer field, the other four helicopters began circling the field, like they had the day before.

The wheels of the first helicopter touched the grass, and a Stinger missile leaped out from under the bleachers at the adjoining baseball field. With a 'wooosh' and a plume of smoke, it headed toward the closest attack helicopter. A second Stinger missile launched from the woods on the other side of the field immediately after in a burst of rocket fire. Calvin's pulse, already pounding, quickened further as battle was joined.

Inside the IAB, University of Washington, Seattle, WA, 1050 PDT

"Time to move!' Master Chief said as the last of the students ran out the door. "We've got helicopters inbound!" Before the door could close, five more Rangers came into the building, bearing grenade launchers and extra rifles.

"LT Hobbs thought you could use some support," the lead soldier, Staff Sergeant Dave Kowalski, said.

"Thanks," Master Chief said as he took the offered M-16/M203 grenade launcher combo. "Shuteye and Jet, lead the way back to the main part of the building." The beating of the helicopters grew louder. "Quickly!"

Master Chief hoped that seeing the uniforms would give pause to any soldiers they came across; however, he also realized 'hope' wasn't a very good operational strategy. At least all of the Americans in the building now had weapons.

The Americans reached the corner prior to the front door, and Sergeant Chang and Private Li walked out as if they belonged there. All 20 or so Chinese soldiers in the Fitness Center could be seen over the shoulders of the two guards manning the door. Their heads were turned to look out the floor-to-ceiling glass wall that faced the intramural soccer fields as the two giant helicopters flew in, flared and landed.

Chang and Li motioned, and Master Chief led the rest of the men around the corner as two missiles streaked upward toward the circling helicopters. Two of the helicopters exploded and plummeted out of control. The Chinese soldiers shouted in shock and disbelief, and went running to grab their weapons. Returning to the window, they looked for a shot at whoever brought down the helicopters. They never saw the Americans form up behind them in a firing line.

Master Chief counted in a whisper, "1...2...3...Now!" Eight rifles roared, and five launchers threw grenades into the concentration of men by the wall, blowing out the glass and throwing several of the Chinese soldiers out the window. They fell 15 feet onto the pavement below, out of the fight. The two door guards started to turn, but were cut down in a hail of bullets as the firing line refocused on them.

It was a one-sided massacre, until one of the guards from outside the building fired an extended burst on full auto, hitting several of the Rangers. The Americans returned fire at the two guards, killing them in a spray of blood. It was too late for Staff Sergeant Kowalski, who was dead, and Private First Class Justin Richardson, who had been shot in his right shoulder.

"Medic!" Richardson moaned as he tried to stop the flow of blood coming from his shattered shoulder. One of the Rangers went to assist him.

"All right, guys," Master Chief said. "We've got to find the nukes, and we've got to find them now! We need to hurry; the Chinese know we're here, and they probably won't fall for the navy uniforms again."

Master Chief split his men into two search parties to investigate the corridors that led from the Fitness Center. "Look for ways to get downstairs," he ordered. "They had to bring them in by pallet and probably didn't bring them up the stairs." He looked at the men. "We've got to hurry. The Chinese will be here soon!"

Outside the IAB, University of Washington, Seattle, WA, 1055 PDT

Calvin watched as two of the attack helicopters were hit and went spinning out of control. Faster than he would have believed possible, the closest attack helicopter spun toward the baseball field and began shredding the trees and aluminum stands with 25mm shells. A piece of shrapnel hit the missileer, Corporal Matthew Evans, ripping through his left bicep as he hid under the stands. He screamed in agony as it shattered his humerus, and he clasped his right hand over the wound to staunch the flow of blood. As the helicopter's gunner walked the gun back across the stands, he was hit by another round, killing him where he lay.

The other attack helicopter spun toward where the second missile had launched, but he couldn't find the source of the attack. The pilot brought the aircraft to a hover, and his gunner scanned the area with his infrared scope, trying to find the missileer before he could launch again. Forgetting that 'speed is life' in combat, the attack helicopter pilot brought his aircraft to a standstill, and the gunner began to fire the cannon intermittently at the trees, hoping to flush out the missileer.

"Got him?" Private First Class Jamal 'Bad Twin' Gordon asked as he slid the round into the Ranger Anti-Tank Weapon System (RAWS).

"Yeah, I got him," Corporal Austin 'Good Twin' Gordon replied, looking down the barrel of the 84mm shoulder-fired anti-tank system. "It's only 50 meters. Even you could hit him from here."

"Well, you better make it count, dude," Bad Twin replied. "Master Chief only had four rounds and there's still four helos left."

"Yeah, the next time we go up to his cabin, we need to take more rounds," Good Twin said. "Like, what's the purpose of an anti-tank rifle if you don't have any rounds to shoot with it?"

"Loaded," Bad Twin said, closing the rear of the weapon.

"Ready to fire," Good Twin advised.

Bad Twin moved to the side and checked behind them. "Back blast area clear."

"Firing!"

With a kick that felt like a full-body punch, the 84mm rifle fired, and the dual-purpose, armor-piercing round struck the side of the attack helicopter, penetrated and exploded, killing both the pilot and the gunner instantly. Out of control and on fire, the helicopter crashed to the ground.

As the third attack helo plummeted from the skies, the transport helicopter pilots were struggling to get their aircraft back into the air and away from the killing ground. The helo motors shrieked as their pilots slammed the throttles to full power.

"Now!" Calvin urged silently as the six-bladed rotors began to find purchase, and the helicopters slowly lifted off the ground. Right on time, the aircraft were engaged by the rest of the platoon and bullets slammed into the helicopters at the rate of over 80 a second. The soldiers in the back of the helicopters tried to provide covering fire, but couldn't see the hidden Americans.

Wounded or dead, all four of the helicopter pilots were quickly put out of action, and the helicopters crashed back down to the ground, spilling Chinese soldiers out both sides. Several of the soldiers tried to get up and charge the trees where the Americans were hiding, but a barrage of rifle and grenade fire killed or wounded all of them.

The last attack helicopter had finished destroying the baseball stadium's bleachers and returned to the main part of the field to look for new targets. Seeing the rapid muzzle flashes from one of the M240 machine guns, the pilot turned his helicopter to engage it. The maneuver pointed it in the direction of Conibear Shellhouse, where the sniper team was waiting.

"Target!" Private First Class Mike 'BTO' Bachmann called. "Twelve o'clock, above the flag in the center of the field. Single gray helicopter."

"Roger," Private First Class Steve 'Tiny' Johnson replied as he looked through the scope of his .50 caliber Barrett sniper rifle. "Twelve o'clock, above the flag in the center of the field. Single gray helicopter. Target identified."

"Target is pilot in the aft cockpit," BTO said. "Correction, Chinese helo. The target is the pilot in the *front* cockpit."

"Target is the pilot in the front cockpit," Tiny confirmed.

"Wind from three o'clock, six mph," BTO said, giving him the windage correction. "Dial wind right, one point three mils."

"Roger, wind from three o'clock, six mph," Tiny repeated. "One point three mils. Indexed!"

"Send it!"

"Splash!"

BTO could see the air disruption of the bullet's passage through his scope, and he watched as the round went through the front cockpit glass and the pilot's visor. The pilot's head snapped back and the helicopter wallowed, uncontrolled, while the gunner switched from controlling his weapons system to using his auxiliary set of flight controls.

"Target!" BTO said. "Gunner in aft cockpit. Elevation and wind good."

"Target is the gunner in the aft cockpit," Tiny repeated. "Holding elevation and wind."

"Send it!"

"Splash!"

The gunner had recovered the helicopter and just decided to leave when the .50 caliber bullet hit him in the chest. Having already been deformed by hitting the canopy, the bullet nearly tore him in half. Unmanned, the attack helicopter crashed into the baseball stadium's press box and exploded.

The field was quiet, except for the screams of the wounded Chinese soldiers in the middle of the field, and the popping of exploding ammunition from one of the burning attack helos.

"Quickly!" Calvin said. "Weapons squad, take care of the dead and wounded; everyone else go to the IAB to help with the bombs.

With all the destruction and smoke, someone is sure to notice. We've got to get the weapons and get out of here ASAP!"

He spared a couple of seconds to look out at the battlefield and shook his head. The fight had only taken a few minutes, but it would be a long time before any college students played soccer on the field again. He ran to get the sniper team; he had a new task for them.

Inside the IAB, University of Washington, Seattle, WA, 1105 PDT

"Fuck!" Master Chief said, unconsciously ducking as a bullet hit the wall next to his head. "I think we finally found them." He looked down the long hallway that ended in a door. A Chinese rifle poked through one of the holes in the door to spray bullets down the corridor, and he dove back into the cross-passage.

"I'm hit!" Private First Class Nick Borneo said, trying to put pressure on the hole that had just appeared in his thigh.

Master Chief could see the bullet had missed the bone, but Borneo wasn't going to be running any marathons in the near future. Or walking unassisted very well, either.

"Fuck," Master Chief said again. He was down to four combat effectives, including himself, and he didn't have time for this shit. "Everyone get back," he ordered, motioning them to go further down the corridor.

The troopers pulled back further, with Corporal Beck helping PFC Borneo, and Master Chief grabbed two grenades, pulled their pins and lobbed them down the corridor toward the door.

The first grenade hit the door and bounced back a couple of feet. The door opened a crack, and a shout of surprise was heard from inside the room. The door opened a little further and a hand extended as the second grenade bounced off the door. The soldier froze, momentarily stunned at the shock of seeing a second grenade appear. Master Chief dove back around the corner as the first grenade detonated, with a second explosion immediately following the first.

"Let's go!" Master Chief yelled as he charged down the hallway. The door had been blown off the hinges, and he ran through the doorway to find himself in a room with a large swimming pool. The soldier who had opened the door had caught the majority of both blasts and been blown into the pool; what was left wasn't pretty and stained the water red.

Seeing the remains of his comrade and stunned by the blasts, the second Chinese soldier in the room put up his hands and surrendered as Master Chief entered.

Six large crates sat next to a set of double doors that appeared to go outside, their exteriors marred by shrapnel from the grenades. Holy shit, Master Chief thought as he examined the boxes. Thankfully, they had been far enough away from the explosions that they didn't *appear* damaged, he realized things could easily have gone horribly wrong. Next time, consider the circumstances and *don't fucking rush where nukes are involved!*

The rest of his group arrived in the room, and he had them secure the prisoner and check the other doors that led into unexplored portions of the IAB. Top's group entered through one.

"Glad you could make it," Master Chief said as Top approached. "What kept you?"

"Thanks," Top replied. "We ran into a squad of Chinese soldiers not too far from here, and it took a few minutes to get past them."

"They must have come from here," Master Chief said. "There were only two soldiers guarding the nukes when we found them. How many men do you have left?"

"Three," Top replied, "including me. We lost one killed and another critically injured during our firefight with the Chinese. He needs a hospital immediately."

"Well let's get these damn things loaded and get the hell out of here," Master Chief said. He directed the men to load the crates onto the wheeled pallets nearby and take them to the double doors that led outside.

"Hey, Master Chief," called Corporal Beck, who had been watching the doors. "It sounds like something's coming...something big and loud."

"Get away from the door and into cover," Master Chief ordered. Taking his own advice he hid behind the crate he had been pushing, then realized he was hiding behind a nuclear weapon. He looked around and shrugged; there was no other cover in the room besides the boxes. Hiding behind the weapon was practical...but it didn't make him feel any better.

"Hey," said Corporal Beck, "that sounds like another one of those Chinese LCAC things."

"There could be troops on this one," Master Chief said. He had already done a check of the men and knew they were all running low on supplies; his armory had only held so much. "Watch your shots and conserve your ammo," he said. "Army resupply is running a little slow today!"

Judging by the noise, the LCAC pulled right up to the door and shut down there. After a few seconds, there was a knock on the door in the classic 'shave and a haircut' rhythm. Master Chief tapped out the 'two bits' and opened the door to find Calvin standing in front of the captured LCAC.

"It's amazing how helpful people will be if you stick a .50 caliber rifle in their face," Calvin explained. "I had PFC Johnson point the sniper rifle at the LCAC craftmaster, and he decided that he really, *really*, wanted to drive us wherever we wanted to go. Of course, he wet himself, too, but at least he did that outside of the LCAC."

"Out-*standing*, sir!" Master Chief said. "Give us a minute to get these loaded. I know just the place to go."

Master Chief detailed some of the Rangers to load the weapons onto the LCAC and sent the rest to get the SUVs they had driven to the university. They would need the vehicles for transportation once they were done with the LCAC and to take the wounded to a hospital.

"Hey LT," Master Chief said as he finished, "could you get your driver to fire this pig up so we can get going? I've got a feeling that it's going to get ugly here really soon, and we need to be *gone!*"

Calvin looked over to Shuteye, who had been assigned to guard the craftmaster, "Time to go, Sergeant!" Calvin said.

"Yes, sir!" Shuteye agreed, turning to the driver. The LCAC was quickly on its way.

* * * * *

CHAPTER TWO

Afternoon,
August 20

White House Situation Room, Washington, D.C., 1500 EDT
(1200 PDT)

"They lost three Rangers and had several more wounded, but LT Hobbs and his men were able to recover the nukes," the CNO said to the president.

"Thank God!" the president said with a sigh.

"Amen!" the Army Chief of Staff agreed.

"You're never going to believe where they took them, either," the CNO said.

"You can tell me all about it later," the president said. "First, let's talk about how we're going to get our cities back."

"Yes, sir," the CNO said. "My staff has already drawn up some options. First, though, there are some things that still need to be done..."

61

Boeing Airplane Programs Manufacturing Site, Renton, WA, 1205 PDT

"This place is HUGE!" Calvin said, looking around Boeing's Airplane Programs Manufacturing Site. Located in Renton, WA, the plant was adjacent to Lake Washington, just to the southeast of Seattle. One of the plant's earlier products was a seaplane, and Master Chief knew the plant had a ramp that led down to the lake for seaplane launch and recovery. A quick 8-minute ride at 50 knots was all it took to get the LCAC from the University of Washington to shelter, and the ramp provided easy access to drive it up and into the hangar where it wouldn't be seen by the Chinese. If needed, they could get a navy LCAC driver to come and move it into one of the smaller buildings once it was dark. They didn't *think* they had been seen by the Chinese...but it never hurt to be sure.

"Yes sir," Andrew Brown, the plant's manager, said. "The hangar has over 4.3 million square feet of building space and was the birthplace for some of commercial aviation's most well-known airplanes. Most of the facility is currently dedicated to building our Next Generation 737 airplanes, including the 737-700C convertible freighter, the Boeing Business Jet, and the latest member of the 737 family, the Navy's new P-8A Poseidon multi-mission maritime aircraft." Calvin could see one of the planes nearby painted with all of the standard U.S. Navy markings.

The Navy's newest ship, a *Yuyi*-class LCAC, was parked behind it, somewhat hidden between the plane and the wall. The platoon had renamed it the USS *Ranger* in honor of Staff Sergeant Kowalski,

Corporal Matthew Evans, and Private First Class Steven Shad who had been killed in their recent operations against the Chinese.

"Thanks for letting us store our boat here for a while," Calvin said. "Of course, you never saw us, and we were never here." Calvin didn't mention the six boxes sitting on the concrete floor next to the LCAC. He hoped the plant manager would assume the 10 armed Rangers standing in the vicinity of the LCAC were there to guard the captured boat, even if the Rangers knew otherwise. Only having 10 men left them dangerously unprotected, but that's all the Ranger unit had been able to come up with.

There was a quiet 'beep,' and Calvin pulled Master Chief's phone out of his pocket. He read the incoming text and turned the phone back off again. Looking back at the perspiring man in the suit in front of him, Calvin said, "The president says to give everyone the day off with pay. Before you let them leave, though, make sure everyone knows their lives depend on NOT knowing this vessel is sitting here."

"I believe it," Mr. Brown said, glancing around to make sure no one was close by, "especially since all of the writing on it is in Chinese." He paused. "Wait," he said, "did you say the president? Of the United States?"

"Yeah," Calvin agreed, "that president. He'd like it very much if the word didn't get around that this boat was sitting here. I'd prefer it didn't either." The manager nodded his agreement and Calvin turned and walked over to where the Rangers' executive officer (XO) stood waiting for him.

The XO, First Lieutenant Odysseus Bollinger, had met them at the plant with the additional soldiers after Top had reported they needed a guard detachment for the prisoners they had taken. The

Americans couldn't release their prisoners because the Chinese soldiers knew the United States had recovered the nuclear weapons, how they had escaped and where they had gone. All the Chinese leadership would be able to determine now was that there had been a big fight at the university, all their helicopters had been destroyed and the weapons were gone. They'd also know one of their LCACs had gone missing, but they wouldn't know if that was related. They might *think* it had been destroyed, but they wouldn't know.

"You did a great job so far," the Rangers' XO said. "I have to tell you, I thought this whole idea was lunacy, but you pulled it off. Are you planning on something for an encore, or can I have my troopers back now?"

"Actually, I have another task from the Joint Chiefs of Staff I need them for," Calvin said. "I'm pretty sure I'll be able to return them to you tomorrow, though, if that's okay."

"I don't think it really matters whether it's okay with me or not," the XO semi-growled, "since the Chief of Staff has already told us to shut up and do it anyway." A touch of a smile flashed across his face. "That being said, you guys have done pretty well so far. I'd just ask that you try to bring my men and woman back in one piece."

"I know," Calvin said, already feeling responsible for the deaths of three Rangers and the wounding of another three. "I'm terribly sorry about getting your men killed. The Chinese attack was so sudden, and we didn't have prepared sites to shoot from..." His voice trailed off, and the XO could tell Calvin felt the loss of the soldiers on a deep personal basis.

"I know, sir," said the XO. "Losing men under your command is never easy. Just make sure you do your best by them and make their sacrifice worthwhile. In this case, it certainly was, as you were able to complete the mission and recover the weapons. You also destroyed a whole lot of equipment the Chinese won't be able to replace very easily."

"For what it's worth," the XO added after a pause, "Top was very impressed with your courage under fire and ability to adapt the plan to the changing situation. For your first time in combat, real combat on the ground with people trying to kill you, you did very well. Top even said you'd make a good Ranger, once we got you into shape."

Calvin chuckled, his mood lightening a little. "Yeah, I know. I intend to start getting into the gym more once this is over."

The XO smiled. "Well let me know," he said. "I still have the Chief of Staff's personal number from when he called me earlier; maybe something can be arranged." He turned serious again as he started to walk back to the rest of the group. "Is there anything I can do for you before I take these prisoners somewhere a little safer?"

"Well, XO," Calvin replied, "you wouldn't happen to have a bunch of ammo you're not using just sitting around, would you?" Handing off the Chinese prisoners had solved one of their problems, but it did nothing to help with the ammunition situation. They still had tasks they needed to complete, but without additional supplies their weapons were useless. Master Chief's armory was no longer an option, either; the initial attack had depleted most of its stores.

"The only place I know with a big store of ammunition is the armory on base," said the XO, "but the Chinese are holding it pretty tightly. I know it was heavily guarded last night when we looked."

"Yeah, that's what I was afraid of," Calvin said. "We may need to borrow the rest of the unit in order to get onto base and break into the armory."

"Well, that can certainly be done," the XO said. "That would pretty much fall right into our line of work. Rangers lead the way!" the XO added in a loud voice, quoting the Ranger motto.

"Hoo-ah!" all of the Rangers within earshot shouted. Calvin realized the XO had probably said it for their benefit, just to get them pumped up. They may not like their CO, thought Calvin, but they like their XO. He was a leader who men would willingly follow into battle.

"Before you go and do that, sirs, how about we just go to The Marksman?" Private Li asked.

"The marksman?" Calvin and the XO asked.

"We already have enough shooters," Calvin added. "We need ammo."

"Not, the marksman," Jet said, "but 'The Marksman,' with capital letters. It's a store just to the east of Fort Lewis in Tacoma." There was a collective, "Oh, yeah," from the majority of the Rangers, who obviously knew what he was talking about. "The Marksman is a giant gun store," Jet continued. "It's got everything you need to shoot. It services military customers, the reserves, the National Guard, the police...just about everyone. It's got a big shooting range, tons of rifles, shotguns and pistols, and, more importantly, *tons and tons* of ammo. They even have ammo to fit most of our rifles and machineguns, although they don't carry grenades. Their motto is, 'Where Professionals Train,' or something like that. They may not be able to supply us for World War III, but they might get us through the day."

"Yeah," said the usually withdrawn Tiny, "I go there a lot. They won't have any fifty caliber ammo for me, but I didn't use a whole lot at the university, so I'm still set. About the only rifle ammo they won't be able to get us is the machine gun stuff, because it's belt fed, and all they have are individual bullets in boxes."

"Okay," said Calvin, coming to a quick decision, "here's what we're going to do. All of the Rangers will go to The Marksman and clean them out." He looked at First Sergeant Smith, "Top, I don't care what you have to promise, but I want you to get everything they have. Tell them we'll make good on it once this is over...have them run a tab for us or something. You never know; we may be back. They've probably got contacts and suppliers they can reach out to, too. Have them bring in everything they possibly can."

First Sergeant Smith nodded and said, "I know the owner somewhat. I don't think it'll be a problem. He'd probably *give* us the ammo if it meant kicking Chinese ass; for an IOU, he'll probably put bows on it as well." He smiled. "Does this go on the Navy's tab or the Army's?"

"Having talked to the CNO today, I feel pretty confident I have carte blanche from the Navy's budget," Calvin said. "Put it on my tab."

The Ranger XO was impressed with Calvin's ability to make decisions when they were needed. He could see why the Master Chief had recommended he lead the joint special operations force instead of the Rangers' CO (who *was,* he had to admit, a pain in the ass.)

"All right, the Rangers will go get the ammo and anything else we need from the store," said Calvin, "and Master Chief and I will head back to his cabin." He had already talked to the Master Chief and knew that Master Chief wanted some more explosives. "The command team will meet up after that back at the Sommers' house."

He hated using their house as a rallying point, because he didn't want to draw attention to them, but it was convenient to their next mission, and the Rangers knew where it was.

"Okay," said Calvin, looking around to make sure everyone was in agreement. "Let's get it done!"

Main Street Grill, Ames, IA, 1230 PDT

"Take that, you motherfuckers!" David Anderson shouted.

"Excuse me?" the waitress walking by asked.

"Oh, I'm sorry," Anderson said, in a much more normal tone of voice. He blushed. "I was playing a war game and got a little wrapped up in it."

"I understand," the waitress said, shaking her head. A lot of college students came by the restaurant to use the free wi-fi, and they played a variety of online games. They didn't buy much, and they tipped even less, but at least they usually had good manners. Usually. She looked at his empty glass. "Can I get you something else?"

"No, thank you," the young man said. "Just the check please."

When the young man had come in, his eyes had been red and watery, and he looked like he had been crying. Over the last hour, he had appeared to go from sad to angry as he worked on some program on his laptop. All he had ordered during that time was one diet cola. With two free refills. The waitress left the check and sighed as she walked off. He probably wouldn't tip her for it, either.

As the waitress left, David Anderson looked back at his laptop screen. A graduate student in the computer science department at Iowa State University, he had been studying computer network defense for several years. Today, he had used every last bit of that knowledge, plus some tricks a few of his hacker friends had taught him, to go on the offensive.

He wasn't a destructive person by nature. In fact, everyone always told him his biggest flaw was he was 'too nice.' Whatever that meant.

But not today.

Today he was an only child. Yesterday, he had a younger sister, who was in the hospital in his home town of Algona, Iowa. She had been on life support, having survived a car crash two days before. The doctors had saved her life, but just barely, and she had only been hanging on by the slimmest of margins.

Then the Chinese cut the power throughout the United States.

Of course, the hospital had an emergency generator that should have come on to provide power to patients on life support. Unfortunately, the last time it was tested, someone had failed to turn it back off, and it had continued to run until it exhausted its fuel supply. When the power failed the day before, there was a period of 30 minutes where the hospital was without power while the staff diagnosed the problem, and then someone went to get gas for the generator. During that time, his sister died.

They wanted to attack without warning? He would do the same.

He smiled at his handiwork. He had just taken control of the Xiaolangdi Dam, the biggest dam on the Yellow River, and had locked open all of its spillways. He had read somewhere that there were millions of people that lived along the banks of the Yellow River. He hoped they could swim. "No," he thought with a scowl as he closed his laptop and went to pay his bill. "I hope they *can't* swim."

He was so distracted, he didn't leave a tip.

PLAN LHD *Long*, Pier D, Naval Base Kitsap, WA, 1245 PDT

"Where are my nuclear weapons?" Admiral Zhao Na, the Chinese fleet commander, roared. "How did this happen?" He looked around the conference table of his briefing room onboard the PLAN *Long*.

"That is unknown," Lieutenant Commander Lin Gang said. "When our helicopters got to the university grounds, the helicopters we sent previously were all on the ground burning. All of the army guards had either been killed or had disappeared, and the nuclear warheads were gone. The marines couldn't find any indications of how they had been removed. All they could determine was there had been a big battle, our side had lost and some unknown group had taken possession of the nuclear weapons."

"Apparently, there is an armed group within our perimeter," the admiral said. "Advise Colonel Zhang Wei of this fact and see what the ground force commander's plan is to hunt them down and destroy them."

Admiral Zhao looked at Captain Chan Ming, the Commanding Officer of the *Long*. "Make sure we raise the alert level for the marines ashore," he added. "If there are enough armed Americans running around to destroy six helicopters and a platoon of soldiers, our marines need to be on guard."

"Yes, sir," Captain Chan said. "It will be done."

Admiral Zhao looked back to Lieutenant Commander Lin. "Since the army has so carelessly lost our nuclear weapons, we will need more. Put together an assault package to go and retrieve another six from the storage facility."

Lieutenant Commander Lin nodded. "Aye aye, sir."

Cyberspace, 1300 PDT

The cyber war waged on, unknown and unseen by most, except where it spilled into people's everyday lives. The electricity went out, came back on and then went out again. The internet and phone service were similarly up and down, as were many other commercial and governmental services. Most civilians never knew why these things happened; they just assumed a line was down or something else of a transitory nature had happened. They expected the systems would be operational again shortly...like they always had before.

Hackers as a group are generally proud and somewhat egotistical, though, and the ones in both the United States and its allies did not take well to Chinese hackers taking down their power grids and internet sites. No one told them not to, so they fought back, and warfare was no longer just the province of uniformed soldiers.

Hackers both in and out of uniform fought across cyberspace. The allied hackers made inroads into Chinese society, turning off *their* power grids and opening up their dam spillways, flooding the Chinese countryside.

Chinese civilian hackers also joined the fray. A country with over a billion people, China had as many honor students as the U.S. had students. It also had many excellent hackers who had been operating under quasi-governmental approval for a long time, and it wasn't long before systems were failing planet-wide. No society was safe from the battles in cyberspace. People living in the wilds of Alaska or the jungles of the Amazon might not have noticed the cyber war, but it touched everyone else's lives.

Banks and stock markets world-wide took down their own sites, rather than lose them to hackers. Before they could do so, several servers were completely wiped and had to be rebuilt from back-ups.

No one will ever know how many people were killed in the man-made disasters of March 20; the intentional flooding of the Yellow River alone killed tens of thousands of indigent people living along its banks. When the devastation was made known, it was so horrific that the person or people responsible never took the credit (or blame, for they would likely have been tried for war crimes) for the attack. Never again would society be 'safe' from the perils of war.

Snoqualmie National Forest, WA, 1300 PDT

Calvin and Master Chief had borrowed one of the Ranger's cars to make the trip out to Master Chief's cabin to get more explosives. In addition to rifle ammunition, Master Chief's armory had been depleted of both hand grenades and grenades for the M203 grenade launchers, but there was still a large supply of C4 explosive and the equipment necessary to detonate it. Master Chief thought they would need it to give the missile launchers a little more 'permanent' damage. As Master Chief was the expert on 'killing people and breaking things,' Calvin chose to defer to his assessment and went with him to get the explosives.

The drive to the cabin was uneventful. They took the back roads they had used earlier in the morning and returned to where Master Chief always left his jeep (before it was destroyed), then they walked into the woods to his cabin. Although it was only a mile and a half journey, they had to cross a number of hills, which made it take longer.

Master Chief stopped as the cabin came into sight. The note he'd left on the door was gone. The windows were open, and he could hear the sounds of voices. The voices were calm and relaxed, though, and they were speaking English. After a moment, he began walking again. As they approached the cabin, Calvin grabbed his arm. In a whisper, he said, "The note's gone from the door."

Master Chief laughed. "Yeah, and if they wanted us dead, they'd have shot us when we cleared the tree line. They're watching us through the windows right now." He laughed again. "Nice situational awareness."

"Sor-ry!" Calvin said. "I was thinking big thoughts. I count on you for the tactical stuff."

The door opened, and six men came out. "Hey, Senior Chief! What's going on? Where the hell have you been? Bad guys have taken Seattle and Tacoma. Go do that SEAL shit and take it back for us, would ya?" Their camaraderie and esprit de corps were welcome after what had already been a long and eventful day.

Master Chief introduced Calvin to his friends from the 160th SOAR, and he filled them in on the day's activities. The aviators weren't able to add much intel; they hadn't been able to get onto the base or discover anything else the navy men didn't already know. They were, however, excited to hear about Master Chief's promotion and looked forward to the ceremony formalizing his new rank. They expected Master Chief to throw a party and, with five years of back pay to support it, they expected it to be epic.

Although they joked with Master Chief, it was also evident they were frustrated. The army aviators had to watch as the war for their country continued; they wanted to get into the fight. Just like Calvin, though, they were hampered by a distinct lack of aircraft.

That was about to change. "I spoke with the CNO on the way here," Calvin said, giving them the good news, "and he asked what help we could use. I told him that it would be really convenient to have about a squadron of helicopters and a couple of divisions of soldiers. He said he had talked with the Chiefs of Staff of the Army and Air Force and, although it's going to take a little while to get the men in place, the Chief of Staff of the Army said that he was hoping to have six Blackhawks and six Little Bird helicopters here by late this afternoon."

"How the hell is he going to do that?" asked one of the pilots. "They're going to have to fly cross country from Fort Campbell, Kentucky. That won't happen quickly; with that many helos in the group, just the refueling stops alone will kill the crew day."

"You may be surprised," Calvin replied. "He's got several KC-130 tankers that are going to lead them here, so they won't have to stop. They will stay low behind the mountains as they approach and will top off their fuel just before they arrive. They're going to land at Lower Garfield Mountain Lake, just down the mountain from here. The pilots will be spent by the time they get here, and they don't know the mountains like you do, so they will just be ferrying the helos here for your use. They'll be fully loaded on arrival and ready to go. Think you can find another 18 pilots to man them?"

Calvin was unprepared for the overwhelmingly affirmative response. The aviators *really* wanted into the game. "Good. If things go the way I think they're going to go, we'll need them tonight or tomorrow at the latest."

While the aviators tried to track down more assistance using the satellite phone in Master Chief's cabin, Calvin and Master Chief organized the supplies they needed, said some quick good-byes and were on their way.

The walk back to the car was uneventful...until they reached the final hill. Looking down from the crest of the hill, they could see a squad of Chinese soldiers. Three of the men were looking at the car they had driven.

"Well, this is going to complicate things," Master Chief said.

"Yeah," Calvin agreed; "no shit."

Master Chief and Calvin put their gear down and slithered forward so they could watch the Chinese soldiers without being seen. "Damn," Master Chief said, "I think they've found our footprints." The two men looking at the footprints signaled to the others, who came over to where they were.

"That's going to complicate things, too, right?" Calvin asked.

"Yeah," Master Chief agreed. "I would have hidden the car better if I'd have known they were going to come up this far. I didn't think we were going to be here long and cut some corners so we could get back faster. Looks like we're going to pay for it now."

The Chinese soldiers seemed to be massing as they looked up the hill toward where the men were hiding. Master Chief unslung the rifle from his back and took the covers off his scope. "I'm going to see about evening up the odds," he said. He slid forward on his stomach and pointed the rifle downhill. He paused, looking through the scope. Calvin watched, holding his breath, as Master Chief stopped moving. Master Chief's finger slowly pulled the trigger, and then 'blam.' Master Chief fired twice more in quick succession, and then he jumped backward with a curse as the sounds of return fire came from the other side of the hill. "Damn, that kid is good," he said. Calvin could see blood starting to well up on Master Chief's cheek.

"You're hit!" Calvin exclaimed.

"Yeah, I think a piece of rock or a fragment of the bullet hitting the rock in front of me got me," the SEAL said. "If this had been the bullet, I'd be dead." He wiped off the blood. "I think I got their lieutenant and their platoon sergeant, but then their sniper almost got me."

"You shot their lieutenant?" Calvin asked.

"Well, I shot the one I *thought* was their officer, anyway," Master Chief said. "The way he was gesturing, they were organizing for a patrol, probably to come look for us. All things considered, I'd rather not have them looking for my cabin. The odds of them actually finding it are pretty small, unless they have some world-class trackers, but I figured it was easier to distract them than to count on it." He grinned. "Besides, I have a problem with officers and authority, remember?"

"I'm trying to keep that in mind," Calvin returned.

Master Chief moved a few feet over and then took a quick look over the hill. Rifle fire greeted him. "C'mon, we gotta go," he said. "What's left of a squad of really angry soldiers is coming this way, and I think it's time we should be leaving."

"Okay," said Calvin, bowing to Master Chief's experience, "what do you want me to do?"

Master Chief pointed to the left. "You go that way. Go about 100 steps and then kick a branch and say "shit" or something. Then run like hell for five minutes. I'll hunt them down from behind. Go!"

Calvin went down the back side of the hill to the left, counting as he went, while Master Chief went around to the right. Calvin got to "100," and he looked back in time to see the first Chinese soldier come over the hill. Realizing nothing needed to be said as their eyes met, Calvin jumped like a surprised deer and took off running into the woods. The soldier fired once, missing him by inches. Calvin heard the bullet smack into a tree next to him, and he tried to run faster. Risking a glance back, Calvin saw several other members of the squad in pursuit.

Master Chief waited until the soldiers were all chasing after Calvin and then fired, hitting the last man in the shoulder. He went down hard, slamming face-first into a tree. Most of the others dove to one side or the other. One man continued straight after Calvin; the next bullet hit him in the spine, dropping him like a marionette with its strings cut.

The squad was down to six, but Master Chief saw the flaw in his plan as the squad split; two men continued to pursue Calvin while the other four took cover and began returning fire. Calvin would be forced to face two of the soldiers by himself. Master Chief knew Calvin was screwed. He didn't have time to dwell on it, though, as three round bursts began striking the trees near him, far too close for his liking. Using a large tree for cover, he ran straight away from the soldiers, slapping in a new magazine as he went. When he was out of sight, he crossed over the crest and circled around behind them, hoping to catch the Chinese in the flank.

Master Chief slowed down so that he could move more stealthily and catch his breath. Despite being in excellent physical shape, most of his normal exercise was anaerobic, like chopping wood, and he found himself panting heavily.

Fuck, he thought. Maybe the navy was right and I am getting too old for this shit. He shook his head. No I'm not, and the damn Chinese aren't going to get Calvin after I used him as bait, either. Not if Mrs. O'Leary's boy has anything to say about it.

A burst of adrenaline hit, and he was ready to go again. Deeming he had passed the soldiers' location, he crawled on his stomach up to the crest of the hill. He could see two of the soldiers walking away from him. The furthest of the two looked to his right and said something; there must be a third one over there, Master Chief thought. Hopefully, the fourth one was even further in that direction. Quietly, the SEAL took aim at the soldier on the left. The soldier stopped, scanning the woods. Master Chief put the crosshairs on his heart and fired. He was close enough that there was no drop in the bullet's flight; the Chinese soldier slumped, already dead. Master Chief quickly adjusted his aim to the right.

The second soldier hadn't heard where the shot came from. He tried using a tree for cover, but his silhouette was still visible. Master Chief shot him in the head, and the Chinese soldier fell to the ground.

Switching his aim again, Master Chief saw a flash of movement but couldn't find the third soldier through the scope. Finally, the SEAL saw the Chinese soldier's leg sticking out from behind a tree. Aiming at the shin, Master Chief fired, striking the bone and shattering it. The soldier fell to the ground, screaming. Master Chief looked for a killing shot on the trooper, but heard a small 'snap' behind him just as he was about to fire. Forgetting the shot instantly, he pushed himself off the ground and dove to the right.

The Chinese soldier sneaking up on him saw him move and fired, and Master Chief's side felt like it had been lit on fire as the bullet grazed his ribs. Master Chief dove to the right a second time as the soldier fired again, this time missing. Master Chief turned the dive into a roll and came up into a crouch behind a large tree. He faked as if he were going to continue out from behind the tree to the right, and the Chinese soldier fired again on auto, emptying his magazine into the air.

Master Chief popped back out to the left side of the tree with his knife held high in his right hand and threw it with all his might. Unprepared for the sudden attack, the Chinese soldier watched as the knife spun toward him, and time slowed down for him. The knife completed its final spin and buried itself in his chest. He sank to the ground, his life draining out of him.

Master Chief kicked the rifle away from the soldier and saw it was the Chinese sniper. The kid had been good, but not quite good enough. Master Chief's side burned. The sniper may not have been *quite* good enough, but it had been way too close for his comfort. He shrugged and checked his side; he'd had worse. Master Chief wiped off his knife, picked up his gear and went in search of Calvin.

Calvin was in trouble. Not in the best shape to start with, he was spent and couldn't run any further. He used the last of his reserves to make it up a small hill. A bullet whined past his ear as he crested the hill, and he threw himself down on the other side. Breathing heavily, he spun around and looked back over the hill, just in time to see the Chinese soldier coming after him start climbing up the hill. Aiming hastily, he fired, and the Chinese soldier went down. Calvin reveled at his shot until the soldier jumped back up and threw himself behind a large rock, apparently unharmed. Calvin watched through his scope, looking for a shot. He saw a flash here, then a flash there, but the soldier didn't show himself enough for Calvin to get a shot. Sliding back until he was out of sight, Calvin rose in a crouch and ran about 100 feet along the crest, before sliding back up to the top of the hill. He looked through the scope and saw he had moved far enough; he now had a view of the unsuspecting soldier behind the rock.

Calvin put the crosshairs on the soldier's head. As he started to pull the trigger, he paused. He had never killed anyone before. Even earlier, when he had shot at the Chinese, they had been shooting back at him. That seemed like combat; this seemed like murder. He thought about his friends in the air wing being shot down by the Chinese without warning; this was no different. But this was war...and at least *this* soldier knew he was in combat.

One of us has to die, thought Calvin; no, one of us *will* die. Better him than me. Sighing slightly, he fired. Not a combat soldier, he hadn't allowed for the drop of the bullet. Instead of hitting the soldier in the head, it hit him in the chest. The round expanded when it hit him, ripping out half a lung as it exited his body. He fell to the ground, coughing weakly as he died; Calvin had killed him.

Calvin felt like he wanted to vomit and rolled onto his back, his eyes shut tight. As he opened them again, he looked up to see a Chinese assault rifle pointing into his face from about six inches away. The opening in the barrel was cavernous, far larger than anything he had ever seen in his life.

Looking up past the rifle, Calvin saw the soldier's face. He looked angrier than anyone Calvin could ever remember seeing in his life, even Calvin's father the time Calvin had borrowed his sports car without asking and totaled it. This guy was madder. Calvin couldn't know it, but Calvin had just killed the soldier's best friend. The soldier's thoughts warred within him; his orders were to capture if possible, not kill. Colonel Zhang had said they needed info on the group operating behind the lines, but the American had just killed his best friend, and no one would ever know...

He decided to kill the American, and his finger began to tighten on the trigger. Calvin could see the decision in the soldier's eyes and knew he was dead. He wanted to pray, but nothing came to him except, "Help me, Lord."

Calvin started to close his eyes, but then saw the soldier's head explode as a bullet hit the Chinese soldier between the eyes. The soldier's finger spasmed on the trigger, and the gun fired. Calvin jumped as the bullet buried itself in the ground, an inch to the left of his head.

After a pause, Calvin started to breathe again and watched as the soldier's body toppled over. He laid there panting as Master Chief jogged up.

"Are you hurt, sir?" Master Chief asked.

"No, I'm not," Calvin groaned. "Thanks to you. Another second or two later, though, and I'd have been dead." He looked at the blood stain on Master Chief's side. "Oh, shit! You've been hit!"

"That?" Master Chief asked, looking down at his side. "That's only a flesh wound. Now, if you're all done resting, sir, we really have other things we ought to be doing than just lying around." He helped Calvin up.

"Yes we do, Master Chief...indeed we do."

Joint Base Lewis-McChord, Tacoma, WA, 1445 PDT

Colonel Zhang Wei was frustrated. The special forces commander had more tasks than he had people. Too many things to do and not enough assets to do them with. He could feel the momentum slipping away from him...and it was only the *second day*! He had almost 12,000 men and women in-country, but it wasn't enough. Two thousand to guard this avenue of approach, one thousand to guard this base; pretty soon there was no one left.

How his men had lost the nuclear weapons was beyond him. Yes, he would have liked to have had more men to guard them, but he needed men to guard the roads, he needed men to guard the surface-to-air missiles, and he especially needed men to guard the bases. He absolutely could *not* allow the Americans to get their weapons or their aircraft; that would change the balance of power immediately.

He had to find the group who had taken the nuclear weapons and put a permanent stop to their activities. They could not be allowed to undermine Chinese authority; if the Americans thought they could fight back, there were far too many of them for his men to stop. He had sent out a squad of men to follow up on a lead but hadn't heard back from them yet. It had also just been reported that someone had set up a road block on I-5. That could not be permitted!

The whole plan was predicated on having the nuclear warheads to hold the Americans hostage. Without them, the U.S. forces were free not only to attack here in Seattle, but also to help in the defense of Taiwan. He *had* to get the nuclear weapons back, or he had to get more. If he didn't, the Chinese were going to lose, and he was going to be the one to blame. That was not acceptable. The navy was going to go get more of the warheads; they'd better not return empty-handed. For his sake.

He'd handle the road block, himself.

Sommers' House, North Bend, WA, 1500 PDT

"Hey sir, we've got a present for you!" Private Li said as Calvin and Master Chief walked into the Sommers' house. The Rangers had returned from the gun shop about 45 minutes earlier and were working on options for destroying the HQ-19 battery. Currently waiting for the navy men were Top, Shuteye, Tiny, BTO, Deadeye, and Jet. There were also several staff sergeants and a corporal in attendance. Unlike before, all of them were now in uniform.

"You got a present for me, Jet?" Calvin asked. "Why does that scare me?"

"Yes sir," Jet replied. "The Colonel thought that if you were going to be our platoon leader, you ought to look the part." He nodded at the corporal, who was one of the people Calvin had seen but hadn't really met yet. He was about six feet tall and deeply tanned. Calvin didn't understand why the Colonel was wearing the insignia of a Corporal.

"He's a *Colonel?*" Calvin asked. "Then why isn't he in charge?"

The Colonel looked a little sheepish and quickly developed a blush that was visible even under the tan. "No, suh," he said with a pronounced Southern accent. "That ain't mah real name." The way he pronounced them, both 'real' and 'name' had two syllables. "Mah real name is Jimmy Sanders; the boys just call me 'Colonel' 'cause ah likes my chicken. And prob'ly 'cause of mah last name, and ahl, too, ah 'spose."

Top, seeing Colonel open his mouth to continue talking, broke in. "As slowly as the Colonel talks, we'll be here all day if he explains. The bottom line is Corporal Sanders thought, and the rest of the platoon agreed, that we can't have you running around in clothes that don't fit you. It's bad for our image." Now Calvin was the one to blush. Top continued, "So we got a few things for you while we were out."

He handed Calvin a bag. When Calvin looked in, he saw a camouflage uniform and boots like what the Rangers were wearing. "That will help you look the part," Top said. "They're actually the Colonel's, since you two are about the same size. If we ever have time to get you a name tag, we'll get that put on too, but for now you'll just have to be 'Sanders.'

"Thanks," Calvin said. After he had time to think about it, he realized the group should have uniforms on if they were going to be engaged in combat operations, and had told Top to have the troops get theirs. "That'll work."

"Oh, that's not all," Top said. "Officers are supposed to have pistols, so we picked you up one. It's a Glock 20C, chambered for 10mm rounds, with a 4.6 inch barrel. We figured you'd want something with a little bit of stopping power. The best part was, since we didn't know if you could shoot or not, it came with two 15-round magazines; hopefully, that will be enough to hit whatever you're aiming at. We picked you up an extra two magazines, too. Sixty rounds ought to be enough to make you dangerous." He handed Calvin a big shopping bag containing the box the pistol was in, as well as a holster, the extra magazines and several boxes of ammunition. "Dangerous to the enemy, that is, and not to us. If you need more than that, we're not doing our jobs very well."

"This is cool," Calvin said. "Thanks, guys."

"No worries, sir. We just put it on your tab, since you were paying for it and all, but that's still not it. Wall, front and center!" A huge man came forward. Though not as big as 'Tiny,' Calvin could see how the Staff Sergeant who came forward could be called 'The Wall.'

"Hi, sir," Staff Sergeant Patrick Dantone said. "They call me 'The Wall' because people are always trying to hide behind me in combat."

"I can see why," Calvin said. "You're not Tiny, but you're not tiny, either." Calvin smiled at his own play on words.

"Yes sir," The Wall said without inflection. He had heard that joke, or a variation on it, about a thousand times. "I didn't figure you had a lot of time with the M-16 or any of the combat rifles we have, being an aviator and all, but I wanted you to be able to defend yourself. So, since you were buying, I picked this up for you, too." He handed Calvin a shotgun he had on a sling.

Calvin took it with a word of thanks. As he looked at it, he saw that it looked nothing like any shotgun he had ever seen. "That has to be the shortest barrel I have ever seen!"

"Yes, sir," The Wall explained. "The Marksman has a gunsmith in the store who does repairs and modifications, pretty much anything you need. I had him cut the barrel down to make it into what I like to call the 'Street Sweeper.' It isn't going to be much good at a distance, but you've got us for the distance work. If someone gets up close it's going to give you a big blast pattern that ought to give you a little room for error. With the barrel sawed off, it's also pretty easy to handle." He chuckled. "More importantly, it also comes with a 10-round drum magazine, so you've got a good number of shots with it before you have to reload. We loaded it with double-ought buckshot, but we also got you a couple of boxes of slugs, too, in case that's the way you want to roll."

"That's awesome." Calvin said. "Thanks."

Top smiled. "Well, before you get all mushy on us, sir," he said, "most of this is so that you aren't a hindrance to *us*. We all have our own jobs to do, and we wanted you to be able to take care of yourself without having to detail someone to babysit you. My job is to make sure you don't come face-to-face with the bad guys, but if you do, you need to have the ability to deal with them."

"I get that," Calvin said, somewhat chastised. "I just had a close encounter of the way too personal kind with a Chinese soldier. If you want to keep them off my back, I'm *way* good with it." He explained what happened on the way back from Master Chief's house. Even though the clean-up process had been expedited by the arrival of the SOAR aviators, who had come out to help when they heard the shots, the attack had delayed their return to the Sommers' house by over half an hour.

When he finished, Top gave the two navy men the details of the Rangers' trip to the gun shop, which had been a huge success. In addition to the weapons they had brought back for Calvin, they had also acquired rifles for the men in the platoon who were out of belt-fed ammunition; they had picked up several Bushmaster rifles and a Century Arms C93, all of which were chambered for the 5.56mm NATO round. They had also bought every round of ammunition that fit any of their weapons, including the Varmint Express and Zombie Max brands.

Several of the soldiers were looking forward to trying out the specialty loads, especially the ones labeled for the zombie apocalypse. Those bullets were heavier and should possess a lot of stopping power, especially at shorter ranges. If they worked on the undead, they ought to work on the living, too. What they gained in weight, though, they lost in muzzle velocity, which would somewhat decrease their effectiveness at longer ranges.

The Rangers had put their extra time at the Sommers' house to good use. Although all of the Rangers were physically fit, BTO in particular was an excellent runner and had been sent out on a jog to locate all of the HQ-19 missile system's components. As part of a sniper team, he was conditioned to lie hidden for hours, or even days, if needed. In the lead up to a mission, though, he was like a little terrier, full of boundless energy. He needed an outlet, and the long run did him good. Although the Chinese security had been tight around the park, and BTO had been forced to run a wide loop around it, he had been able to determine the whereabouts of most of the Chinese vehicles. As the spotter on a sniper team, he was also used to looking at something and describing it so someone else could understand.

A former intelligence specialist before becoming the army's first female Ranger, Deadeye Taylor gave them the information on the missile system. "A Chinese Growler battery, like the Russian S-400 system from which it was derived, consists of eight missile launchers with four missiles each, a truck-mounted 'Big Bird' acquisition radar, a truck-mounted 'Grave Stone' engagement radar, three support vehicles and a mobile command post," she told them. "While blowing up the missiles would ensure they couldn't be fired, it is more important to blow up the radar and the command post trucks, leaving the system blind and dumb. It would also be a lot easier to blow up a couple of radars than to target all eight of the missile launchers."

"Any chance of waiting until tonight to do this?" Top asked as they started looking at their options. It was obvious the mission would be far easier to accomplish at night, through stealth, than during the day. Unfortunately, it wasn't going to be dark until about 2200, which meant losing most of the afternoon.

"If we can't get it done any earlier than that, we will," Calvin answered. "I know my air wing and the Air Force are trying to get in here, though, and it will be a lot easier if the missile system is gone."

"All I'm saying is it would be a lot easier to attack at night, and we'd probably lose fewer men," Top replied, looking Calvin in the eye. "If we have to do it now, though, we have to do it now."

Calvin's phone buzzed as he got a text. He read it, frowned and looked at Top. "Looks like you're going to get your wish. Our tasking just changed." He turned to Master Chief. "What do you know about taking over a ship?"

"Taking over a ship?" the SEAL asked. "We've done some things involving ship take-downs. How big is the ship?"

"Ummm, I think it's pretty big," Calvin answered. "Would you consider a LHD to be big?"

"Since we don't have any LHDs in the area, I'm guessing you mean the Chinese one," Master Chief said. "If so, yeah, it's pretty big. It's almost as big as an aircraft carrier. What is the mission?"

"Apparently, the Chinese had a party yesterday onboard the *Long* that all of the local big wigs and senior brass in the area attended. When the invasion started, they captured the governor, a couple of senators and all of the navy leadership in the area. The Chinese are holding them onboard the LHD, using them for propaganda. The Joint Chiefs of Staff wondered if there was any way we could get them back."

Master Chief considered. "So, they want the group of us to break onto a base being held by the *Chinese*, sneak onto a *Chinese* boat full of *Chinese* soldiers, find where the hostages are being held, if indeed they *are* still being held on board, break out some unknown number of them, sneak them out past the aforementioned *Chinese* soldiers and bring them to safety? Does that about sum it up?"

Calvin looked as sick as everyone felt after hearing Master Chief describe it. "Ummm, yeah," he said with a sigh, "I think that about covers it. I'll tell them to forget it." He pulled out the phone.

Master Chief grinned. "Now, sir, why would we want to do that and miss out on our chance to be bona fide heroes?" he asked. "Of course we can do it. Nothing could be easier. We can probably even be back by dark so Top can get his night direct action strike on those missiles out there."

"Wha..what?" Calvin asked, incredulous.

"SEAL, *have you lost your mind?*" Top exclaimed. "You must be woozy from blood loss!" The rest of the Rangers just stared at Master Chief with their mouths open, wondering whether he was insane or just having some fun with them.

"Okay," Master Chief said, "I agree that infiltrating their base, storming their ship and trying to find and release an unknown number of hostages would be pretty near impossible on a normal day, especially with the entire Chinese navy after us." He looked at Sergeant Chang. "But what if I could magically get you onboard the ship without anyone knowing you were there? Would we have a chance then?" A small smile appeared on Shuteye's face.

"Well, yeah, maybe," said Top with no small amount of exasperation. "How are we supposed to get onboard without anyone knowing, though? Hide in boxes and Fedex ourselves onboard?"

"Nope, I've got a much better plan, one that our esteemed lieutenant might even call a 'tactically elegant' solution." He looked back at Sergeant Chang to see him grinning. "Hey Shuteye, do you sup-

pose Private First Class Wu Tao would drive us there for
$1,000,000?"

Sergeant Chang nodded, seeing where this was going. "He might
just do that if you asked nicely."

"I don't get it," said Calvin. "Who is Wu Tao?"

"Gee, sir, you should learn to make more friends, get around a
little more, maybe even spend a little time with the people you
meet," Master Chief said. "You actually met Wu Tao today. He is a
poor, disenfranchised young man who was drafted and made to
leave his home and everyone he loved." Seeing that Calvin and Top
still didn't get it, he added, "He used to drive a LCAC in the service
of another country's navy."

Both of the other men smiled, catching on. It might be possible
after all.

"You're just going to have to make one little phone call first..."

48th Street Underpass, I-5, Tacoma, WA, 1600 PDT

"That's it!" yelled Trooper Bob Davidson to the log-
ger, who shut down his truck. With the addition of
this truck, the blockade of I-5 was now complete.
The city police might be stymied by the invasion of a few thousand
Chinese, thought Davidson, but not the Washington State Patrol.
District One had *always* owned the highways in the Tacoma area...*and we always will.*

Made up mostly of retired military veterans, the State Patrol had
strong ties to the local National Guard unit, and every one of them
owned at least one rifle. With a liberal in the Oval Office, most of

them now owned at least three and had stockpiled thousands of rounds of ammunition...just in case.

The Chinese weren't taking *their* city without a fight.

They had barricaded the 48th Street underpass of I-5 as their ambush site. It was a natural chokepoint, with 20' high hills and fences on both sides of the highway, and a concrete divider between the northbound and southbound lanes. Seeing the State Patrol blocking the road with their squad cars and armored SWAT vans, several loggers driving past stopped and offered the services of their logging trailers to help with the barricade. The trucks had been incorporated into the barricade, and the logs they carried provided excellent firing positions for the troopers to hide behind.

Trooper Davidson of the Special Weapons and Tactics (SWAT) team commanded the road block. His men were trained to assault and dismantle methamphetamine labs, as well as many other high-risk situations. Not only were the SWAT troopers armed to the teeth, but they also had several skilled snipers on the team as well. He had deployed his men and some National Guardsmen they had been able to get hold of along the hills ringing the barricade, closing off northbound travel on I-5. No Chinese were going to venture north from Joint Base Lewis-McChord on *his* watch.

So far, the road block had been a success, and they had already bagged one vehicle full of Chinese soldiers. During the course of their duties, his troopers had noticed the Chinese were using black civilian vans to transport their troops in addition to their military vehicles. When his spotter two miles down the road radioed that one of the black vans was coming, they had been ready for it.

The driver tried to escape when he saw the road block, but the snipers had shot out the van's tires while he was turning around.

When the soldiers in the van came out shooting, they had been met by over 50 American riflemen, nearly all of whom had military marksmanship training. The firefight hadn't lasted long. The Chinese were surrounded and in the open, while his men all had prepared firing positions. The Americans had taken captive the two wounded Chinese who surrendered; the other ten had been killed. No Americans were even wounded in the action, except for one National Guardsman who fell down and cut himself on a piece of broken glass on the roadside.

The next engagement was shaping up to be more difficult; his spotter had just reported a column of military vehicles approaching from the south that included two tanks. Looking south from the end of the overpass, he could see them approaching. There was a tank in the lead, followed by what looked like an anti-aircraft gun and nine infantry fighting vehicles (IFVs). The second tank brought up the rear of the column.

Davidson had expected the tank would stop a little way down the road and use its gun to blow up the trucks, so he wasn't surprised when the tank commander did just that. It stopped about 1/4 mile down the road and fired four shots into the trucks that were blocking the northbound lanes and then a final shot into the SWAT van that completed the barricade. That hurt, as it had cost the department *a lot* of money to purchase. Although it was 'armored,' it was never expected to have to face a Chinese main battle tank. The shell that hit it destroyed it.

Davidson had known his men wouldn't be able to take on the tank with just their rifles, so he had pulled everyone from the barricade. None of his men were hurt in the barricade's destruction. He watched as the tank stopped about 100 yards short of it and moved to the side of the road, allowing several of the IFVs to pass. As the IFVs reached the remains of the barricade, their back doors opened and a couple squads of soldiers got out. At the same time, the rest of the soldiers dismounted from the other six IFVs that were still on the other side of the tank. He smiled when he saw that three of the vehicles were sitting on a patch of asphalt that looked wet, even though it hadn't rained in several days.

The Chinese soldiers dismounting those vehicles knew instantly something was wrong. He could see from their expressions they smelled it. Some began to run; others climbed back into their vehicles.

"*Fire!*" he yelled, and all of the troopers and guardsmen began firing at the dismounted soldiers from the hills along the road. Glass jars of napalm arced out from the overpass, smoking as they fell, to burst on the vehicles and roadway below them. With a "wumpf," Trooper Maya Chandler lit the stream of gasoline that had been jetting down the side of the hill from a tanker truck they had 'borrowed.' The gas had been streaming for the last several minutes, and it had begun to pool on the roadway. The three IFVs parked in it were instantly engulfed in flames, as were the two IFVs near the barricade that had been hit by napalm. All of his men began firing at the soldiers who were trapped between the two fires, killing most of them in the first few seconds.

With a "boom" that was magnified by the enclosed area, the tank fired its main gun into the overpass. Huge chunks of concrete were thrown into the air, as well as several of his men he had placed there to throw the napalm jars. The guns from the IFVs also began firing up the hills toward where his men were hiding, and he saw several more of his troops get hit.

"Get off the overpass!" he yelled to the troopers who had survived the first blast, and they began running to the west. One paused to light his last jar of napalm and was caught in the detonation of the second tank shell. What remained of him was blown off the back of the overpass. Davidson winced.

He looked back down at the road and assessed the situation. Four of the IFVs were out of commission. Two were burning fiercely from the napalm bombs and two more from the gasoline trap. The third IFV had crawled forward out of the gas, but was on fire. As he watched, some of the ammunition inside it blew up from the heat. That one was done, too, he decided. Unfortunately, the same couldn't be said for the tanks and the rest of the IFVs, which continued to blaze away at the Americans with both their main guns and their machine guns. The anti-aircraft gun also joined the fight, and its four-barreled cannon made a ripping noise as it fired hundreds of rounds up the slope. The shells tore through a sniper team picking off Chinese soldiers on the roadway. What was left of the men when the gun moved on wasn't recognizable.

His men had destroyed five IFVs and killed about 30 Chinese soldiers, but it was time to go as the battle began to swing very much in favor of the remaining armored vehicles. The remaining Chinese soldiers who had dismounted further down the road also looked like they were gathering to make an assault up the hillside. The State Patrol had done what it came to do, and he could see there wasn't much more to be gained.

"Retreat!" he yelled, and his men began to melt away back to the civilian world. The troopers on the west side of I-5 ran north toward the Tacoma Mall, where they had parked their cars, while the ones on the eastern side ran toward Giaudrone Middle School. Within seconds, they were indistinguishable from the rest of the populace.

Not a bad day's work, thought Davidson as he headed toward his car and the rendezvous. He regretted the loss of seven of his troopers, but knew the Americans had given far better than they had received. This was *their* town, damn it, and the Chinese would pay for coming here. He had some good ideas for their next engagement, too.

Boeing Airplane Programs Manufacturing Site, Renton, WA, 1620 PDT

The USS *Ranger* roared out of the Boeing hangar and onto Lake Washington with a smiling Wu Tao deftly guiding it on its way. His new best friend, Master Chief O'Leary, had promised him $1,000,000 if he would drive the LCAC up to the *Long*, get them onboard and then bring them back to the hangar. He hadn't believed Master Chief when he said the President of the United States would personally guarantee the money...until he had spoken to the president on the phone himself!

He was very excited to be driving the LCAC again. When he and his crew had been captured, they had expected to be shot once they got back to wherever the Americans had come from. That was what his officers had told him to expect if they were captured, anyway. At a minimum, the Chinese soldiers were going to go to a prisoner-of-war camp for a long time, as he didn't believe his country would ransom him back. But when they got back to the giant hangar with all of the aircraft in it, two of the Americans had come and talked to him. Not to question him on things they could use to attack the Chinese, but just to talk to him and see how he was. One of them, 'Shut-eye,' could speak his language and translated for the other, whose name was Ryan.

After finding out about how he had been conscripted by the navy and dragged off from his home, Ryan asked if Wu would be interested in becoming an American citizen. Would he? Very much so! He didn't have any money, though, and couldn't speak the language. Those were big problems. The American had said he would think about it. When he had come back later, Ryan had offered him $1,000,000 plus citizenship in the U.S. if he would just help them get their people back from where they were being held. Wu had to admit the way they were captured was not honorable, so helping the Americans get them back was actually the honorable thing to do. All he had to do was get the Americans to the *Long* and back, and he was set for life! A new name, a lot of money...set for life! In China, he had been drafted because his parents didn't have enough money to send him to college or to bribe the officials; now he was going to be a millionaire!

He hummed merrily to himself as he navigated the LCAC back to the ship.

"Have you ever seen someone so happy with himself?" asked Calvin in a loud voice over the roar of the jet engines.

"No, sir," yelled Sergeant Chang in his ear. "He's getting a great deal. He even got to speak to the president—do you suppose he ever spoke to the president of the PRC? Unlikely!"

They were interrupted by BTO, who came into the port pilothouse. "Sir!" he yelled, handing his scoped rifle to Calvin. "Take a look at the ship!"

They were just rounding Point Glover, and the base was visible four miles away down Sinclair Inlet. Calvin looked through the scope. Although he couldn't hear them over the roar of the LCAC, he could see a lot of helicopters with their rotors turning on the deck of the LHD...with *a lot* of men getting into them. If they're coming for us, he thought, we're doomed.

Tapping Wu Tao on the arm, he gave him the signal for slow down. As the throttles came back, the level of noise went down from 'skull splitting' to merely 'mind numbing.'

"Places everyone!" he yelled out the door.

PLAN LHD *Long*, Pier D, Naval Base Kitsap, WA, 1630 PDT

Lieutenant Commander Lin Gang looked out the tower window as the helicopters began launching and sighed.

"You look worried," the Assistant Air Operations Officer, Lieutenant Wong Bai, noted.

"I am," replied Lieutenant Commander Lin. "I have a very bad feeling about this. When we drew up the original plans to capture the Americans' nuclear warheads, we had overwhelming force and surprise on our side. I was sure we could get away with it, and we did."

He shook his head. "But now it is over 24 hours later, and no one has been back to Bangor since the initial attack. It is impossible to know what our troops will find. One helicopter went by the field earlier in the day on its way to Everett. The pilots didn't see anyone in the field, but couldn't be sure about the forest around it, which was heavily wooded."

"Shouldn't we have left some troops there to guard it?" Lieutenant Wong asked.

"I wish we could have," Lieutenant Commander Lin replied, "but we only have so many troops, and they can't be everywhere at once. Our marines are currently guarding the base here at Bremerton, the Seattle-Bremerton Ferry stop and the city of Bremerton, as well as a few checkpoints on Highway 3, both north and south of here. The only way we could scrape together 60 soldiers for this mission was by using the marines we had guarding the hostages we captured yesterday. Now they're being guarded by sailors from the ship, instead."

"There is plenty of combat power in that force, though," said Lieutenant Wong, nodding at the window where the last helicopter could be seen taking off.

"Yes, if nothing else, I convinced Admiral Zhao Na that this mission should be 'maximum effort,' and the admiral authorized the use of four Z-15 helicopters to transport the troops, two Z-8 heavy-lift helicopters to carry the weapons and all four of the remaining Z-10 attack helicopters to provide security. If the Americans have fortified the area, hopefully the attack helos can keep them at bay while the marines secure the additional nuclear warheads we need. This plan is based on having the Americans' warheads in our possession; we have to get them back!"

While the men watched the helicopters depart, a call came over the radio on the well deck operations frequency. "Long *Well Deck Control, this is* LCAC 1, *over*," said the voice of the coxswain.

"LCAC 1, *this is* Long *Well Deck Control*," replied the well deck supervisor. "*Where have you been?*" Lieutenant Commander Lin knew the LCAC had gone missing hours ago; it hadn't been heard from since it went to go pick up one of the original nuclear weapons for return to the ship. The admiral assumed the LCAC had been sunk by whoever had taken the weapons; they hadn't had time to search for it yet.

Lieutenant Commander Lin looked up Sinclair Inlet and couldn't see the LCAC...wait, there it was...he could see it following the Seattle-Bremerton Ferry, but the ferry blocked most of it from sight.

"*We had an electrical system failure,*" replied the coxswain, whose voice he recognized from long association. "*We had to go ashore on the island to the east of Bremerton to conduct repairs. We have a temporary fix in place right now and are returning to the ship for a new LCAC to go complete our mission.*" Fat chance, thought Lieutenant Commander Lin, the weapons are all gone. Good thing you weren't at the university. You'd probably have been killed, too.

"LCAC 1, *Well Deck Control, that mission was aborted. Return to the ship and tie up inside so you can get your problem fixed.*"

"*Well Deck Control,* LCAC 1, *we are returning to the ship and will proceed inside for maintenance, out.*"

USS *Ranger*, Naval Base Kitsap, WA, 1635 PDT

The coxswain hung up the radio's transmitter and smiled at Shuteye, saying something in Chinese. The sergeant translated, "He said, 'See? No problem. These things have electrical problems all the time.'"

"Okay," Calvin said, "It's your show, Master Chief."

"I've got it, sir," Master Chief replied. "Don't worry."

"It's my job to worry, remember?" Calvin asked. He went outside to hide under the tarp with the rest of the platoon, leaving Master Chief, Shuteye, and three other Americans visible. The Americans only had four sets of Chinese naval uniforms, plus two sets of coveralls that had been found on the LCAC. Wu Tao was wearing his own uniform, and both Shuteye and Jet were wearing the captured uniforms they had used previously. That left one uniform for Sergeant Daniel "Dreamer" Nguyen, who was of Vietnamese descent and the two sets of coveralls for Master Chief and Top. Neither of these men looked Chinese; hopefully, with hats on and slouched over like they were working on broken machinery, no one would notice before it was time.

It had been Master Chief's idea to follow the ferry up the inlet. With the big ship in between them and the *Long*, it would be difficult for anyone on the ship to get a good look at the LCAC until the ferry pulled off at the terminal. They would have to go the last 1,000 feet or so without cover, so Jet had positioned himself between the ship and the two men in coveralls. As they got closer, he gave them a running commentary on the approach to the well deck.

"The stern gate is down," Jet said, "and we have the green light to enter. It looks like there is about three feet of water in the well deck. The rest of the well deck I can see is pretty much empty, except for three people on the catwalk on the right and two on the left. We are going to tie up on the right, where the three men are. Two are holding ropes for us. The other one is supervising. Both men on the left are leaning on the railing; they look like they are just watching. Don't look up. They're watching us. They don't look concerned yet."

Shuteye and Dreamer looked up for the men to throw the ropes down to them. As the ropes were coming down, Jet could see the brows of one of the men on the left start to furrow. He was a friend of one of the original sailors and knew the LCAC had departed with a crew of four; now there were six. "We're blown!" Jet said. "NOW!"

he yelled. Instantly, all of the Americans grabbed their weapons and began firing. Master Chief got both of the men on the left side, while Top shot two on the right and Dreamer killed the third. All five used pistols with suppressors; the muffled reports of the pistols firing couldn't be heard over the noise of the LCAC's jet engines shutting down. The rest of the Americans sprang from under the covers and tarps, and they quickly scaled the ladders and secured the control room which looked out onto the well deck through two windows.

"Ask him why he shut down," Calvin ordered.

After a brief conversation, Shuteye translated, "He was told to shut down. If he keeps the motors running, the admiral will get mad about the noise and send someone down to find out what's going on."

"That's fine, then," Calvin said, as the rest of the people exited the LCAC.

The platoon split up. Nine people stayed to ensure they had a ride home. Eight members of the platoon, led by Shuteye and Top, left to go retrieve the dignitaries. Master Chief took another six to complete a different mission.

Bangor Naval Base, WA, 1645 PDT

Colonel Bart Williamson watched as the attack helicopters came in first, ready to unleash their overwhelming firepower at the first hint of trouble. The commander of the 7th Infantry Division was normally a jovial man, but this morning's situation was anything but funny. His men and women were out-gunned, and he needed to do something to even the odds.

The Chinese would *not* be allowed to take any of the nuclear warheads. Not while he was in command.

The helicopters circled the edges of the field, looking for something to shoot, but failed to find his camouflaged men and women hiding in the forest. After several trips around the field, they called in the transport helicopters, and the ones carrying the marines came in first. They touched down and, as the first marines jumped out of them, all hell broke loose.

Colonel Williamson wasn't able to get all 12,000 men and women of the 7th Infantry Division to the field like the Army Chief of Staff promised. He didn't even get half, or even a quarter of the division in the time available. He did, however, get 2,895 people to the field, and all of them were armed with rifles. Most carried their own deer rifles or those of their friends; others had to go shopping. There wasn't a sporting goods store or pawn shop within 20 miles of the base that still had a rifle or ammunition left on its shelves. At the signal, nearly all of them fired at once.

Three quarters of the soldiers had been designated to target the attack helos, with an average of over five hundred rifles shooting at each of them. Hitting a moving target is hard, and the helicopters were not only moving quickly, but they were also built for combat. Composite armor protected the bottom and the sides of the cockpit, as well as the engines and the fuel tank. The aviators were well-protected, too, with thick, bullet-proof glass in the canopy. With that much lead in the air, though, the Americans were bound to hit the helicopters, and some of those rounds were eventually going to hit something vital. He hoped.

Two helicopters were critically hit within the first few seconds. The first had the drive shaft to its aft rotor cut. Without the ability to counter the main rotor's torque, the pilot lost control and the helo began to spin round and round, its gyrations ceasing as it impacted the ground just inside the tree line. Its rotors disintegrated on impact, throwing pieces of shrapnel that killed two soldiers and wounded another five.

The second helicopter had several bullets hit close together on one of its main rotor blades, causing it to fail, and it snapped off and flew through the air like a scythe. The attack helicopter went out of control, crashing into the trees and killing the three soldiers who had the misfortune to be underneath it. The rotor blade hit once and cart-wheeled into the cockpit of one of the transport helicopters that had just landed, severing the right arm of the pilot-in-command and destroying most of the cockpit's instrumentation. The copilot bailed out of the cockpit as black smoke began to engulf it.

The other two attack helicopters returned fire, and Williamson's soldiers began to die. Each helicopter carried 16 rockets, and both pilots began to walk them down the tree line of the field where the soldiers were hiding. The gunners did the same thing with their 25mm Bushmaster cannons, using their thermal sights to find and kill the American soldiers as they exposed themselves.

The transport helicopters on the ground were not so lucky. Originally built as civilian helos, they lacked much of the armor and shielding of the attack helicopters, and they were also sitting targets. Although only a quarter of the American troops were firing at them, their fire was far more effective, and a second transport helicopter was quickly destroyed. The pilots of the Z-15s did not have bullet-proof glass to hide behind, and the pilots of a third transport helicopter were killed before they could get their aircraft off the ground.

The final transport managed to get airborne and its pilot struggled to get it out of the killing zone, his efforts made more difficult by the dead weight of his copilot as he sagged forward onto the control stick. As the pilot reached over to pull back his partner, he too was hit, and the helicopter slammed into the ground, injuring most of the marines in the back who hadn't jumped out on its initial touchdown.

The troops still in the helicopters tried to use their fuselages as cover, and the marines who had dismounted took what cover they could find and returned fire. Even with most of the Americans continuing to shoot at the attack helicopters, the Chinese were still greatly outnumbered, and they were rapidly put out of action by the Americans who had good cover behind trees they had cut down to make firing positions.

The heavy-lift Z-8 helicopters, unarmed except for a door-mounted 20mm cannon, hovered out of the way of the attack helicopters as they continued to battle the forces on the ground. One of the remaining attack helicopters swooped lower into the field to get a better angle on the soldiers and negate the cover of the trees. It fired its final two missiles, killing another six soldiers and wounding 13 more, but took a round through the engine's cooling system. Fluid began streaming down the side of the helicopter and, within seconds, the engine began to overheat.

The pilot struggled to get the helicopter away from the bullets that continued to ricochet off it, including one that hit the canopy in front of his face. As the helo strained to climb higher, heat continued to build up in the engine. The pilot wrestled the helo away from the field and had just turned back toward Bremerton when the motor seized; the helicopter crashed into the forest several hundred yards away, eliciting a ragged cheer from the Americans who had been shooting at it.

The pilot of the final attack helicopter was a veteran, and he kept his helicopter further back from the incoming fire. This forced the Americans to shoot at the most protected areas of the helicopter, while the helicopter's cannon chewed up the tree line and the soldiers who were hiding in it. Eventually, though, an incoming round hit the ball bearings in between the swash plates of the main rotor's drive shaft, and the pilot felt his controls get mushy. Barely able to control the craft, and with no one left on the ground to support, he pulled his aircraft back up and around to return to the ship. The Z-8s, unable to do anything on their own, and facing a tremendous increase in fire as the attack helicopter withdrew, turned and followed.

Seeing their support and transportation flying away, the few remaining Chinese marines in the field quickly put their hands up and surrendered. The Americans had held the field, although they had lost 287 dead and another 426 wounded, almost 25% of their forces.

Task Force Top, PLAN *Long*, Naval Base Kitsap, WA, 1645 PDT

Shuteye led the team forward into the ship from the well deck. He knew from Wu Tao that he needed to go forward, down a couple of decks and then back aft again to find the brig. Wu had never been in trouble so he didn't know exactly where the brig was, but he knew it was somewhere on that deck. Seeing no one in the passageway as he opened the watertight door, Shuteye went in, and the rest of the team followed. Just inside the door he saw what he needed; a diagram on the wall showed the ship's layout.

Shuteye found the "You are here" dot and then the symbol for the ladder going down. He needed to go to the next cross-passage and then right. As he reached the passage and turned right, he ran into a PLAN sub-lieutenant, the equivalent of a U.S. Navy lieutenant junior grade.

"Watch where you are going!" exclaimed the sub-lieutenant in Chinese. Seeing the white men behind Shuteye, he opened his mouth again to shout or yell, but was cut off as Shuteye jammed his pistol into the officer's chest.

Shuteye backed him into the wall with the pistol. "Say nothing and lead us to the brig, or I am going to repaint this passageway with your blood!"

The officer saw all of the pistols pointing at him, and his eyes opened wide. Each looked huge with its attached suppressor. He slowly turned around and went back the way he had come.

As he reached the ladder well, which had stairs going both up and down, he started to go up. "Wait!" said Shuteye. "The brig is downstairs."

"No, it's up," the officer said, sprinting up the stairs. He drew a breath to yell for help, but was struck in the hip by a round from Sergeant Chang's silenced .45 caliber pistol. It shattered his hip, and he fell backwards down the stairs. A second shot missed and ricocheted up the steel ladder well. As he hit the deck, there was a loud crack, and Shuteye could tell his neck was broken from the unnatural angle of his head. If he wasn't dead, he soon would be. The puddle of blood starting to pool around him was of greater concern.

"Fergie, get the body out of the ladder well," Top said to Corporal 'Fergie' Ferguson. "Everyone else, try the doors further down the passageway and see if you can find one that's open."

"Got one," PFC 'Woody' Woodard said, opening a door. "Looks like it's a storage room. It must be for the marines; it has a bunch of camping gear inside."

Fergie pulled the dead officer inside while Woody found a towel inside the storage area and wiped up the blood trail leading to the room. It was impossible to clean up all the blood in the ladder well without wasting too much time; they locked the storage room door and continued down the ladder.

Shuteye paused two decks down on Deck 5. There were two doors leading out of the ladder well. One door was labeled 'Armory' in Chinese characters; the door on the other side of the ladder well was labeled 'Brig.' "Give me a second to check," he said. Receiving agreement, he slid out the door marked 'Brig' and into the empty passageway beyond. It led to a door about 15 feet down the corridor, with a closed door on both sides about halfway down. The door at the end of the hall had Chinese characters identifying it as the brig. Shuteye tested the door and found it locked; he went back to the ladder well to get the rest of the group.

"It's locked," Shuteye said as they approached the door.

Top saw the door was just a normal door, not a watertight door with a seal. He realized he had two choices, knock on it and alert them to their presence, or try to smash it and charge in guns blazing. While the first option was potentially stealthier, whoever answered the door might ask for some sort of password. Failing to get it, they would have problems and might have to charge in, anyway, but now everyone would be prepared. The other option, while offering the element of surprise, was a huge unknown. They might smash the door in to find Chinese soldiers in with the prisoners, complicating their targeting and potentially leading to the deaths of some of the hostages. Neither were great options, but he had to choose one.

"Okay," he whispered, "here's what we're going to do." He looked at the biggest man in the group, "Wall, I want you to kick in the door. I'll be on the left; Fergie will be on the right. We'll go through the door in standard combat spread. Shoot any Chinese soldiers, but be careful of any hostages that might be there. Everyone understand?"

Everyone nodded agreement, and they took their places. The Wall took a deep breath, focused, and used every bit of his 256 pounds to kick the door. The door sprang, slamming open to the right. Top and Fergie ran into the room, guns drawn, searching for targets, with the rest of the squad pouring in behind them.

Top pulled up in surprise. Beyond the door was a large 30'x30' jail cell with a small desk and office area on the Rangers' side of the bars. The entire room was empty; there were neither hostages nor guards.

Task Force SEAL, PLAN *Long*, Naval Base Kitsap, WA, 1645 PDT

Four decks above Top, Master Chief was in a ladder well looking at a diagram of the ship. Not seeing what he wanted, he went up another deck to the 01 level. In a bizarre naming convention he didn't understand, the highest deck that went the length of the ship was labeled the '1st Deck.' Every deck below that was a sequentially numbered deck, '2nd Deck,' '3rd

Deck,' etc. Every deck above the 1st Deck was called a 'Level' and was sequentially numbered going up, starting with the '01 Level,' then the '02 Level,' and so on. The well deck was on the 3rd deck; Top had gone down two decks to the 5th Deck while he had gone up two decks and now a level. He went up another ladder to the 02 Level and looked at the diagram.

"Yep, there it is!" he exclaimed.

"What are you looking for?" Jet asked, looking at the diagram. "I don't know all of the Chinese characters on it, but I know some of them."

"I'm looking for the Flag spaces where the admiral would be," Master Chief said. "See this area here?" he said pointing at the diagram. "It's marked in red, which probably means for the normal enlisted soldiers and sailors to stay out. I'm guessing, but I think that's either weapons or the admiral. Weapons' spaces are normally lower in the ship and more to the interior so they don't blow up if the ship takes damage; this *has* to be where their admiral is. It's also about where our admiral would be on a similar U.S. ship, and it's got some bigger rooms nearby for standing watches and having conferences. I would bet money these two rooms here, joined together, are the admiral's quarters."

Jet looked at the diagram. "I think you are right," he said. "One says bedroom."

"It's down this passageway," Master Chief said, indicating one of the doors out of the ladder well. "You go first, look like you belong, move fast and we'll follow." He took one last look at the diagram, memorizing the schematic. "Go!" he ordered.

Jet strode purposefully out the door, nearly running into someone who was just about to open the door. As he stepped back in surprise, Master Chief shot him three times in the chest, and then pushed Jet on down the passageway, leaving the Chinese lieutenant to bleed out on the floor.

"We've got to rely on speed," Master Chief whispered. "Let's go!" The two men continued down the passageway with the other four Rangers close behind them.

Thirty feet further down the passageway, two leather curtains in bright red blocked the passageway with big Chinese lettering.

"My guess is it says something like "Stay Out! Authorized Personnel Only!" Jet translated.

"Great!" Master Chief said. "This is the place!" Pushing past Jet, Master Chief opened the curtains to find two Chinese officers standing outside a door, a junior lieutenant and a captain. He shot them both and moved on, changing out his magazine for a fresh one. He stopped two doors further down the passageway at a door with a lot of official-looking markings on it.

"This is the admiral's office," Master Chief said. "I just hope he's here!" He tried the door, quietly. Finding it unlocked, he whispered, "One, two, three!" and threw it open, charging in. Sitting behind a large, official-looking mahogany desk was a Chinese admiral, with a U.S. Navy captain sitting on the other side of the desk from him. Although there was a pistol on the desk, it wasn't needed; the navy captain was handcuffed to the chair.

The Chinese admiral, a large man who was both tall and stout, started to grab for his gun, but slowly withdrew his hand when he saw he was outnumbered. Seeing the people bursting into his office were Americans, he smiled and said in English, "Can I help you?"

"Yes," Master Chief said, "you're coming with us." Pointing at the captain, he told Jet to free him. There was a small key on the admiral's desk that looked like it would fit the handcuffs.

"Thanks," the captain said. "How'd you get here? Are we winning?"

"No sir," Master Chief replied, "we're not winning yet, and how we got here is a long story that I'd rather tell you once we're somewhere safer. I've got a group getting the rest of the hostages out of the brig. Do you know if there are any being held anywhere else?"

"No one is being held in the brig," the captain answered. "There were too many of us, so they put us in one of the marine enlisted berthing areas."

"Shit!" Master Chief said. "I guess Top will have to figure it out." Looking at the admiral, he motioned with his pistol toward the door. "Let's go."

"And if I refuse?" the admiral asked, stalling for time.

Master Chief cocked the gun and looked at him. "You can come with us, or you can die."

A shout was heard from the passageway. "We just ran out of time. Move!" Master Chief ordered the admiral.

The admiral was just starting to get up when two Chinese officers ran in through the door, yelling something in Chinese. Both were met with a fusillade of bullets as six pistols fired on them simultaneously. They fell to the floor, both of them struck several times. Master Chief turned back to the admiral, who was reaching for the pistol on the desk. He fired once, striking him in the middle finger and removing the last knuckle. The admiral wailed something in Chinese as he balled his fist, protecting it with the other hand.

112

"Unless you want another one through the head," Master Chief told the admiral, "*get moving!*" He looked at the captain, "If you're ready to go, sir, I'd suggest we go quickly."

"This is your show," said the captain. "Just tell me where to go."

Master Chief instructed the massive Tiny to take charge of the admiral and BTO to help the captain, who didn't look entirely steady on his feet. Tiny grabbed the admiral by his collar. Even though the admiral was a large man, and more than a little gone to fat, Tiny lifted him to his tip-toes. "Don't be givin' me no problems, suh," Tiny told the admiral. "Ya hear?" Bleeding and in pain, the admiral didn't say anything, although he did nod slightly. Tiny lowered him a fraction, allowing him to breathe, and said, "Good. Then we may just get along."

Opening the door, Master Chief quickly stuck his head out and then back in. A gunshot sounded in the corridor. "We don't have time for this shit," Master Chief said. He dove into the corridor, surprising the pistol-armed marine 20 feet down the passage. He fired three times before he crashed into the other side of the passageway, hitting the marine in the chest twice. The marine went down.

Master Chief stood up grimacing in pain. Fresh blood began welling from the earlier gunshot to his side. "I'm getting too old for this shit," he growled. "Follow me." He led the way back to the ladder well, followed by the captain and BTO, Tiny and the Chinese admiral, and Jet. Master Chief had the Gordon twins bring up the rear. As stealth was no longer an option, the twins had pulled out their rifles and were ready to 'rock and roll.' Master Chief had no idea which was which, so he just said, "you two bring up the rear," and they did.

The group made it back through the leather curtains and down to the ladder well. As Bad Twin was going through the door, the curtains parted slightly, and someone looked through. Bad Twin fired a three round burst into the curtain and was rewarded with a grunt, as at least one bullet struck the person. The curtains closed, and Bad Twin joined the rest of the group hurrying down the stairs.

Task Force Top, PLAN *Long*, Naval Base Kitsap, WA, 1650 PDT

One of the primary military axioms is to never split your forces. Along the lines of, "if some is good, more is better," the thinking is that it is better to keep your troops together and have enough power to overwhelm the enemy.

Top violated the rule and split his group.

He didn't know where the hostages were being held, or if they were even on the ship any longer, but he did know where the armory was and knew they were low on ammunition. He led his squad into the armory, killing the two Chinese soldiers who were supposed to be on guard, but were playing cards instead.

Top was unimpressed with the armory. Until that point, he had thought they were just lucky that they hadn't run into many soldiers while going through the marines' spaces onboard the ship. Seeing how empty the armory was, he realized they had all disembarked, taking most of their weapons and ammunition with them. The only things remaining in the racks were a few rifles and RPG-69 launchers. As they went into the storage room, he was a little more encouraged to find a variety of boxes and crates. Shuteye only recognized a few of the labels (as most children were generally *not* taught the characters for things like 'grenades' and 'explosives' as a matter of course). Top didn't have time to spend looking in all of the boxes; his mission was to find the hostages.

Taking Shuteye, Corporal Cornelius Hill and Private First Class Hector Carrasquillo with him, they left the other four Rangers to go through the boxes and take a shopping list of things back up to the well deck. As the RAWS gunners were low on ammunition, he instructed them to bring back at least a couple of the RPG-69s, as well as plenty of ammunition for them. Grenades would also be handy, he told them, as well as bullets to fit the three remaining light machine guns still in the rack. With The Wall leading them, he knew they would make good choices in what they requisitioned from the armory. He also knew they'd be able to carry a lot of it, too.

Top led his group back to the ladder well. Looking at the schematic of the ship there, he didn't see any other large, open areas on the 5th deck that would be indicative of a jail. On a hunch, he didn't think they would be further down in the bowels of the ship. If anything, they were more likely to be higher up, closer to the Chinese leadership. With that decided, he went up one of the flights of stairs.

Reaching the next landing, he looked at the schematic for the 4th Deck. The only spaces he saw that looked big enough to hold all of the people the Chinese had captured were labeled as barracks spaces (as closely as Shuteye could translate, anyway). He didn't see anything that was identified as a jail, brig or anything similar. Failing that, he went up another ladder to the 3rd Deck. Avoiding the puddle of blood at the bottom of the ladder well, he looked at the map, but didn't see anything that looked like it would be a holding cell, either.

With most of the 3rd Deck and 2nd Deck devoted to the well deck and vehicle storage, the hostages would have to be on either the

1st Deck or on one of the levels. The 1st Deck was also probably used as hangar space for aircraft maintenance, so that was out, and the levels would all be for operations and administration if they were anything like U.S. ships. He was missing something, but he didn't know what it was. Where could they be?

The only big spaces on the ship were the berthing areas, the well deck and the hangar deck. The flight deck had a lot of space, but it wasn't a confined space, so they would need more guards, and it was exposed to the elements. That was out. Other than sitting in chairs for long periods of time, the conference rooms didn't work very well. There wasn't enough room for sleeping, and toilet facilities would be problematic. There was enough room on the hanger deck for mattresses, but once again, it wasn't enclosed, so the Chinese would need a lot of guards, and toilet facilities would again be problematic. That only left the berthing areas, where the soldiers and sailors slept, but the Chinese would have been using them...he smacked his head. "I'm so stupid!" he said.

"Why's that?" Shuteye asked.

"Where can you put a group of people that has beds as well as bathroom facilities?" Top asked in return. "In the berthing spaces," he explained. He could see Shuteye start to ask a question and went ahead with the explanation, "If the marines have disembarked, all of the marine berthing is available!"

All of the Rangers nodded their heads in agreement. Top looked at Shuteye. "What is the closest berthing area to the well deck?"

"There was some enlisted berthing on the 4th Deck," he remembered.

"Let's go!" Top exclaimed, leading them back down the ladder. As they reached the 4th Deck, a noise began to sound loudly in the passageway. It sounded a lot like the General Quarters alarm of a U.S. ship. Just like its American counterpart, it was followed by a man's voice talking over the ship's intercom.

"We're blown," Top said, "We've got to hurry!" He looked at the ship schematic again and urged Shuteye toward one of the doors. "It's down this hall." Shuteye slid through the door and went running down the hallway. People running through the halls with the General Quarters alarm sounding wasn't out of the ordinary; it was expected. He came upon two men with rifles who looked alert as they stood outside one of the doors in the hallway. Shuteye looked down past them and yelled, "Look out!" as he pointed with his left hand. As the guards looked to see what he was shouting at, his right hand came around from behind his back with his pistol. It coughed four times, and the two guards slumped to the floor.

"Top!" Shuteye called, and the other three men came down the passageway from the ladder well.

"Hurry!' Top shouted. "I heard people coming down the stairs!"

Shuteye opened the door and saw 24 pairs of scared eyes looking back at him from the bunks in the berthing room. They had found the hostages.

Well Deck, PLAN *Long*, Naval Base Kitsap, WA, 1650 PDT

"Shit!" Calvin shouted as the ship's intercom system started to sound. "Bong! Bong! Bong! Bong!" This was followed by a man's voice saying something, but he had *no* idea what. He looked at Wu; the sailor looked terrified. "This can't be good," he thought. "Okay, think...what happens at General Quarters...hmmm." As an aviator, Calvin didn't have a station he had to man during General Quarters; it was expected that during any battle he would be off flying his FA-18, trying to stop whoever or whatever was inbound to the ship. When General Quarters sounded and he wasn't airborne, that was normally a good time for a nap while all of the sailors did their 'boat stuff.'

He knew people would be going throughout the ship during General Quarters, closing all of the watertight doors and hatches. He wasn't worried about holding the well deck unless a tank drove in from outside. He had nine heavily-armed Rangers covering all the doors into the well deck and was in control of the monitoring station. He fully expected someone to try to close the stern gate, but they would need to get into the control room to do so, which meant getting past the Rangers first.

Wu Tao came running up to him, jabbering excitedly while pointing at the LCAC and gesturing frantically out the back of the boat. Apparently he thought it was a good time to leave. While Calvin agreed, they couldn't leave without the rest of his men and the hostages. He shook his head, pointing at the deck of the ship; they were staying.

He looked around in time to see Master Chief's group come struggling in through one of the doors. They had what looked like a U.S. Navy captain and a large Chinese man with a lot of gold braid on his uniform with them, but Calvin didn't have time to find out who they were. "Get in the LCAC and start manning up the guns!" he yelled to Master Chief, trusting him to do what needed to be done. Master Chief continued shepherding his group into the LCAC and then came back to stand by Calvin once they had loaded.

"Anything I can do to help?" Master Chief asked.

"Yeah, Master Chief," Calvin replied. "Have Jet take Wu into the boat, and let's get it fired up. As soon as everyone gets back, we need to get the hell out of here!" Master Chief left to take Wu to the boat. The interior of the well deck had quieted after the General Quarters alarm was given, but the stillness was soon broken by the roar of the LCAC's jet engines starting up.

"Hey sir, I hate to tell you this," Sergeant Jose 'Boom Boom' Morales said, running up to Calvin, "but I think I heard the helos returning before the motors started."

"Yes, I..." Calvin paused as gunfire sounded. Two Chinese soldiers tried to make it into the well deck. Neither made it all the way in, and one collapsed in the doorway, jamming it open. "I heard the helos, too," he finished. "I hope the team gets back with the hostages soon, or we're gonna be screwed."

As he finished, one of the doors further aft opened, and the team transporting ordnance came through. This was their second trip, but it would have to be their last. Three of the Rangers staggered through with big loads of ammunition, followed a couple of seconds later by Sergeant Jacob 'Paris' Hylton, who was walking backward and firing his rifle.

Paris continued to fire as he backed his way through the door. As he reached through the doorway to close it, he was suddenly tugged to the side as he was hit high on his left arm. He fired back through the door one-handed and yelled, "And stay down!" Paris tightened the latching mechanism with one hand and jogged over to Calvin with blood dripping down his left side.

Saluting, he said, "We're back sir, and we got some good stuff."

"Welcome back," Calvin said. "Get in the boat and get that arm looked at."

Paris looked down at it. "Bah, that's just a scratch," he said.

Calvin sighed. Rangers, he thought, as more gunfire sounded from across the well deck. Calvin couldn't see what his troops were shooting at, but they must have gotten it because they stopped shooting. From his shoulder, Master Chief yelled over the roar of the LCAC, "They're just probing us so far, but they know we're here. It looks like most of the marines were on the beach, but they'll be calling them back as fast as they can. You should get under cover, sir; you're too valuable to lose." He pointed to the control room with one hand, a big chunk of plastic explosive in the other.

"Why don't you use that as your command post until we go?" Master Chief advised. "It will give you some cover, at least."

Gunfire erupted from two places in the well deck as the probing continued.

"On second thought," Master Chief said, "we can't hold this much longer. You better get in the LCAC. I'm going to leave the Chinese a little present, and then we'll start falling back to the boat." He went around to the other side of one of the tanks with Tiny in tow. He could see they were busy doing something there.

Sustained gunfire sounded from one of the port-side passages, where the Chinese appeared to be putting together a sustained assault into the well deck. If they got through, the Americans would be wiped out. Calvin could see one of the Rangers get hit in the leg; it looked like Sergeant Logan 'Lawyer' Hale, one of his squad leaders. He crawled back to cover, and one of the Rangers ran up from the boat to help him get down the ladder.

"Screw this!" yelled Boom Boom. Pulling out two grenades, he pulled their pins and threw them as hard as he could. The grenades vanished through the open doorway, and Sergeant Morales heard a short scream before they both detonated. Firing from the passageway ceased abruptly.

One of the doors on the starboard side of the ship that hadn't been used previously suddenly popped open, and two Chinese soldiers charged out. Before they could orient themselves and shoot, Corporal Berron 'Reggie' Wayne triggered a long burst from the starboard 14.5mm machine gun on the LCAC, killing them both. A third person followed them out the door, but fell forward, dead. Corporal Wayne kept the gun pointed at the doorway, ready to repel the next Chinese attack. Before he could fire, a white hand waved in the doorway, followed by Corporal Hill and Sergeant Chang, and then all of the American hostages. Top brought up the rear of the group.

"*Run!*" yelled Calvin, waving and indicating the boat. The hostages ran to the LCAC while Shuteye and Corporal 'Boot' Hill took up covering positions. As the civilians and military hostages loaded the boat, soldiers led them to cover. Calvin looked up to the coxswain shack and saw Wu gesturing feverishly at the bow door. With a massive 'clank' the stern gate shifted. Wu indicated that it was about to shut, trapping them in the ship. "*Let's go Rangers!*" Calvin yelled.

All of the soldiers who were in covering positions pulled out grenades, jerked out the pins and threw them at the same time into the passageways. Once the grenades were airborne, they turned and began running for the LCAC, with Master Chief and Tiny joining them. As the soldiers hurried to get aboard, the stern gate started rising. Although it was three feet underwater at its furthest end, the water immediately began bubbling and frothing as the gate began displacing it. Two soldiers remained on the LHD as Wu Tao advanced the throttles of the LCAC, and the boat started backing out of the well deck.

Shuteye, who was coming down the ladder, jumped the remaining four feet when he saw the boat start moving, rolling when he hit to cushion his fall. Before Boot could join him, he was hit in the back of his left knee by one of the soldiers coming through the door. He fell to the catwalk and began crawling toward the ladder. Master Chief knew he wouldn't make it in time.

"Tell him to stop!" Master Chief yelled, pointing at the coxswain's compartment, but no one was close enough to do so. The stern gate was level with the surface of the water; it began picking up speed as it no longer had to contend with the additional weight of the water. Wu knew if he didn't gun the engines, he wasn't going to get the LCAC out before the gate closed. His million dollars, and probably his life, depended on it. He wasn't stopping.

Standing at the rail of the LCAC, Master Chief was the only one with a chance to save Corporal Hill. If he didn't do something, Boot would be left behind. 99.9% of Americans wouldn't have gone back to get the downed Ranger at the risk of their own lives, but Master Chief wasn't 99.9% of Americans. He was a SEAL, and SEALs did *not* leave men behind. He was up the ladder in a flash and back onto the catwalk where Corporal Hill lay struggling to reach the LCAC as it pulled away.

Master Chief scooped up the injured soldier in a fireman's carry, with the soldiers on the boat providing covering fire. Bullets from the machine guns ricocheted throughout the well deck, turning it into a buzz saw. Very few Chinese soldiers attempted to enter the well deck with the bullets whistling around; the ones that entered, died.

As the LCAC approached the end of the catwalk, Master Chief looked down and saw The Wall and Tiny waiting, ready to receive Corporal Hill. Master Chief tossed the soldier as far as he could. The two men reached out and just...just got a hold on him, drawing him onboard. Master Chief looked up to see that the back of the LCAC was even with the end of the catwalk; he was going to, quite literally, miss the boat.

Master Chief took a couple of steps to build up speed, jumped onto the railing at a run, and dove out over the water toward the LCAC. Although close, he hadn't *quite* timed it perfectly; his left hand grabbed the guard rail of the boat, but his right hand missed. He tried to get his right hand back up, but the blast of the LCAC's giant fans was too much as it backed out; his left hand slipped before he could grab onto the boat with his right hand. He fell.

Two strong hands grabbed his wrist as the LCAC leaped over the end of the stern gate like a car jumping from a ramp. With a crash and a splash of water like Niagara Falls, they were out of the ship and into open water.

"I've got you, son," Governor George Shelby said. Several other hands grabbed hold of Master Chief's other wrist and, with Tiny and The Wall joining in, pulled the SEAL aboard. "Can't have a registered voter getting left behind now, can we?" the governor asked.

Master Chief lay on his back on the deck of the boat, breathing heavily. Getting. Too. Old. For. This. Shit. As what he heard sank in, he swiveled his head to look at the governor. "Thanks," he said, "but I don't think I voted for you, sir."

The governor smiled. "That's okay, my boy," he said with a twinkle in his eye. "Maybe next time, you will."

Top walked up to stand over his friend. "Thanks for grabbing Hill," he said, then chuckled as he helped Master Chief up. "About that jump, though..." His voice trailed off, and then he exclaimed, "Shit!"

"What?" Master Chief asked, climbing to his feet.

Top looked back at the amphibious assault ship. "The helicopters are back, and it looks like the Chinese are getting them ready to come after us."

Master Chief stood up, flexing bruised muscles and battered tendons. He could feel his side leaking again, too. "You're really going to like this," he said looking back.

The assembled group looked back. Nothing happened, except that the first helicopter lifted from the deck of the ship and started in pursuit of the fleeing LCAC.

"What am I going to like?" Top asked.

Everyone looked at Master Chief. He looked back at the ship. Nothing happened.

"Wait for it," he encouraged.

The second helicopter began to lift.

Nothing happened.

And then the ship exploded.

It didn't just detonate with a 'bang,' but with an earth-shattering ka-BOOM that not only could be heard above the roar of the LCAC's jet engines, but could be *felt*, as well. The force of the blast caused the ship to heel over, and one of its antennas went into the rotor blades of the second helicopter as it lifted off. The rotor disintegrated; shrapnel and cart-wheeling pieces of rotor blade ran the length of the flight deck and splashed into the bay. Without the rotor, the helicopter crashed back down to the deck thirty feet below, and additional shrapnel went flying as its rear rotor hit the deck and fragmented. Black smoke began to billow as the helicopter's fuel caught fire.

A second geyser of water erupted as the force of the explosion caused the retaining mechanism on the stern gate to fail, and the entire back of the ship unhinged and splashed into the bay. Water poured into the ship, and it began to sink.

"What the hell was that?" one of the U.S. Navy captains asked with awe in his voice.

Master Chief looked around. The wonder he saw on the faces of the people as they watched the destruction of the massive ship was obvious, making the sight of the former flagship sinking into the mud even more satisfying. It was good to be back in the military, he decided; how many people get to do *that* kind of stuff in their daily jobs?

"That was a little trick I learned from some of my 'associates' in Afghanistan," Master Chief explained. "You've heard of an improvised explosive device, right?" Everyone nodded in agreement. "What I did was to just make a bigger one, using a bunch of Chinese explosives and tank shells. I was hoping to penetrate the hull of the ship; it looks like I succeeded."

"No time for that now," Top said. "We've got to take care of that incoming helicopter!"

Calvin looked up to see the helicopter had closed to only a couple of miles away. The 20mm cannon in the helicopter's doorway was manned, and he did *not* want to play 'dueling machine guns' with it, especially with the LCAC's deck covered in civilians. Before he could start getting the former hostages under cover, there was a dual

'woosh' from the front of the boat, and smoke filled the main compartment of the LCAC.

"I launched first, dude," one of the twins yelled as two missiles
streaked upwards from the bow of the LCAC.

"Like, no way," replied the other. "You know mine beat yours."

There must have been surface-to-air missiles in the ordnance the
platoon had appropriated from the *Long's* armory, Calvin realized,
although he didn't know why everything had to be a competition
with the twins.

Shaking his head, he turned to watch the missiles streak toward
the helicopter. Even though it tried to jink out of the way at the last
minute, the missiles were much more agile than the large helo; one
missile detonated on the left engine and the other destroyed the
right. As both engines lost power, the rotor blade slowed, and the
giant helicopter fell slowly from the sky to splash into the Puget
Sound like an oversized rock into a pond. Calvin could already hear
the twins arguing about who hit it first.

"So that's what getting shot down looks like," Calvin said, standing next to Master Chief. "I have to say I like it a lot more when
someone else is doing it." He could see that people were spilling out
of the helicopter as it started sinking. "Do you suppose we ought to
go back and fish them out?"

Master Chief pointed to the shore. "Those strange-looking tanks
moving toward the water's edge are Chinese amphibious tanks.
Since they're 'amphibious,' they can swim out to where we are.
They're also 'tanks,' which means they have a big gun on the front
that blows shit up. Judging from the size of the detonation I made
using some of their shells, there's a lot of explosives in them. I vote
we let the Chinese pick up their own people today. In fact," Master

Chief concluded, "I think we should leave *now*, before anyone else arrives."

"I'm with you," Calvin said. He walked over to Shuteye and pointed to Wu in the pilothouse. "Tell him to take us home!"

Boeing Airplane Programs Manufacturing Site, Renton, WA, 1730 PDT

Calvin looked at his watch as the LCAC shut down inside its hangar at the Boeing Airplane Programs Manufacturing Site. He couldn't believe it had only been five hours since the last time they had shut down the LCAC here. So short a time, and yet, how many times had he almost been killed? This ground combat stuff is for the birds, Calvin thought. Or the SEALs. *Not aviators!*

With people able to hear themselves speak again, all of the former hostages wanted to thank their rescuers for coming to get them. The politicians and spouses were probably a little more enthusiastic in their praise; they had never prepared themselves mentally for combat or to be hostages. A momentary calm descended on the hangar, and Calvin left Master Chief to supervise the debarkation while he went to see if the plant's manager was still around. Before Calvin could find him, however, he heard a disturbance from where the recovered hostages were exiting the LCAC.

A man was yelling in an authoritarian tone. Calvin sighed; as the senior officer of the platoon, he knew the care of VIPs and senior officers fell to him. He went back to investigate and saw a large man wearing an admiral's uniform berating one of the troopers. The man's nametag read 'Barnaby,' and Calvin realized he was Rear Admiral Dan Barnaby, the Commander of Navy Region, Northwest. In this position he was also Calvin's boss, although he was several steps (or more) up the chain of command.

Calvin could hear him from a long way out. He hadn't enjoyed his captivity, and he was ready to start getting some revenge. As his feet hit the hangar floor, he began bellowing orders. "Soldier, who is in charge here! It was nice of you to bring us here, but this is not where our command headquarters are! We need to get to the base, so we can begin running the resistance and get the Chinese kicked out of our country! I need to speak to your commanding officer, right now! Point him out to me!"

Calvin hated people who only spoke in exclamation points. He sighed again; he *would* have to handle the problem. Although there were a number of captains from the admiral's staff standing around, none showed any inclination of getting in the admiral's way.

The only thing saving the situation at the moment was that the admiral had found the perfect person to talk to, Corporal Jimmy 'Colonel' Sanders. "Well, suh," Jimmy said, with at least two syllables in the first word, "Ah'm shur dat him's around here som'place, n'all, 'cause he was cert'n'ly on dat bargey thang wid us. If'n y'all'd relax yahrselves, suh, and fix yahrselves a seat, Ah'll try to hunt up the lieutenant, suh."

The admiral looked slightly bewildered at the Colonel's speech. He decided to try again. "Soldier, what is your name!" he bellowed. "Who is this lieutenant! Is this an army organization or a navy one! *Who is in charge here!!!!*"

The Colonel looked right back at the admiral, with the same look a puppy gives you when you accidentally step on its tail, the 'Why did you hurt me? What did I do?' look. His accent only got worse as he got flustered and tried again. "Now suh, Ah'm fixin' to git the lieut'nt fuh y'all. T'ain't no need to git rowdy n'all. Ah knows he's aroun' here somewhere or n'udder." Seeing Calvin walking over, his eyes lit up at the solution to his problem. "Suh, Ah'm..."

"I got it, Jimmy, thanks," Calvin said as he approached the admiral and saluted. "Hi, sir, Lieutenant Shawn Hobbs at your service. This little organization is...um...mine."

"Lieutenant Hobbs! Why are you wearing an army uniform with the name Sanders on it! Wait! The last man had one too! What is going on here! How come I don't know about this organization! Where are we! I've got places to go and things to do!"

When the admiral took a breath, Calvin spoke up before the admiral could continue, speaking louder than normal in the hopes of distracting him. Also, seeing that all of the former hostages had wandered over to see what the commotion was about, he tried to pitch his voice so everyone could hear it and save himself the trouble of having to repeat it.

"Here's the short version of the story, sir," he said, looking around to include everyone in the story, "China invaded the Seattle area yesterday. I was flying at Fallon, Nevada, and was sent here to see what was going on. I got shot down by a Chinese missile and was rescued by a SEAL who lived here in the mountains." Calvin thought he heard Master Chief snicker the word 'helicopter;' the fact that Calvin's jet had been shot down by a helicopter was a source of great amusement to the SEAL. Calvin continued, "The SEAL also happens to have some good friends in the Ranger community and a lot of weapons, and when you add that all together, you end up with this group, which has been doing its best to give the Chinese some payback all day. We were asked to drop what we were doing to come rescue you, so we did, but now we have to head back out again. That's the short version; unfortunately, it's also the only one we have time for right now. I also have some wounded men to see to…"

"Unacceptable!" the admiral interjected. "I'm in charge now, and you work for me! I'm the senior officer present! No one is leaving until I get some answers! I'm setting my staff up here, and you are going to provide security for this building while I work!" He finally noticed that the LCAC was Chinese. "We also have Chinese technology here that must be protected! How did it get here!"

"With all due respect," Calvin said, cutting in again when the admiral took another breath. "We have to be going." Seeing Master Chief approaching, he asked, "How are our wounded men doing?"

"Good, sir. We're all loaded up and ready to go." It wasn't difficult to see his amusement at Calvin's situation. "Would you like us to come back later and get you?" he asked with a grin.

The admiral saw Master Chief's rank insignia, and he finally had a piece of normalcy he could grab a hold of. "At last! A proper navy man, dressed as a navy man! Senior Chief! Set up a perimeter around this building, so that we can begin planning the return to our base! I have my staff, and we are ready to get to work!"

"Sorry, sir," Master Chief said with a smile. He didn't look or sound particularly sorry. "I can't do that. The president has already given us additional tasking we need to complete." He didn't feel like trying to explain that he was now a Master Chief, especially since his uniform still had the insignia of a Senior Chief Petty Officer.

"The president!" the admiral exclaimed. "Right! He's in Washington! I'm right here! I need you to come with me and help re-establish some order from this chaos!"

"With all due respect, sir," Master Chief said, sounding about as respectful as he had sorry, "we have other tasks we're supposed to be working on."

"No! I need you here right now!"

Calvin sighed. He hated having to do this, but he could see that everyone else was loaded up and waiting for him to go to the next job. "Um, Master Chief, can I borrow your phone, please?"

"With pleasure," Master Chief said with an evil grin. "Here sir, let me put it on speaker for you."

"I don't think that will be necessary," Calvin said. He spoke into the phone for a minute and then handed the phone to the admiral. He met the Master Chief's eyes as they walked a short way off and frowned. "Really, Master Chief? You know what's about to happen to the admiral, right? You think that embarrassing him in front of all of these politicians and his staff is going to help with anything?"

"No, not particularly," Master Chief said, "but it sure would be fun and, you know..."

"Yeah, Master Chief, I know *all about* you and authority," Calvin said, sighing. "Intimately. Speaking of which, I've been meaning to ask you. Did I see the Chinese admiral you brought back was missing a finger? Was that your doing?"

"Hey, that's not fair!" Master Chief exclaimed. "The admiral tried to grab a gun. It was self-defense! I didn't break him on purpose! And besides, it was just the tip of his finger, not the whole thing."

Calvin looked at him in mock disbelief, "Couldn't you have grabbed his wrist or something? He's like 250 pounds and more out of shape than even I am. Surely you have better reflexes than him, right?"

Master Chief winced. "Well, yeah, but other people were shooting at me, and I just didn't have time!"

Calvin pressed, "So, what you're really saying is the out-of-shape admiral is faster than you?"

"No, I'm not saying that at all! I was ten feet away from him!" Master Chief exclaimed. Calvin raised an eyebrow. "It may have even been more like twelve or thirteen feet!"

Calvin grinned. "Now you sound like our admiral; all your sentences are starting to end in exclamation points. Are you sure you're not getting too old for this, Master Chief?"

"*No sir!*" Master Chief said emphatically.

"Okay," Calvin said, the grin now a full-fledged smile. "Just checking."

* * * * *

CHAPTER THREE

Evening, August 20

White House Situation Room, Washington, D.C., 2130 EDT (1830 PDT)

"What are you thinking? Are you sure you even *are* thinking? If so, you are obviously having delusions of adequacy! Now stop bugging the platoon, give them whatever assistance they require and then *get the hell out of their way! "DO I MAKE MYSELF PERFECTLY CLEAR?"* shouted the President of the United States, Bill Jacobs. Apparently, the person on the other end of the phone replied in the affirmative because the president grunted a brief "Good," and then hung up the phone.

"Thank you, Mr. President. The team was going to have problems getting anything else done with Barnaby running amok," Admiral James Wright, the Chief of Naval Operations, said.

"My pleasure," the president replied. "It was actually kind of fun, once I got warmed up to it. Now, you said the team actually *sank* the Chinese amphibious assault ship?"

"Yes sir," Admiral Wright said with a chuckle, "as much as you can sink something that is tied up to a pier, anyway. Not only did they get the hostages off the ship and then sink the ship at the pier, they also brought back the Chinese admiral who was in charge of the naval portion of the operation."

"Those guys don't do anything by half, do they?" asked the president. "What was it they were calling themselves?"

"The lieutenant leading the group said they were the '1st Joint Special Operations Platoon.'"

"Okay," said the president, changing subjects; "Back to business. Where do we stand with Taiwan?"

"We're still in danger of losing the island," the Navy Intelligence captain said. He had been briefing the president when the call from Seattle came in. "We have some really good news, but we have some really bad news, as well. Once the team in Seattle recovered the nuclear weapons, we commenced operations for the defense of Taiwan. We had two submarines in the area, the USS *Seawolf* (SSN-21) and the USS *North Carolina* (SSN-777); they have both gone on the offensive."

"Our initial report from the *North Carolina* is outstanding. She caught an invasion wave in the middle of the South China Sea. Apparently, the Chinese thought holding Seattle hostage would freeze us for longer than it did, and they sent over a wave of eight amphibious assault ships with only a *Jiangwei*-class frigate and a *Luyang*-class destroyer for protection.

The *North Carolina* started by sinking the destroyer and the frigate with its initial torpedo volley and then proceeded to sink all eight of the transports. After the fourth one went down, the rest started abandoning ship rather than waiting to go down with all hands. The *North Carolina's* commanding officer gave them time to abandon ship and then sank the remainder of them. Most of the people in the last four ships will survive, but all of the equipment is at the bottom of the South China Sea, and their soldiers are in rubber rafts. When we last heard from the *North Carolina*, they said they had indications the Chinese aircraft carrier was nearby. It was the commanding officer's intention to find it, track it and sink it. That's the good news."

"Things did not go so well for the *Seawolf*," he continued. "Her patrol got off to a good start, with her sinking a Chinese *Yukan*-class tank landing ship she found out on its own. Later, she found a convoy of eight Chinese transports and started shadowing them, looking to get a shot. The convoy appeared to be guarded by a *Luyang*-class destroyer, a *Luzhou*-class destroyer and a *Sovremenny*-class destroyer. The problem was the *Sovremenny*-class destroyer was not a Chinese ship, but a Russian destroyer shadowing the Chinese convoy.

The Russians have always shadowed our ships to watch how we trained so they would be better prepared to fight us in a war. Apparently, they were doing the same thing to the Chinese, and they were shadowing the convoy to see how the Chinese conducted amphibious operations. Unfortunately, the *Seawolf* sank the convoy. All of them, including the Russian destroyer. The State Department is on the phone with the Russians right now, and they are *pissed*. They don't care that their ship was in a war zone. They want blood..."

Sommers' House, North Bend, WA, 1845 PDT

"I'm not sure I can do another mission," Calvin complained, lying down on the couch. "I don't think I have an ounce of adrenaline left in my body. I am *beat*. How do you guys *do* this all the time?"

"Generally, we don't do this many missions in a row," Master Chief said. "Don't worry, though, sir. Once the bullets start flying again, I think you'll be favorably impressed with how quickly your body can make some more adrenaline for you."

The command team was back at the Sommers' house for some final intelligence collection and mission planning, prior to meeting up with the rest of the platoon for the mission brief. Mrs. Sommers had put together an elk stew that had refreshed them, but now Calvin was in danger of going into a food coma. This was more than he had exercised in the last six months combined. When added to the near-constant terror of combat for most of the day, he couldn't remember ever being this tired. Still, the missile system needed to be put out of action so the U.S. forces could operate in the area. He rolled back vertical again and went over to the kitchen table, which had been cleaned off and was now covered in a variety of maps and drawings. Calvin had never realized how complicated a missile system was until he actually saw all of the components of one laid out across the landscape. It was impressive...in a really awful sort of way.

Most of the maps showed North Bend's E.J. Roberts Park and the area around it. The park was a 4.9-acre recreational area located in the northeast portion of the town. A family-oriented facility, it had a playground, two tennis courts, a basketball court, restrooms, and paved walkways. It also now had a bunch of missiles. Calvin knew of at least five missile transporters hidden among the trees in E.J. Roberts Park, including two that were next to each other on the tennis courts. The tennis nets still lay on the courts where the transporters had rolled over them.

In addition to the park, some of the missile system's components were hidden in a field to the south of it. The mostly-open field was about four times the size of the park and had once been cultivated, but it had been allowed to lie fallow for several years, and trees were starting to take over again.

Located to the east of the park was a neighborhood with about 50 houses. Two of the cul-de-sacs had new residents; the Chinese had parked missile transporters in the middle of them. It would be hard to do anything about those transporters without damaging the houses surrounding them. Probably why the Chinese parked them there, Calvin realized.

The soldiers had an excellent view of one of the transporters. Sara had a friend who lived in one of the cul-de-sacs, and Sara had set up a Skype connection with her. Her friend had then turned her laptop to face out the window; they now had continuous streaming video of the deployed transporter. Nothing was happening with it at the moment, although two Chinese soldiers were constantly patrolling the area.

Of all the missions they had conducted so far, this was the one the Rangers were the most prepared for. That didn't mean that they were taking the Chinese lightly or being complacent with their planning, though; this was combat, and they were planning as if their lives depended on it. They did.

The platoon was down to 21 effectives, 22 if you counted Paris, who was 'iffy.' He tried to make light of the wound he had received on his upper arm. It had taken 10 stitches to close, but he said that he didn't have any long-term effects from it. He had refused pain medication to show how small it was until Top ordered him to at least take one of the 800 milligram Motrins that most Rangers kept somewhere close by. The giant Motrins were so much a part of Rangers' daily lives they were also known by the slang term, 'Ranger Candy.'

Even with 22 personnel, they were still pretty thin to go up against what looked to be a guard force of at least a company (around a hundred men) in size.

On the good side, Calvin thought, they weren't forced to do battle with them one-on-one; all they really needed to do was figure out a way to destroy the HQ-19 system hiding in and around the park. They had considered several ways to accomplish the task. The first was to destroy all of the missiles. While that would keep from being used, it wouldn't prevent the Chinese from bringing in additional missiles if they had them. It was an option, but not the best one.

A second option was to target the command and control portion of the SAM network and destroy the system's radars and the command and control vehicle. Without that equipment, the missiles were just a bunch of rocket motors and high explosive; they could neither be launched nor guided. While the Chinese might be able to bring in additional radars or command vehicles, the odds of them having many more of those were a lot smaller, as they weren't made to be replenished. This option would also be easier, as they would only need to blow up three vehicles rather than the eight missile transporters. The final option was to kill all of the missile technicians and operators. Without the people to run them, the missiles were worthless. This option was the hardest, because it was impossible to know which people in the area were the missile system operators and which were the missile system's guards. And the Chinese could always bring in more.

The obvious choice was to go after the radars and the command and control vehicle; any missile transporters they destroyed along the way would be gravy. When they looked at the maps, though, they saw they had a problem with collateral damage, as both radars were in the backyards of houses on Merritt Place and the command vehicle was alongside a house on Taylor Place. Depending on the blast radius and direction, the houses on Merritt Place *might* not be destroyed; the house on Taylor Place, however, was doomed.

Calvin looked a little closer and noticed the house on Taylor Place had a small kiddie pool in its back yard. No, Calvin thought, not gonna happen. Whatever else we do today, I am *not* going to blow up a kid. Looking around, he realized this was why he was in charge.

"Okay, guys," he said, getting everyone's attention. "Here's the problem. See this picture?" He pointed to the pool. "That house has a little kid in it, and I am *not* blowing up a house with a kid. Nor am I filleting him with broken glass when I blow in the windows of his house while he's sleeping. We can't just blow up all of these houses. *They're Americans, damn it!* We're not in downtown Fallujah or somewhere in Afghanistan where all of the people are actively trying to kill us. These are our people and we will *not* kill the very people we are here to protect!"

He looked around and could tell no one else had made the connection before him.

The soldiers and the SEAL looked at each other, looked at Calvin, and then looked at each other some more. Finally, Master Chief turned back to Calvin and said, "Okay sir, granted, I don't want to kill Americans any more than you do; however, we have targets we need to destroy." He paused, then asked, "With all due respect, sir, how do you propose we accomplish our mission of blowing them up, if we can't actually blow them up?" Calvin was surprised; Master Chief actually sounded respectful.

"Well, Master Chief," Calvin replied, "I have absolutely *no* idea how we're going to do it, but I can tell you we're going to sit here on our asses, all night if we have to, until someone figures it out. So, don't give me any shit; just figure it out. You're the ones with all of the experience killing people and breaking things. Just fucking *do it.*"

Top looked at the photo. "Hmmm...," he said. "I guess if we infiltrated down the tree line from Boxley Place, we might get close enough to open up the door to the command vehicle and toss some grenades into it. That'll wreck it without damaging the house behind it. Would that work?" he asked. "It wouldn't be my favorite way of doing it, and it would probably lower our chances for overall mission success, but if we have to keep it within those parameters, we can try to make it work."

Even though he hadn't intended it, Calvin could hear BTO say to Tiny, "Ouch. I'm glad *we* won't be the ones to get stuck with that."

"Okay, I get it," Calvin said, "I'm making this harder than it has to be. The bottom line is that people aren't going to appreciate their houses being destroyed, even if the government fixes them afterwards. For example, my sister has this photo album she has spent literally hundreds of hours on. It's irreplaceable. She'd probably rather lose *me* in a fire than that book. If we start blowing up people's houses, we're going to destroy those things. And if we kill a kid..." He paused, and a funny look crossed his face.

Master Chief had never seen that look before. "Are you okay, sir?"

Calvin rubbed his temples as he looked at the cabinet where Taylor Sommers, Sara's mother, was putting something away. He removed his hands, and everyone could see he was smiling. "Maybe we're going about this all wrong," he said slowly. Everyone waited. He paused, savoring the feeling of accomplishment. Calvin looked at Sara, who was sitting behind the soldiers. "Have you ever wanted to be a Girl Scout?"

The apparent non sequitur had everyone confused, Master Chief most of all. "Sir, are you feeling all right? Did you happen to hit your head earlier?"

"No," Calvin said, "I'm fine. I did, however, have an epiphany."

"What's an epi-phony?" BTO asked.

"The lieutenant's just using a big word to say that he had a bright idea," Master Chief said. "Whatcha got, sir?" he asked.

"We're looking at this the wrong way," Calvin replied. "The people in these houses are Americans. We can talk to them. Why don't we just ask them to leave?"

Everyone looked confused, but Tiny most of all. "Sir," the laconic sniper said, "I'm afraid I don't have any idea what you're talking about."

"Okay," Calvin said. "How about this? We don't want to kill Americans, right? What if we have someone go door to door, posing as a salesperson, and tell everyone to leave for the night. That way, we get all of the little kids out of the neighborhood, and then we can do whatever else we need to. If we can evacuate the people, and especially the little kids, then I don't mind if there is a little collateral damage. I just don't want some kid growing up with nightmares about bad guys blowing up his house while he was sleeping. How does that sound?"

"Gee, sir," Top said, "that's crazy enough it just might work..."

Joint Base Lewis-McChord, Tacoma, WA, 1955 PDT

Colonel Zhang Wei shook his head. The navy had failed him. Again. They had a simple task, go to Bangor and get some nuclear warheads. They had plenty of marines, and they had attack helicopters. And they had allowed themselves to be defeated. Not only that, but now their command ship had been sunk at the pier, and their admiral taken captive. The incompetence!

He should never have trusted the navy with the mission.

In the morning, he would send some of his own men and would get the never-sufficiently-to-be-damned nuclear weapons himself. The Americans had an appropriate saying, 'If you want something done right, you have to do it yourself.' He would send enough tanks, infantry fighting vehicles and combat troops to destroy whatever force was waiting there, as well as anything they might meet along the way. The helicopters that returned had only reported rifle and machine gun fire. His armor would make short work of the Americans guarding the nuclear weapons, and everything would proceed as planned. They might have an 'accident' with one of the warheads on the way back, just for causing him so much trouble.

He had never failed in anything he had ever put his mind to. He *would* get this mission back on track. His honor depended on it.

Three Doors Down from the Sommers' House, North Bend, WA, 2000 PDT

John Huang looked out his window as the men got into their cars and drove off. This was at least the second time all of them had been at the Sommers' house. He knew there were surface-to-air missiles in the park behind their house; wasn't it just a little bit curious that people in military uniforms kept going into the house closest to them? John wondered what they were doing there. They must be spying.

John wasn't just a person with a Chinese-sounding last name; he *was* Chinese and had come to America many years before as a secret agent. A customs inspector for the port of Seattle, it had been his job to let in a number of containers full of arms and uniforms in preparation for the invasion the day before.

And he remained a loyal agent of China.

He would have to keep an eye on that house. On second thought, maybe it was better to report the suspicious activity to the chain of command, just in case. He continued to worry that the ground force commander would consider him a loose end, now that his part in the invasion was over, and he knew what happened to Zhang's loose ends. He desperately wanted to show he was still an asset...

North Bend Premium Outlet Mall, North Bend, WA, 2030 PDT

The platoon met for their final briefing at North Bend Premium Outlets, a big outlet mall located less than a mile west of the Sommers' house, where they had taken over the stock room of the Carter's outlet store. Top had approached the manager of the store, and he had agreed to allow them to use it. All of the employees had been warned to stay out of the back.

While business had gone on as usual in the front of the store, nearly 30 men were resting and recovering from missions in the back. All of the stock had been stacked along the walls, and the shelves were being used to store arms and ammunition. It looked eerie to Calvin to see a RPG-69 rocket launcher sitting alongside 'Mr. Cuddle Bunny.' He had seen similar things before in post-apocalyptic role-playing games; he never thought it would happen in America.

Looking at the men assembled in the room, intense concentration evident on their faces, Calvin had a random thought. In the history of warfare, what was the most unlikely place a major military operation had ever been planned? If it wasn't in the back of a store that sold baby clothes, Calvin wasn't sure where else it could be. Maybe if the campaign maps had been spread out on the altar of St. Peter's Basilica at the Vatican, perhaps.

Calvin, Master Chief and Top quickly detailed the plan for destroying the HQ-19 missile system, and everyone began final checks on their weapons. Although their manning was getting low, they were once again flush with arms and ammunition, courtesy of the armory on the *Long*. There were enough rifles and ammunition to go around, and all of the troopers who had previously carried American machine guns were now re-armed with the Chinese equivalent. Although they were without the punch of a heavy machine gun and the Ranger Anti-tank Weapon System, they had been able to capture several grenade launchers, and they had a good number and variety of grenades to use with them. The twins had been playing with one of the RPG systems and were looking forward to trying out all of the different types of grenades.

In addition to their haul from the ship, the owner of "The Marksman" had been able to call in some favors and had acquired almost 30 grenades for their M203 grenade launchers. He had cheerfully provided them to the team with only a 20% mark-up added to Calvin's bill. Calvin didn't care; with the capability they added, he was happy to get them...and besides, it wasn't *his* credit card they were using.

One of the other benefits of having their operational headquarters at the outlet mall was it had allowed Staff Sergeant Dantone to go shopping at the local toy store. He was looking for something that would give them the ability to communicate as a group and synchronize their actions, something they had lacked. While he wasn't entirely successful, he was able to come up with a potential workaround he hoped would provide at least some of the needed capability.

He had bought out the store's entire supply of Motorola Talkabout hand-held radios. Billed as the "ultimate communication tool for the serious outdoor enthusiast," the MR350 had an advertised range of up to 35 miles. What had sold The Wall on the MR350 radio was its silent vibrating ringer; they could use it to synchronize their operations without giving away their presence.

They were as ready as they were going to be.

Sommers' House, North Bend, WA, 2200 PDT

"Oooh, mom, did you hear his speech about how 'These are our people, and *we will not kill the people we are here to protect?*'" Sara asked, her voice a little on the dreamy side. "Isn't he soooo cool?" Sara had just completed her rounds of the neighborhood, and the Sommers' family was relaxing in their living room.

"Yes," her mother replied, seeing where this was going. "I wouldn't get too attached to him, though. He's doing a very dangerous job and might not make it through the night, much less into next week."

"Oh, *mom!*" Sara exclaimed. "Why do you have to *say* something like that? Besides, did you see the way all those men, all those *tough Rangers*, looked up to him and did what he said? He's soooo cool," she repeated.

Tom Sommers looked up as someone knocked on the door. A hard banging, it was nothing like what the soldiers used when they came by. A little concerned, he went to the door and opened it just enough to be able to see the squad of Chinese soldiers waiting outside. He started to say, "Can I help you?" but was knocked backward as the door was kicked in, and the soldiers stormed into the house.

They raced through it, finding and subduing his wife and daughter. As he watched their progress, he was happy the soldiers had taken their stack of maps and pictures with them when they left. They would have been hard to explain, perhaps even fatal. There were already stories circulating about people who had confronted the occupiers and disappeared.

Another person walked into the house. While Tom didn't recognize the uniform of the person, he *did* recognize the aura of authority emanating from him. He carried himself like someone who was used to being in charge and to being obeyed. The man came to stand in front of the Sommers family and said in good English, "I am Captain Du Jun. One of your neighbors has indicated to us you have had some military men here today, and we would like to know what they were doing."

Sara spoke up impulsively before either her mother or father could say anything. "One of them is my boyfriend," she explained. "He came over with a few of his friends to say 'hi.'"

"I see," the captain said. "And why were they in uniform?"

Sara hesitated slightly and said, "They were in uniform because they were out camping over the weekend in the woods. They didn't realize you had taken over, and it would look odd for them to be in uniform. We told them to go change, so they left."

"So, you have to be in a military uniform in order to camp in the United States?" the captain asked.

"No, you don't," Sara said, "but it helps to be in camouflage if you are out stalking deer to get ready for the upcoming hunting season. That way they can't see you as easily."

"I'm sure it does," the captain replied. He almost believed her, but something about the story seemed a little wrong. When you added to it the slight hesitation she showed when she answered, it seemed like she might be hiding something. Perhaps the Chinese agent who had reported this family had been correct; they could very well be subversives. If so, a night of sleeping on a concrete floor, followed by a session with the interrogation squad, ought to loosen up their tongues.

"Okay, I believe you," he said. The family sagged visibly. "That is why I am going to take you to our headquarters, so you can call this boyfriend and prove to my major you are telling the truth." He could see it in the way their faces fell; they were hiding something. Whatever it was, he was sure they would get every last bit of information out of them in the morning.

"Take them back to headquarters!" he ordered.

KIRO-TV, Channel 7, Seattle, WA, 2305 PDT

"I n local news, workers in Seattle and Tacoma celebrated their liberation from the oppression of the American government," KIRO's anchorman, Danny Rizzoli, read. The broadcast showed a large Chinese flag being unfurled from the top of the Space Needle in downtown Seattle, and then it cut to a group of Americans cheering and applauding. "Workers are also looking forward to better pay and working conditions under the Chinese, as well as a better standard of living for everyone in the region."

Rizzoli looked up from the papers on his desk. "I'm not going to read any more of this crap—" A burst of rifle fire hit him in the chest, interrupting him permanently. In the control booth, the Chinese Public Affairs Officer (PAO) pushed the 'kill' button before Rizzoli's words reached the end of the seven-second tape delay. Based on some of Rizzoli's earlier comments, the PAO had kept his finger over the button the entire broadcast, ready to terminate it at a moment's notice if Rizzoli said something he shouldn't. The show went smoothly to a commercial.

When the audience came back from commercial, only the co-host, Anna St. Cloud, was at the anchor desk. Although she looked scared, she followed the script for the rest of the broadcast, and there were no more problems. The cameramen kept her face in close, so that the audience couldn't see the red stains on her white blouse. The PAO was sure the drying blood provided an excellent reminder for Ms. St. Cloud to stick to the script.

* * * * *

CHAPTER FOUR

Morning, August 21

Team Calvin, E.J. Roberts Park, North Bend, WA, 0100 PDT

The neighborhoods around Roberts Park had been prepared as much as possible for the coming conflict. Sara had done her impression of a Girl Scout Cookie salesperson on Merritt Place, warning the four families who were closest to the potential danger zone. Instead of walking around in the two cul-de-sacs where the missile transporters were, which might have raised the Chinese suspicions, Sara called her friend who lived there and had her warn the neighbors. Over the course of the next couple hours, families went out for walks and just kept going, or went out to the movies, or to get groceries or a variety of other errands that had suddenly become important.

The neighborhood families left lights on and set timers, where able, to make it seem like they had returned, especially in upstairs windows where the Chinese wouldn't be able to see. While the houses seemed occupied, there was only one person still remaining in the 25 houses closest to the battle zone. Tyson Schattenkerk, a part time reporter for the local paper, had stayed in his house overlooking the missile transporter in the Taylor Place cul-de-sac. He also had a good view of the large field behind his house, where some of the other missile vehicles were, as well as the tents of the 100 or so Chinese soldiers who had taken up residence in the area. He had his low light cameras out and was hoping to get some good photos of the conflict he could sell and make a fortune on.

The members of the platoon had left the mall an hour and a half earlier after getting a short nap. Marginally better rested, they had split up to go to their starting points in small groups. They didn't want to attract attention, so they had to be off the roads by the midnight curfew.

Calvin waited on a roof in the northeast corner of the area of operations. Untrained in this method of warfare, he would have been more of a hindrance than a help. Still, he had a rifle with a night scope and could help spot movement. He was also far enough out of the way he could run for it if things went badly, while the rest of the platoon 'tactically egressed.' From where he lay, peering over from the opposite side of the roof's peak, he was able to see the majority of the large field in which the Chinese were camped. The field extended to the left of him for about 1,000 feet, with the neighborhoods and then E.J. Roberts Park to the right. He couldn't see into the park or the neighborhood because of the trees, but had a good view of the field.

Now that they'd had a little more time to study it, the platoon had found all of the main pieces of the missile system. The system's radars were located on the far side of the field from Calvin; from there, they had a good line of sight down the valley to the east which would prevent aircraft from attacking along that axis. The command truck, as they had noticed earlier, was still located along the tree line of the neighborhood in front of him, tucked up into the backyard of one of the houses. The missile transporters were scattered throughout the area in good cover, with two hidden in the trees of the park, two more on the park's two tennis courts, two hidden in the tree line next to the field and the final two located in the cul-de-sacs of the neighborhood.

The supply trucks were parked in the southwest corner of the field, inside a shed that was part of a cluster of three large metal farm buildings. Those buildings seemed to house the majority of the comings and goings of the troops; the local command structure appeared to be located in the barn that was the largest of the three buildings. There was also a farmhouse located to the south of the buildings. It was unknown whether the Chinese officers had taken it over and were sleeping there, or if they were staying in the barn.

Calvin looked at his watch, 0114.

"I wish you'd stop doing that," BTO whispered from a little further along the roof. "Every time you look, you make a small bit of light. Sooner or later, someone's going to see it, and we're pretty exposed up here."

"Yup," Tiny agreed, lying next to him.

The sniper team was used to waiting; sometimes missions called for them to be in position for days prior, where they had to wait patiently on the chance they *might* get a shot. Sometimes the target never showed, and it was all for naught. Sniper teams either learned patience, or they found a different warfare specialty. Being a sniper wasn't for everyone.

"Sorry," Calvin said. "Never done this before, and I'm kind of nervous."

"Good; you should be," BTO whispered back. "Now, shut up!" He thought about it a second and realized what he had just said. "I mean, please shut up, *sir!*" he corrected in a whisper.

Rather than say anything else, Calvin just nodded slowly, showing that he got the point. BTO re-focused his attention on the field, scanning for targets. Calvin watched for a couple of seconds and then nearly wet himself when the walkie talkie vibrated in his pocket.

"Be ready," BTO advised quietly. "Here we go."

Team Twin, E.J. Roberts Park, North Bend, WA, 0115 PDT

The twins initiated the attack. Located near a little league baseball diamond to the south of the field, they had already loaded their two RPG-69 launchers. Both of them would fire a rocket in the initial barrage; after that, it was Bad Twin's turn to be shooter, and Good Twin would load for him. Bad Twin looked down the infrared sight at the barn, going through everything he'd been able to find out about the system and its ammunition on the internet. Just like the venerable Russian RPG-7, from which the Chinese had reverse-engineered the RPG-69, the system was a low-cost, easy-to-use weapon. The launcher had a 40mm tube, but could fire a variety of projectiles that were much larger. The launcher and sight mechanism were fairly light, weighing only 18 pounds. The standard 85mm anti-tank rocket would have weighed an additional five pounds...but that wasn't what he had loaded.

Instead, both he and his brother had 120mm WPF 2004 rockets, which would get the attack off to a really big bang. The WPF 2004 was a recent introduction to the Chinese arsenal that weighed two pounds more than the normal rocket and had a fuel-air explosive warhead. These rockets detonated with the same power as five pounds of high explosive and were devastating in close quarters, especially if fired into a building.

Both brothers were aiming at buildings.

Bad Twin was shooting at the big barn on the left, and Good Twin at the vehicle storage building on the right. Bad Twin counted down, and they launched at the same time. The rockets functioned as designed, arcing over the road and penetrating the sides of the thin aluminum frames. With a tremendous explosion, the building holding the support vehicles was leveled. The other weapon detonated in the barn, and the left half of the barn collapsed, although the beams at the right end of the barn still held up that end.

Both brothers paused a second to take in what they had just done.

"Cool," mumbled Bad Twin, in a voice full of awe.

Then they were back at it, firing rockets as fast as Private First Class Hector 'Macho' Carrasquillo, the fourth member of the team, could spot for them.

Although the maximum range of the system was listed as 500 meters, accurate firing was difficult at ranges over 300 meters. They had closed to about 150 meters to make sure they hit the farm structures on their first volley, which meant they were also well within range of return rifle fire, and shots began to ring out.

The first reload Good Twin fed into the launcher was an anti-personnel incendiary rocket. Meant for killing enemy soldiers, the weapon had 900 steel balls and 2,500 incendiary pellets that scattered over a 15-meter radius on detonation.

Bad Twin fired the rocket-propelled grenade, and it burst within 10 meters of the guard he had seen at the still-standing end of the barn. Rifle fire from that direction ceased, and a brush fire started. He handed the empty tube back to Good Twin and got one with a Type 69 warhead in return.

Macho had seen troops coming from the farmhouse and had called for the anti-personnel round. The rocket landed just to the left of the three soldiers but did not explode. Instead, it hit the ground and then bounced back up six feet, where it detonated in an airburst, scattering 800 steel balls that scythed outward from the blast. All three of the soldiers went down.

With no more soldiers in sight, Macho called for another WPF 2004 round to finish off the barn, and Good Twin's next reload had the large thermobaric round on top. Bad Twin took his time, aimed and launched the weapon into the part of the barn still standing. It detonated inside, blowing out the rest of the building and flinging away pieces of the soldiers who had been going into it to rescue their comrades.

Macho called for more of the airburst rounds as soldiers began coming out of their tents across the field and running toward them. Although the soldiers couldn't see the rocketeers, as they were on the other side of the fires burning at the buildings, every time Bad Twin launched a rocket, the back blast lit them up, and they were starting to draw more and more return fire. Reggie responded with a three-shot burst at every muzzle flash he saw.

Macho had the brothers fire one more air burst, and then everyone ran to the south, stopping behind the home dugout at Turguson Park's baseball field, where they had pre-positioned three more rockets. Bad Twin put the first of these, an airburst round, into the nearest concentration of soldiers, and then both brothers loaded and fired a high explosive/high explosive anti-tank round simultaneously. Although originally designed to give an anti-tank capability, the rounds exploded into 1,500 pre-fabricated fragments if they didn't hit the steel armor of a tank.

The two brothers dropped the rounds 10 meters apart between the two buildings, and the entire team left the field at a jog while the Chinese were picking themselves up from the force of the twin detonations.

They didn't stop after that; it was never their intent to get into a pitched battle, but to draw the Chinese to the south. Any casualties they caused along the way, though, were quite all right.

Team SEAL, E. J. Roberts Park, North Bend, WA, 0115 PDT

"Holy shit!" Master Chief thought as the buildings exploded. Even though the blast was contained within the buildings, he could still feel the 'thump' of the concussion as the rounds detonated. One of the buildings completely blew out and collapsed to the ground, burying the missile supply vehicles he could see inside. Although one end of the larger building remained standing, the Chinese wouldn't be able to use it again any time soon. It looked like it would probably be easier to knock it down and start over. The next round detonated in a sheet of flame that looked like a white phosphorus round. Flames began to lick the side of the barn and caught the dry grass on fire. The level of light increased dramatically near the farm buildings, ruining the night vision of anyone in the area.

As he watched, a second thermobaric round hit the barn and leveled it. The concussion of the round and its ability to use up the oxygen in the air had a smothering effect on the fire still raging in the area. As he watched, soldiers from the camp started heading toward the source of the attack. He could tell where the brothers were; the back blast from the RPG launcher was obvious when they fired it.

The brothers' spotter was doing an outstanding job; any time Chinese soldiers gathered, anti-personnel rounds dropped in on top of them. The rounds looked like giant shotgun blasts that shredded everything within 50 feet of them.

The battle was going far better than he had hoped. By his count, the Chinese had lost at least 30 soldiers killed and a similar number maimed by the time the RPG team left for the rendezvous point. If the Americans had followed up the RPG bombardment with a full-force attack, they might have been able to kill or capture the entire company's worth of troops. Maybe not, he decided as he watched. More soldiers continued to pour from the farmhouse, and more men than expected came running from the tents. The Americans were probably up against two full companies of troops, not one.

As the RPG team withdrew, the Chinese soldiers were solely focused on the southern end of the field; no one was looking at the radar vehicles. Even the guards who were posted by them were looking south as explosion after explosion devastated their comrades. Master Chief and Corporal 'Becks' Beck snuck around the vehicles from the north and shot them both with silenced pistols.

With the guards out of the way, Master Chief got to work. Starting first with the truck-mounted 'Grave Stone' multi-mode engagement radar, he pulled the high explosives out of his pack and began attaching them to both the vehicle and the radar's antenna mast.

Master Chief was an expert in most facets of the SEAL trade. He was both an outstanding pistol and rifle shot, and he could run and swim all day long, even better than kids half his age. But where he truly excelled was with explosives. As he had demonstrated onboard the *Long*, he was a creative genius with them. He had sunk the *Long* primarily with explosives he had found on the ship; now he had explosives from his own private cache, and he had spared no expense.

While the rest of his five-man team dropped off the explosives they had carried and then provided over watch support in case someone came their way, he wired the engagement radar and then the truck-mounted 'Big Bird' acquisition radar, as well. Some rifle fire sounded from the northeast, but it was not directed at him so he continued working on the truck, smiling happily to himself when he found that both trucks' gas tanks were full. He finished attaching the explosives, and his team withdrew back into the shadows.

Team Top, E. J. Roberts Park, North Bend, WA, 0115 PDT

"**W**ow!" Top thought as he felt the buildings blow up to the south. Those must be pretty good explosions to feel them this far away, especially since they went off *inside* the buildings.

He and his team of six were infiltrating the park from the north. Theirs was the most difficult mission of the evening, and the reason for the diversion. He and The Wall were within two meters of their targets, two guards patrolling around the missile transporters in the park.

Team Calvin, E.J. Roberts Park, North Bend, WA, 0115 PDT

"Impressive," rumbled Tiny at the force of the concussion.

Calvin continued looking through the scope. Unlike Tiny's, his rifle did not have a suppressor on it. If he shot, there would be a muzzle blast visible to anyone who was looking, which would also highlight them on the roof. As that was a 'bad thing,' he did not intend to shoot at anything unless one of his troop's lives depended on it. It was, however, interesting to watch professionals at work. Tiny fired, his rifle sounding like a light cough next to Calvin.

E.J. Roberts Park, North Bend, WA, 0115 PDT

The two Chinese guards looked at each other in surprise as two explosions came from the south. Their squad was on duty at the northern end of the field, guarding the missile system command vehicle and the missile transporters in the park and neighborhood. More blasts came from the south, and they stopped their patrol around the command vehicle and watched as the detonations lit up the night sky.

With a 'thwack,' one of the guards spun forward, with most of his left shoulder separated from his body. Knowing his partner had been shot, the other guard dove to the side and spun around to look for the shooter.

Tyson Schattenkerk, a part-time reporter for the Snoqualmie Valley Record, had been watching out the window all night, and he had started taking pictures of the guards patrolling around the truck to stay awake. He was looking through the viewfinder of his camera when the guard was shot, and he saw an explosion of blood as the giant bullet hit him. Tyson pulled out another camera with a longer lens to get a close up of the soldier on the ground; unfortunately, he forgot to turn off the flash, and it strobed as the remaining soldier turned to look in his direction.

The soldier saw the flash and knew the shooter was hiding on the second floor of the house to the north of him. He sighted down his rifle as best he could with partially flash-blinded eyes, and he fired his rifle through the large window on full automatic, going through most of the magazine before Tiny's next round caught him in the chest. It was already too late for Tyson Schattenkerk, though; three of the soldier's rounds hit him in the chest, and he was already dead.

It was also unfortunate for the platoon. Now the Chinese were aware something was also going on at the north end of the field.

Team Top, E.J. Roberts Park, North Bend, WA, 0115 PDT

Top and The Wall paused as the gunfire sounded to the east of their position, and the men they had been about to grab jerked in surprise. The two Americans were equally surprised; there wasn't supposed to be any firing in their area. As they were aware of the attack in progress, the Americans reacted more quickly than the Chinese. Like snakes striking, they leaped forward to grab their intended victims. Both men had fashioned garrotes with wire taken from the Sommers' piano, and they looped them around the two guards' throats and pulled them tight.

Taken by surprise, the guards neither made a noise nor fired their weapons. Top and The Wall lowered the dead men to the ground without a sound. With the first two down, there were only six more guards left in the park, the two guards at the tennis courts and two pairs of guards in the cul-de-sacs with the missile transporters.

The guards at the tennis courts were being watched by Private First Class Adam 'Nine' Severn and Corporal Suzi 'Deadeye' Taylor. The two pairs of guards in the cul-de-sacs were similarly being watched by Corporal Jimmy 'Colonel' Sanders and Private First Class Christian 'Woody' Woodard. If the Chinese soldiers left their posts, the Americans would kill them before they could interfere; otherwise, they would be shot when the command vehicle detonated. Having disposed of their guards, Top and The Wall continued to infiltrate toward their objective, the missile command vehicle, while explosions continued to hammer away to the south.

They crept up to within 80 meters of the command vehicle, and Top pressed the walkie talkie twice, giving the signal. The three machine gunners and Deadeye took out the remaining guards, and The Wall fired their last RPG-69 rocket, sending a tandem-warhead anti-tank grenade into the side of the missile system's command vehicle. Although the anti-tank grenade was unable to penetrate the armor of most modern tanks, it *was* able to destroy lighter-skinned vehicles like armored personnel carriers and armored fighting vehicles. It also did a terrific job against trucks, like the missile system's command vehicle. It was destroyed in one shot, killing everyone aboard.

Having completed their mission, Top's team withdrew to the north. Fire began lashing out at them from the soldiers in the center of the field as the missile command vehicle burned brightly, highlighting everything in its vicinity. The team vanished into the woods and jogged north past the Sommers' house. They did not go into it, or even near it, so as not to draw undue attention; however, as they went by, Top saw what looked like a Chinese man exiting the front door. The man looked furtively left and right before running off down the street to the west.

Something was wrong.

Top sent The Wall to check on the Sommers and chased after the man. The chase didn't last long; the man went into a house three doors down. Top jogged up to the door and tried the knob. It was locked. The fire was slackening to the south, and Top knew he didn't have long before soldiers came investigate the destruction of the command vehicle. He kicked the door in to find the man drawing a pistol from a desk in the hallway. As the door slammed in, the man spun and fired.

Top dove back out of the doorway, the bullet ripping a hole through the bottom of his uniform pants. Top stuck his rifle into the hallway about a foot off the ground and fired a sustained burst. He heard a scream and then the sound of a body hitting the floor.

He glanced in through the door and then dodged back out of the way. The man was on the ground, holding his stomach. Coming into the house, he approached the man and kicked away the pistol lying nearby. Judging by the amount of blood, the man was probably hit a couple of times. He must have tried to dive out of the way when Top pointed his rifle into the hallway; it hadn't worked.

The man looked up and laughed, despite the obvious pain he was in. "Ha, ha, ha," he said. "They've taken away your friends! I reported them, and they took them. I did my duty!"

"*Who* took them?" Top asked.

"The captain," the man said, losing strength. "You'll never see them again. They went to the command center..." He passed out, dead or dying.

Worried now, Top went out the back door and north one block, before heading east. He had to find the lieutenant.

Team Calvin, E.J. Roberts Park, North Bend, WA, 0130 PDT

Calvin and the sniper team had just climbed off the roof and were about to leave for the rendezvous point on the bank of the Snoqualmie River when Master Chief appeared at Calvin's shoulder, startling him.

"Damn it!" Calvin exclaimed. "Don't *do* that!"

"Maybe you'll forgive me if I give you a present?" Master Chief asked, handing him a little box. The box had a push button on it, with a cage over the top.

Calvin's eyes narrowed. "What's this?" he asked.

"Well, you know how you're always giving me a hard time about being nice to authority? I thought I'd try it out once." Master Chief pointed out over the field to where the outline of one of the radars could be seen in the light of the burning barn. "I'm giving you the honors. Look that way and push the button."

Realizing they didn't have a lot of time to fool around, Calvin flipped up the cover, looked out over the field and pushed the button. He stared in awe as a temporary second sun illuminated the earth. For a few moments, night turned into day as the two radars went up in supernova explosions guaranteed to cook anyone unfortunate enough to be standing in the vicinity of them. Even four football fields away from the twin blasts, Calvin could feel the heat and concussion. The engagement radar antenna, a flat piece of metal about 10'x6'x9" weighing hundreds of pounds, was blown off its vehicle and flung over a 100 feet into the air, fluttering back down like an overgrown steel leaf. The massive tractor that had been carrying it was obliterated, blown into so many pieces the farmer would be finding them in his field for years to come.

When the fireball cleared, there were two small remnants of the radar vehicles and a field strewn with soldiers dead and dying from the shrapnel wind that had just blown through them.

"Holy shit!" Calvin muttered in awe. "What the hell was that?"

"Well, you said you wanted to blow up the radars so the Chinese could, and I quote, 'never use them again.' I was trying to do what you ordered. I don't believe they will *ever* be able to use those radars again." Master Chief looked smugly confident.

"They won't be able to use any of the houses nearby again, either!" Calvin yelled, forgetting that there were still enemy soldiers in the vicinity, even if most of them were currently deaf and flash-blinded.

"Now, sir, you said, and again I quote, 'a little bit of collateral damage is okay if we get the people out ahead of time.' With your great plan, we got everyone out, so I figured a little breakage was authorized. If nothing else, it certainly sent the Chinese a message."

"Master Chief, are you familiar with the term 'passive-aggressive?' It's where you appear to go along with something, but still continue to do what you want. I don't know; maybe you're oppositionally defiant. I'm no psych major, so I can't be sure. Regardless, I'm pretty sure you knew that *wasn't* what I was looking for. I just wanted them unusable, not vaporized."

Master Chief sighed, shaking his head. "You try to do what an officer wants, and look at the thanks you get..." He shrugged and then smiled. "You have to admit, though, the Chinese must have gotten the message."

"Yeah," Calvin said, "they probably got the message that it's time for them to leave. Assuming anyone survived the blast, that is."

As they started egressing east to the rendezvous, Top ran up. "Sir, we've got a problem."

South China Sea, South Pacific, 1700 China Standard Time (0200 PDT)

The war for the South China Sea raged on. The United States Navy had given far better than it had received, but it had lost both of its submarines. The *Seawolf* and the *North Carolina* had sunk 26 transports and nine escorts, including China's only operational aircraft carrier, before being sunk in turn.

The *Seawolf* was caught by surface forces as it attacked its third convoy and went down for the last time with all hands, a victim of a helicopter-borne torpedo. The *North Carolina* had snuck up on the Chinese aircraft carrier *Liaoning* and had put two torpedoes into it and a torpedo into each of her destroyer escorts. Unfortunately, the *North Carolina* hadn't noticed the quiet *Kilo*-class submarine in company with the carrier, and it had fired two torpedoes from close behind the *North Carolina*. Although the *North Carolina* fooled one of the torpedoes with a decoy, the other one hit the submarine. She was also lost with all hands.

Although the situation on the island of Taiwan was dire for the allies, the Taiwanese where able to fortify the northern tip of the island, and they still held both Taipei and New Taipei. Those two cities were extremely important, as they were the largest and fourth largest cities on the island, with over 1/4 of the island's population living in them. If help could arrive soon, they might still be able to hold onto the island. The sacrifice of the two U.S. submarines had curbed, but not stopped the tide of Chinese forces that continued to come ashore on the island. Fighters from the U.S. base at Okinawa were beginning to strike back at the Chinese, although they were taking heavy losses going up against equipment that was nearly as good as their own. Troops were also being forward deployed from the U.S. to the Philippines and Okinawa. Help was coming...if the Taiwanese could hold on long enough for it to arrive.

With the entrance of the United States into the war in Asia, Japan had redefined its treaty obligations and entered the fray. The Japanese Maritime Self-Defense Force was one of the largest navies in the world and the second largest in Asia (after the Chinese PLAN), and they moved five of their large Aegis destroyers to the Okinawa area to provide an air umbrella for the base. The Japanese also launched their attack subs into the South China Sea waters to replace the submarines the United States had lost. Although all 16 were unable to get underway at once, they were able to get 10 on patrol. The Taiwanese wondered whether 10 would be enough to stop the Chinese tide; the Japanese wondered whether the South China Sea would be big enough for all of them to operate at once.

Middle Fork Snoqualmie River, North Bend, WA, 0200 PDT

"All right," Calvin said, "give me the whole story where everyone can hear it." The platoon had retreated northeast and rendezvoused where one of the neighborhood's roads met the banks of the Snoqualmie River. Shuteye and Jet weren't there, but Top had said they should start the briefing without them.

"When we were withdrawing after we blew up the command vehicle, I saw someone coming out of the Sommers' house," Top said. "I asked The Wall to go and check on the Sommers while I chased him down. As it turns out, the man only lived a few doors down, but he was a Chinese sympathizer, who turned in the Sommers for dealing with the military. He said the Sommers got taken away by some 'captain' to some 'command center.' He traded gunfire with me, and my rifle beat his pistol. He died before he could tell me anything else."

Calvin looked at The Wall. "I take it they weren't in the house when you went to check on them?"

"No sir," The Wall replied. "It looked like someone had tossed their house looking for something. I don't know if it was the Chinese soldiers looking for information or the Chinese neighbor looking for their valuables to steal. All I can tell you is they were gone, and their house was a shambles."

"Has anyone heard of this command center?" Calvin asked the group. Some shook their heads, while others just returned blank stares. None replied in the affirmative.

"Damn it," Calvin said. "We're the ones responsible for getting the family taken away. We have to find a way to get them back!"

"I know someone who might have some info on where to find them," Top said.

Calvin followed Top's gaze; Shuteye and Jet were returning.

"Did you have any success?" Top asked.

Shuteye nodded his head. "Top asked us to go back and see if we could find a soldier we could capture and question," he explained. "There were a lot of soldiers around the field who were somewhat dazed after the explosions, especially that last blast, so it wasn't too hard to capture a soldier we could talk to. After a little...persuasion...he decided it would be better to tell us than to make us any angrier than we already were. The command center is where their headquarters is. It's at some sort of truck stop on the highway."

Calvin turned to Master Chief, who lived close by. "Do you know where he's talking about?" he asked.

Master Chief looked thoughtful. "Yeah, I know where that is. Remember when I said I blew up an anti-aircraft gun? It was in the truck stop parking lot." He paused. "If they're being kept in there, they may not be easy to get to."

"I don't care," replied Calvin. "They got taken away because they helped us. We're going to get them back."

"And the fact that they have a young, cute daughter that likes you?" Master Chief asked.

"Has nothing to do with it," Calvin answered. "Wait, she likes me? How do you know?"

Top sighed loudly. "Youth these days are so stupid," he commented to Master Chief. "Still, the Sommers did help us, and we should get them back if possible."

"I know," Master Chief said. "It's the 'if possible' that worries me. That truck stop is going to be a tough nut to crack."

He was interrupted as an HQ-19 missile transporter came roaring up to them and parked close by. The platoon readied their weapons, expecting an attack. A bigger surprise followed, as the doors to the cab opened, and the twins jumped out, followed by Reggie and Macho. Macho was walking with a limp.

"*Dude!*" said the one who had been driving. "How do you like our ride? So, we were like walking along coming back here, and this thing was like, sitting there all by itself. So we said, *dude*, let's like, try to hotwire it."

The other twin chimed in, "But when we jumped into it, the keys were like, right there in the ignition."

The driver finished, "And since, like, Macho was all shot up and shit, we thought we'd drive him back in style." He looked at Macho. "Dude, you *were* style'n, weren't ya?"

Calvin looked at Top and Master Chief. "First an LCAC, now a missile transporter. Growing up, did you guys always steal your friends' toys when you were done playing with them?"

White House Situation Room, Washington, D.C., 0600 EDT (0300 PDT)

"So, as you can see, sir, we've made some gains in the area, especially now that the Japanese and Koreans are engaged, and we are going to take advantage of the cover of darkness tonight to drop in reinforcements to Taiwan." It had taken some time to get things moving, but the United States finally had forces shifting all over the globe. Soldiers were loading onto a variety of troop transports for movement to the Pacific and the northwest United States. When darkness fell on Taiwan tonight, the United States was going to try the largest combat parachute drop since World War II to reinforce the Taiwanese position in the north of the island. In addition to the aircraft headed that way, a massive air strike was being put together at Okinawa. The United States was coming, and there were a lot of pissed off soldiers, sailors and airmen that were ready to give the Chinese some payback.

Just like the animosity toward Japan after the sneak attack on Pearl Harbor, the president appreciated the determination of the American people that this attack neither go unpunished nor be allowed to succeed. The media was filled with interviews of common people on the streets of America who were ready to 'nuke them back to the Stone Age' or just 'kill those commie bastards.'

The Chairman of the Joint Chiefs continued his brief. "With regard to the Seattle Theater of Operations, we have also begun to get forces into place for opening up the region to attack. We believe the Chinese position in the area is somewhat like an egg. If we can just crack the hard outer shell, we should be able to roll up their forces in fairly short order. In fact, we just got word the Joint Special Operations Platoon was successful in taking down the HQ-19 missile system in the eastern portion of the area of operations. We're not sure what they did, but there was an explosion visible from space. They are completing a locally-derived mission and then will be working on another mission for us, which will open up a route into the city along I-90."

TCA Truck Stop, North Bend, WA, 0315 PDT

Master Chief and Calvin looked out from the cover of the forest behind the Edgewick Inn, listening to the sounds of guns firing in the distance. There wasn't a *lot* of firing, but it sounded like the Army was starting to probe the Chinese positions east of town. Good, Master Chief thought. It was about time for them to get into the game. Every once in a while they heard a louder 'boom' as a bigger gun, probably a tank, fired.

The situation at the truck stop was worse than Master Chief remembered. Now, instead of two PGZ-95 self-propelled anti-aircraft systems, there were five in the vicinity. Having gone by Twin Falls Middle School three blocks to the north, he knew there was one located on the baseball field there. Another two vehicles occupied the parking lot across the street at the truck stop and one more was located at the Genie Lift factory a block north of him. Sara had also told them earlier about a fifth one on the other side of I-90 she had seen the day prior. It was probably still there, too.

It didn't appear much was going on at the truck stop itself; most of the activity was at the Edgewick Inn across the street. It made sense for the headquarters to be in the hotel, as that would give the Chinese access to conference rooms, dining facilities and beds to sleep in.

The hotel was closer to the woods, which would allow the platoon to approach it unseen. This was much better than the truck stop; the approaches there were nearly devoid of cover.

Hmmm...nearly devoid of cover was not the same as completely devoid of cover, Master Chief thought as he looked again. Yes, it might just be possible to do this. It would really suck if something went wrong, but just maybe...

"We might be able to do something about the anti-aircraft guns," Master Chief whispered.

"We should, now that we're here," Calvin replied. "The Chief of Naval Operations told me the guns were our next target when I spoke to him on the way here. They want to get a group in here by air, and those things need to go. If we can kill two birds with one stone and blow them up while rescuing the Sommers, we would considerably simplify our morning. Maybe we could even get some sleep."

Without warning, Calvin pulled Master Chief back into the concealment of the trees, as a Chinese soldier came around the corner of the hotel. Apparently, he couldn't be bothered to go inside; he relieved himself behind the hotel and then went back around to the front.

"How did you know he was coming?" Master Chief asked.

"I saw him," Calvin replied. Master Chief didn't see how that could be, but didn't have any proof, so he let it go. He must be more tired than he thought if an aviator had better senses and reactions than he did.

They crawled back into the woods and went several hundred yards deeper to where the rest of the platoon was waiting. Clearing off a small area of the ground to use as a map, Master Chief drew the platoon a picture of the area.

"Okay, there are two of those anti-aircraft guns sitting at the truck stop. Deadeye, do you remember anything about them?" Master Chief asked.

Corporal Taylor thought for a couple of seconds and then answered, "Yeah, the PGZ-95 is a tracked anti-aircraft gun that has four 25mm cannons and four infrared homing missiles on it. The guns are lethal against both aircraft and surface targets as they can fire up to 800 rounds a minute and can be brought to bear on ground targets. The system can also chew up any light armored fighting vehicle short of a tank." Somehow, her voice sounded even higher than normal at 0315 in the morning, if that was possible.

Master Chief nodded his head. "As the lieutenant can tell you, they are also extremely tough on aircraft, and we need to get rid of the ones sitting out there so our aviation units can get in here." He pointed to parts of the map he had drawn. "In addition to the two vehicles at the truck stop, there is one up here to the north at a school, another one a block to the north of the truck stop at this factory and a fifth one down to the south on the other side of I-90. There is also the hulk of a sixth vehicle in the truck stop that burned up yesterday. Don't get confused by it in the dark."

Master Chief paused to ensure he had their attention. "Our high value targets are the Sommers family, who are probably being held in the hotel located here along the tree line. Just like the attack on the missile system we just completed, we are going to have to go with a diversion to lead the troops away, while the main group goes into the hotel to retrieve the family. We believe all three are in the hotel, but we don't know where or if they're going to be together. The odds are that they will all be together, or close by each other, and will probably be in or around the common areas on the first floor. They probably will *not* be up in a hotel room, but if you see soldiers guarding a room upstairs, that is a possibility."

"The problem is going to be in the targeting," Master Chief told them. "The PGZ-95s are in four different places, and we only have three RPG launchers to shoot them with. We're also running low on ammunition, as we only have nine anti-tank rounds and four anti-personnel rounds left. One of the anti-aircraft guns will probably get manned up and operational before we can put a rocket into it. If so, everyone will have to be very careful."

One of the twins put a hand up. Master Chief acknowledged him.

"Okay, so, like, why not take one over and, like, use it against them?" the twin asked.

"That'd be wonderful," Master Chief said sarcastically, "I suppose you're going to drive it?"

"Oh, no," the same twin said, "that's like his job, man; he's the designated driver," he said, pointing at his twin. "Like, it's his turn. I get to be the shooter, dude, 'cause like, he got to fire most of the rockets earlier and, like, it wouldn't be fair, otherwise."

"And he would soooo tell mom, too, if I didn't share, the little tattle tale."

"Dude, that's harsh, 'cause like, you're the biggest squealer I know. You always run to mom."

"Stop!" Top commanded in a harsh whisper to cut them off. He had seen this act before and knew they could go on hours if you let them. Besides, he thought, they were so alike that if one was a tattle tale, the other one probably was, too.

Master Chief just looked annoyed. "But you think you can drive it?"

The twin picked to be the driver shrugged. "Dude, we were like, 'in' tanks before we became Rangers. Both of us could, like, drive them if we needed to. Just because it's Chinese doesn't matter. They probably stole the technology from us anyway, dude, and it'll look a lot like ours." He paused and looked at his brother, who nodded his agreement to the unspoken question. "We can totally drive it," he concluded.

"Firing its weapons might be harder," Master Chief cautioned.

"Prob'bly so," the twin whose turn it was to be the gunner said, "but, dude, what a *rush* if I can figure it out."

Master Chief decided to just accept it and move on. "Okay, the twins are going to capture the one to the north, then roll the gun down to the hotel. If for some reason one of the other guns doesn't get hit, the twins will engage the gun and destroy it. Jet and Dreamer will go with the twins to provide support. Jet can maybe even get close enough to use a suppressed pistol on whatever guards are protecting it."

"The Wall and Reggie will take one of the RPGs and take out the vehicle at the Genie Lift factory. They will have two high-explosive anti-tank (HEAT) rounds, as well as one of the airburst anti-personnel rounds."

"PFC Woodard and PFC Hall will take the second RPG launcher, four of the HEAT rounds, the last thermobaric round and the other airburst round. They will go around to the other side of the truck stop and will approach using this finger of trees that runs down this small creek. If you go slowly, you ought to be able to get within about 150 yards to take your shot. You have to be fast, because you have to take out two of the vehicles. Sergeant Morales will lead this group and Corporal Ferguson will keep the Chinese at bay with his machine gun while the RPG guys do their job."

"Corporal Sanders and PFC Severn will take the last RPG, the last three HEAT rounds and the last HE/HEAT round and will take out the vehicle to the south. No heroics, no trying to kill lots of Chinese. Just destroy the vehicle and boogie back to the rendezvous. If we're not back, we're probably in trouble; meet us at the tree line behind the hotel and provide whatever support you can without compromising your position."

"That leaves Top, Shuteye, Paris, Deadeye and Becks to accompany the lieutenant and me. It's a smash and grab operation. Get the Sommers and exit as quickly as we can. If we're there more than 5 minutes, we're probably dead. The sniper team will be on the roof of the convenience store to the north of the hotel. From there, it ought to be able to support the team at the truck stop and maybe help us out, too." He looked around at the serious, concentrating men and woman. "Any questions?" There were none; they were professionals and knew their jobs. "Stay sharp, stay focused, and we'll get through this just fine. Okay, here's how we're going to time it..."

TCA Truck Stop, North Bend, WA, 0415 PDT

It had taken almost an hour for everyone to get into position. The timing worked out well; they would be attacking at the time of the morning where biorhythms were at their lowest, and it would be difficult for the defenders to respond to an attack.

The twins' group would be leading the attack again. The PGZ-95 they were attacking sat at second base on the Twin Falls Middle School's baseball field. Good Twin had spent the last five minutes working his way closer and closer to the anti-aircraft gun; he was now hiding behind the visitor's dugout on the third base line. The Chinese clustered around the vehicle didn't look particularly alert or 'on guard,' as they had their rifles slung on their backs. In addition to the gun's crew of three, there were three other soldiers standing nearby talking to the crew. The driver was inside the vehicle; the rest were outside.

With a crashing and moaning, Jet came stumbling out of the woods. Mumbling words in Chinese, he limped toward the soldiers before dropping to one knee, and then finally falling to the ground on his stomach. Weakly, he lifted his head up to look imploringly at the soldiers, holding out one hand toward them, before falling again to the grass of center field.

The soldiers, who had drawn their rifles, re-slung them and jogged over with the two crewmen to where Jet lay. One of them knelt down and rolled Jet over, only to have a silenced pistol whip up to his temple.

"Don't move!" commanded Bad Twin as he and Dreamer stepped out of the woods with leveled rifles.

Bad Twin could see the soldiers calculating their chances. There were more of them, but their rifles were slung. The Chinese soldiers made the sensible decision; they surrendered.

Seeing the ambush, the driver tried to get away, and he was reaching up to shut his hatch when Good Twin grabbed it. Good Twin stuck the muzzle of his pistol in the driver's face, and the driver also raised his hands and surrendered.

The Americans used zip ties to bind the hands and feet of the Chinese soldiers and left them tied up at home plate. Bad Twin arranged the gun commander so that it looked like he had just slid into home. "Dude, look, he's saaaaaafe!" he said to his brother.

"Good one, dude!" said Good Twin.

The twins and Dreamer got into the vehicle. Bad Twin sat in the driver's seat, Dreamer in the commander's chair and Good Twin in the gunner's position. Jet walked along outside it, wearing a Chinese uniform.

While Bad Twin started the vehicle and worked out how to steer it, Good Twin began turning on the gun's weapon systems and trying to figure out how to use them. The vehicle had an electro-optic director in the front of the turret, which fed data to the onboard fire-control computer. This information was used to determine how much the gun needed to lead the target when the gunner opened fire, based on how fast the target was moving. While this would have been helpful, Good Twin couldn't figure it out without the ability to read Chinese. The gunner also had a joystick to manually aim and fire the guns, which Good Twin *was* able to operate and looked forward to using. He had fired one round to make sure he knew how to use the system, and he couldn't wait to go full 'rock and roll' with the guns.

As expected, the vehicle's controls were not terribly different from any of the other armored vehicles the twins had ever driven, and Bad Twin was soon steering it toward the south. They crossed the road and entered the parking lot of the Genie Lift Corporation. On the west end of the complex was a large parking lot that normally held the flatbed trailers for transporting the equipment the company made. In the middle of that parking lot was the second PGZ-95. As Bad Twin drove their captured vehicle toward the enemy gun, a blast of flame came from the forest to the south and an anti-tank rocket leaped out, crossed the distance to the Chinese gun and detonated inside it, turning it into a raging inferno.

Although surprised, several of the guards pulled their rifles off their shoulders and started shooting into the woods. If they expected the anti-aircraft gun that had just turned into the parking lot to help them, they were mistaken. Instead, the vehicle continued toward them, and the guns traversed down, flames spitting from its barrels as the 25mm cannons began firing at the Chinese soldiers. The powerful guns fired for five seconds, sending 66 shells toward the troops firing at their friends.

When Good Twin ceased firing, there wasn't much left of the Chinese soldiers; even their rifles were splintered and unusable. "Aw, dude, that's just sick," he said to his brother, looking at the mess he made. "I think I'm gonna spew."

The team at the truck stop fired their first rocket when they heard the explosion of the Genie Lift anti-aircraft gun. PFC 'Woody' Woodard had been ready for several minutes, and the rocket streaked out to the closer of the two PGZ-95s and detonated inside it.

The Chinese soldiers in the parking lot initially looked north toward the sounds of gunfire and explosions at the Genie Lift parking lot, but their attention quickly refocused when the gun blew up next to them, killing and wounding several in a spray of hot metal. As the RPG team hurried to reload, the Americans started taking rifle fire. Sergeant 'Boom Boom' Morales returned fire with his rifle and Corporal 'Fergie' Ferguson with one of the captured Chinese automatic weapons. Fergie's weapon chattered in full automatic as he swept it back and forth across the parking lot, and the Chinese soldiers dove for cover. PFC Trevor 'Mad Dog' Hall slid the next HEAT round into the RPG and slapped Woody on the back to tell him it was ready. As Mad Dog stepped to the side, there was a meaty smack as a 5.8mm round caught him in the chest. He fell backward without a sound, shot through the heart, dead.

PFC Woodard heard the round hit his loader as he fired, and it caused him to jerk to the right. Instead of hitting the second anti-aircraft gun, the rocket flew past it, exploding in the middle of the grassy field to the north of the parking lot.

"Help!" Woody yelled, and Boom Boom ran over to take up the loader's duties.

Corporal Ferguson's rifle went dry, and there was a break in the outgoing firing as he changed out the 80-round drum magazine.

"Let's go, Fergie," Boom Boom said. "We need something to keep their heads down."

Fergie pulled the charging lever to put the first round into the barrel. "Coming right—" he said as another smacking noise was heard.

"Aw, fuck!" Fergie said as he looked down. "I'm hit." He fell backward.

Boom Boom looked up to see Fergie's body shiver once and go still. A little trickle of blood ran down from the corner of his mouth. Boom Boom could tell he was dead, too.

The decrease in outgoing fire resulted in an increase in incoming fire, and more rounds began impacting all around them. Worse, the American soldiers could hear the PGZ-95's motor start up, and Boom Boom knew he only had seconds before the anti-aircraft gun turned them into paste. He looked up to see if the vehicle had started to turn toward the soldiers yet, and the rocket he was attempting to load slipped through his fingers. As Boom Boom fumbled to pick it up, the anti-aircraft gun began to move, and the turret to traverse in their direction.

Tiny had been doing everything he could to reduce the number of people shooting at the RPG team. Able to view the attack from the roof of the convenience store on the other side of the street, every time he fired, someone died. The problem was one of numbers; for every soldier he shot, four or five more came running out of the hotel. As yet, none of them had noticed that some of the soldiers were falling forward, shot from behind. That couldn't last forever.

As the PGZ-95 started to move, BTO saw that he was needed, too. "Shit!" he swore as he scooped up his M203 launcher. He didn't think that he could kill the anti-aircraft gun with grenades, but if he could just distract it a little, he might give the RPG team enough time for another shot.

BTO's first round landed short of the vehicle, raining shrapnel off the side of the gun. He quickly reloaded and fired a second. This one landed in front of the anti-aircraft gun. While it didn't destroy the vehicle, it did get the attention of the weapons system's crew, and the turret began turning toward where he and Tiny were hiding on the roof.

BTO knew the gun would be devastating to them in the open. "Time to go!" he shouted as he slapped Tiny on the back. They ran to the back of the roof and jumped off just as the gun opened fire. The two men hit the ground and rolled, and came up running toward the woods as the anti-aircraft gun's 25mm cannons shredded Ken's Gas & Grocery.

Many of the soldiers turned to see what the gun was firing at, and the incoming fire slackened on Sergeant Morales. He finally succeeded in mounting the rocket on the RPG launcher and slapped Woody on the back. Woody took a breath, released it slowly, and fired at the PGZ-95. The rocket launched and arced across the intervening distance to intersect with the side of the turret. As it blew up, it also caused the sympathetic detonation of the ammunition inside the vehicle, blowing the turret completely off its chassis. It flew up into the air and came to rest upside down, 10 feet away from the body of the vehicle.

"That's it!" Boom Boom yelled. "Let's get the hell out of here!" The two men turned and ran down the tree line, trying to interpose as many trees as possible between themselves and the people trying to kill them. They ran as hard as they could, with the Chinese in hot pursuit. As he ran, Woody succeeded in loading the final rocket into the RPG. He stopped, turned and fired the platoon's last thermobaric round. The weapon hit in front of their closest pursuers; the blast shredded the first two soldiers, and it killed several more of the ones following them. While the pursuit continued, it slowed noticeably; none of the Chinese soldiers wanted to be the next person caught in a thermobaric detonation.

Some of the pursuit also diverted to the south, as an explosion came from the other side of I-90. Corporal 'Colonel' Sanders and Private First Class 'Nine' Severn had taken a little longer than expected to get into position, as they had run into several large concentrations of troops. Since the last time Master Chief had been by the position, a 'whole heap' of men, as the Colonel would later say, had moved into the area. Judging by the numbers they saw, the Americans estimated that at least a battalion's worth of men (over 1,000) had moved into the valley to stop any American advances from that direction.

The two men were still sneaking through the woods when they heard explosions coming from the north. They weren't particularly worried about the gun they were hunting going to help its comrades to the north; if it moved, it would have to go right past them. As they approached it, the men could hear the vehicle's motor fire up, and it sounded like it was coming in their direction. They looked out from the trees, it wasn't long before they saw it headed north on 468th Avenue, going up to help the Chinese fighting at the truck stop.

It didn't make it.

Although Jimmy Sanders may have talked slowly, he was a master with most projectile-firing weapons. The RPG launcher was no different. As he looked through the sights at the gun, he thought to himself, 'It's not going fast...just lead it a little...no real wind to speak of...FIRE!' and the rocket sped toward the last PGZ-95, hitting it in the side. The vehicle's side armor was not enough to stop the grenade, and it penetrated, killing all of the people inside and rendering the gun inoperable. As soon as the RPG launched, the two men headed deeper into the woods, evading the pursuit they knew would soon be after them.

Edgewick Inn, North Bend, WA, 0430 PDT

Hearing the sounds of the anti-aircraft guns' detonations, Master Chief led the team from the woods to the back of the Edgewick Inn. Sloppy, he thought, not to have guards behind the hotel. They must think themselves pretty safe here. *Not in my country, damn it!*

He approached the back door of the kitchen, identifiable by the cigarette butts on the stoop outside where the cooks came to smoke. He tried the handle, but it was locked. As he shook it, he realized that the door, while locked, had been jimmied so it didn't shut all the way. Management must have locked the door so the cooks couldn't smoke without locking themselves out; they, in turn, rigged the door so it wouldn't shut all the way. Master Chief laughed to himself. Sometimes smoking saved lives.

The men snuck through the kitchen as explosions and gunfire continued to sound from outside. Master Chief reached the service door into the dining room and looked out the window. After the day they were having, he couldn't believe his luck. There were the Sommers, all tied to chairs. Unfortunately, there were also four Chinese men in the room with them. As he watched, one of the Chinese, an officer, backhanded Mr. Sommers, snapping his head around and almost overbalancing him in his chair. Master Chief couldn't hear what the man asked Mr. Sommers, but he obviously didn't like the answer Mr. Sommers gave as he backhanded him the other way, this time knocking his chair over.

He felt the lieutenant stiffen at his side. Oh, shit, he thought; it looked like the women had received a similar treatment. That won't go over well. The Chinese officer, who Master Chief could see was a major, started screaming at the man lying on the floor and made a big show of drawing his pistol. Master Chief didn't like where this was going.

Looking around the kitchen, he saw a bowl of fruit. Grabbing an apple, he put it into Shuteye's hand. "Go out there *now* and distract them from this door," he whispered.

Shuteye nodded and walked out the door, nonchalantly taking a bite out of the apple so that he wouldn't have to talk. The Chinese men all snapped their heads around to look at Shuteye as he came through the door.

"Who are you?" the major asked. "How did you get in there?"

Shuteye was still wearing his Chinese navy private's uniform, so he bowed obsequiously as he backed toward the door to the lobby. "I came in the back door from outside," he mumbled. "I was hungry so I went to get something to eat. So sorry to intrude."

"What is the navy doing here?" the major asked. "Who *are* you?"

"I'm the apple man," Shuteye replied. "Want one?" He lobbed the apple underhanded to the major. It arced through the air, and all of the Chinese men's eyes were focused on it as it traveled toward the major. They didn't see Master Chief and the rest of the men pour out of the door behind him.

The major felt a presence behind him and started to turn, but he was too late. Master Chief shot him with his suppressed pistol, hitting him twice in the head. The major dropped, dead. Shifting his aim, he shot a second soldier, the one guarding Mrs. Sommers.

Calvin, the second one in, only had eyes for Sara, and the guard behind her whose hand was starting to draw a pistol from his holster. Calvin's pistol was already in his hand, and he brought it up and fired twice. The guard fell backward, hit twice in the chest.

Paris and Top both fired twice as they entered the room, hitting the final guard in the chest. All four Chinese soldiers were down.

Master Chief and Top checked the guards while Calvin and Paris freed the hostages. Looking at the bullet holes in the guard behind where Sara had been sitting, Master Chief asked Top quietly, "Are both of those yours?"

"Actually, no," Top said. "I shot the other guard. Those are both the lieutenant's. He put them both into the guard's center of mass while on the run into the room." He nodded his approval. "He's a keeper."

"Yeah," Master Chief agreed, "he's not so bad." He paused and then finished, "For an officer."

Calvin gathered the family and was rewarded with a quick kiss on the cheek from Sara after he cut her loose. They went back out through the kitchen with Master Chief in the lead and Top as rear guard. Master Chief looked out the door and, seeing no one, went running out with Mrs. Sommers. Shuteye followed with Mr. Sommers, leaving Sara to be escorted by Calvin, something he was happy to do. They made it into the woods and safety, going deeper into the forest as shots and explosions continued from in front of the hotel. Finally, the gunfire slackened and, after a "wuuump" that could only have been the last thermobaric rocket exploding, things got quiet.

Calvin hoped everyone had made it.

His cheek still tingled.

Snoqualmie National Forest, Washington State, 0545 PDT

Calvin was beat. After rescuing the Sommers, all he could think about was falling down and getting some sleep. When he called the CNO, though, he found out that sleep was still going to be denied him. He was surprised by Admiral Wright's response when told the platoon had destroyed the PGZ-95s ahead of schedule. Sure, he expected the CNO to be happy, but he didn't expect the over-the-top ecstatic response he received.

Nor did he expect to be told to go immediately to Master Chief's house in the woods. Instead of getting some long overdue and well-deserved sleep, he had instead sent the Sommers family off with Top, who would take them to the house of Erika Gardner, one of Sara's friends, where they would hopefully be safe. They ought to be welcome, too, since Erika was one of the students the platoon had rescued from the University of Washington yesterday (was it only yesterday?) morning.

This whole 'war' thing was starting to get in the way of his love life, Calvin thought with a sigh. Maybe the Master Chief did have a point about authority.

After dropping the Sommers family off, all of the Rangers would then go on to the Boeing Hangar, including the twins in their captured PGZ-95. They could get some rest there, as well as hide yet another piece of captured Chinese equipment. They were starting to have quite a collection. Calvin wondered idly what all of it would sell for on the open market. Or the black market. Or the Fresh Market. Damn, he was getting loopy.

As they came over the hill that looked down onto Master Chief's cabin, Calvin was amazed to see the meadow beyond it. When he had spoken to the CNO, Admiral Wright had said something about "the need would be apparent once you got there." It had been too vague for him to figure out at the time, and Calvin way too tired to care, but now he could see that the CNO hadn't wanted to say anything because he was worried about operational security.

The meadow below Master Chief's house was covered with helicopters. Not just a few here and there, but lots of helicopters, and mostly the big, troop-carrying kind. The 'air assault' kind. Black. Army. Like 'Apocalypse Now' with 'Ride of the Valkyries' playing in the background. Damn, he was babbling to himself again. Gotta focus.

Not only were there *a lot* of helicopters on the field, but also what looked like an army's worth of soldiers in and around them. The soldiers looked like they were readying themselves for battle;

they were checking various pieces of their gear, cleaning their weapons and generally standing around looking nervous. Probably like he had been yesterday morning before going into battle...when he had enough energy to stand up straight.

As they approached the cabin, a first sergeant jogged up to them. "Are you Master Chief O'Leary?" he asked.

"Guilty as charged," Master Chief said, sounding annoyed.

The first sergeant looked at Calvin, who was still wearing one of Corporal Sanders' uniforms. "Ummm, there was supposed to be a lieutenant with you. Is Lieutenant Hobbs going to be along shortly?"

"That's the lieutenant right there," Master Chief said. "He had a uniform emergency and needed to borrow one of our troop's uniforms." He looked pointedly at the helicopters. "Can you *please* tell me what the hell the entire 101st Division's doing trampling down my lawn?" He looked at Calvin. "Sir, did you invite your friends over without asking permission first?"

"If I did," Calvin answered, "I'm too tired to remember doing it."

"Well, sir," the first sergeant said, finally understanding that Corporal Sanders was Lieutenant Hobbs, "we've been waiting for you for a couple of hours now. The colonel requests your presence in the cabin as soon as possible. They're holding up the briefing for you."

"Summoned into my own damn house?" Master Chief asked. "See what I mean, lieutenant? Damn officers come, invite themselves into your house, make themselves at home and then summon you into it like you don't belong there. Ain't that some shit?"

"I'm with you, Master Chief," Calvin said. "Personally, I'm too damn tired to be summoned. I think I may just go join the unit at the

Gardner's house." Master Chief could see his eyes looked a little dreamy. And tired. Very, very tired.

The first sergeant looked worried. "Umm, sir, we're kind of holding up a major battle just to wait for you two. People are dying that might not have to. American people. If you could please come inside, I'm sure they'd greatly appreciate it."

Calvin sighed heavily. "All right. C'mon Master Chief, let's go see what the colonel wants." He cocked his head. "Maybe it will be for us to get our crew rest."

"Probably not," Master Chief grumbled.

"You're right, probably not," Calvin agreed. Looking at the first sergeant, he asked, "Who's the colonel, and who are you guys, anyway?"

"The colonel is Colonel Colin Daly, and we're the 1st Battalion of the 506th Infantry Regiment." As the first sergeant said that, five soldiers who were within earshot all chorused the unit motto, "Currahee!" which was Cherokee for "Stands Alone!"

The three men walked into the house to find the main room full of men in uniform. Calvin recognized a couple of Master Chief's Special Operations Aviation Regiment (SOAR) friends, but the rest must have come with the helicopters.

The first sergeant coughed to get the colonel's attention. Looking up, the colonel said gruffly, "Hmph, 'bout time. Glad you could be bothered to join us."

Calvin could see Master Chief bristling. For that matter, he felt kind of bristly, himself. He decided to try and extend an olive branch first. "Gee, sir, we've been pretty busy stealing nukes and rescuing damsels in distress for the last 24 hours. Did we forget an important staff meeting?" Okay, that hadn't turned out to be an olive branch, but he had meant to be nice when he started.

"We have been waiting for you since before dawn. The battle has started out there, and people are dying. You were supposed to give us an intel brief so that we could get into the fight."

"Colonel, let me ask you a question," Calvin said. "How much would you like to fly over five anti-aircraft guns that each have four cannons and four SAMs on the way to the fight? Would that be a lot of fun?" Calvin almost kept the sarcasm out of his voice. Almost. "What we've been doing, while you were 'waiting to get into the fight,' was destroying them so that you *could* get into the fight without dying along the way. Now, I haven't slept in over 24 hours, I've been shot at more times than I can count and I've killed people at close range, something aviators generally don't do. So please don't give me any more shit while I'm trying to help you, and, unless you want to see my next kill up close, tell your sergeant *not to drink the last cup of coffee in the pot.*"

The sergeant in question put down the pot. Master Chief went over, poured the last cup and brought it to Calvin. He tried really hard not to smile at the colonel's sudden embarrassment but failed. Hell, he was tired, too.

Cup of coffee in hand, Calvin sighed. "Sorry, sir," he said, giving the colonel a chance to be back in charge. "What can we do to help you?"

Willing to move on so that he could be about his business, the colonel used a little more moderate tone. "Well, if you got rid of the anti-aircraft guns, you've made my life a lot easier." It was almost an apology, Calvin noticed. Almost. The colonel continued, "I understand your unit also got rid of the HQ-19 missile system, too?"

"Yeah, we did," Calvin said. "Actually, that was pretty fun. You should see what a 100 pounds of explosives can do to a radar vehicle. I understand the explosion was visible from orbit."

"Visible from space? Really?" Master Chief asked with a touch of pride. "You didn't tell me that."

"And give you a big head? Perish the thought." Calvin looked back at the colonel. "Sorry, sir, we're kind of tired. What can we do for you?"

"Well, if you can stay awake long enough, we need to know whatever you can tell us about enemy troop strength, enemy positioning and how we can break through here," the colonel said.

"How you can break through?" Calvin asked. "You're already through. By coming the way you did, you can march right down the other side of the hill and be behind enemy lines. The Chinese can't be everywhere so they are blocking the main valley. We could have left any time we wanted; we were just having too much fun to go."

"Okay, so we can just go down the valley and sneak around the Chinese lines?" the colonel asked.

"Absolutely. It looks like you have transportation," Calvin said, "so you can get down there and hit them from behind any time you'd like. Give me a map, and I'll show you how to get there. Hell, let me ride in the front helo, and I'll help lead you there."

"I thought you were too tired to do anything?" the colonel asked.

"Well, sir, I'm getting my second wind and besides, I'm going that way, too. Oh, yeah, and no one's shot at me in a couple of hours now. I guess I miss the whiz of bullets flying past my ear. Where's a map?"

Calvin showed them the best route to get down to the main valley I-90 ran through. Judging by the sounds of gunfire they had heard when they were at the truck stop, Calvin and Master Chief guessed the line of battle was somewhere around the Olallie State Park.

Looking at the map, there was a quarry about a mile behind the battle line. They could land near the quarry, form up and assault the Chinese battle lines from behind, rolling them up and opening up the line of advance. Once they broke the Chinese line, there was nothing to stop the Americans short of Seattle.

Before the soldiers boarded their transport helos, Colonel Daly addressed the unit. There were about 1,000 men, but his voice had that 'command tone' that carried, like several drill sergeants Calvin had known.

"Gentlemen!" he thundered. "The 101st Airborne Division was born on August 19, 1942. On that day, its first commander, Major General William C. Lee, read his General Order Number 5, promising his new recruits that the unit had 'no history, but had a rendezvous with destiny.'" He looked down at a piece of paper he was holding. "General Lee then went on to tell them,

'Due to the nature of our armament, and the tactics in which we shall perfect ourselves, we shall be called upon to carry out operations of far-reaching military importance, and we shall habitually go into action when the need is immediate and extreme.

Let me call your attention to the fact that our badge is the great American eagle. This is a fitting emblem for a division that will crush its enemies by falling upon them like a thunderbolt from the skies.

The history we shall make, the record of high achievement we hope to write in the annals of the American Army and the American people, depends wholly and completely on the men of this division. Each individual, each officer and each enlisted man, must therefore regard himself as a necessary part of a complex and powerful instrument for the overcoming of the enemies of the nation. Each, in his own job, must realize that he is not only a means, but an indispensable *means for obtaining the goal of victory. It is, therefore, not too much to say that the future itself, in whose molding we expect to have our share, is in the hands of the soldiers of the 101st Airborne Division.'*

Colonel Daly looked up and continued, "Today's mission is indeed of far-reaching military importance, and our need is both immediate and extreme. We come to take back our city that was taken from us ruthlessly and without warning. *We will* fall upon the enemy like General Lee's thunderbolt from the skies, and *we will* snatch victory from the jaws of defeat. *We will* do these things, because you are the finest examples of your generation, and because each of you *is* that 'indispensable means' for obtaining the goal of victory. The future is in your hands today! I know you will not only make me, but our entire nation proud. Give 'em hell!"

One thousand voices all yelled simultaneously, "Currahee!"

With that, the soldiers of the 101st went to their helicopters and off to war.

Onboard *Blaster 205*, Walla Walla, WA, 0600 PDT

It had been a long wait, but they had finally been given the 'go ahead' to launch. Captain Jim 'Muddy' Waters, the commander of Carrier Air Wing 2, was ready to lead his aviators into battle. He was also known as the air wing's 'CAG,' an abbreviation for Carrier Air Group commander, a term used in the early days of carrier aviation. Although the 'Air Group' had become an 'Air Wing,' the term CAG had continued to this day (perhaps because 'CAG' was easier to say than 'CAW').

CAG had lost several of his aviators two days previously on the opening day of the war to sneak attacks by the Chinese, and he was ready to pay them back. With interest.

The key to air wing strike planning, as every aviator knows, is to build a sanctuary in which to operate. Depending on the mission, this might be high altitude (if the threat only consisted of rifles and handheld SAMs), or it might be low level (for aircraft and larger SAMs). Until now, creating a sanctuary around Seattle would have been difficult due to the robust package of both high and low-level threats the Chinese had brought with them.

His air wing had been waiting for the removal of either the HQ-19 or the PGZ-95 threats; now, they had been blessed to have both of them taken out. Could his air wing have removed the threats? He believed they could have, through a process of wearing them away, but it would have put his aviators in harm's way to take them out. He didn't know what direct-action force on the ground had taken them out, nor did he care; he was just happy he got to go hunting for bigger things.

Captain Waters' mission was to take out the Chinese 'eye in the sky.' Somehow, the Chinese had flown one of their giant AWACS planes to the United States, and they were basing it at Sea-Tac airfield. With the AWACS in the air, they had a great picture of everything flying within a 200 mile radius of Seattle. That couldn't be allowed to continue. With it out of the way, U.S. aviators would be able to use the terrain they knew so well to their advantage, without the Chinese being able to look down and see them in the valleys.

Over 20 of the air wing's aircraft had formed up just south of Eugene, Oregon, where they were carefully staying outside the 200 mile exclusion zone the Chinese had declared around Seattle. They were nothing more than a diversion, though. The pilots would periodically fly toward the exclusion zone like they intended to attack, but would then break off at the last minute to stay outside it. It kept the Chinese on edge and hopefully focused their attention somewhere other than where the real threat was. Of course, they had to know this was exactly what the Americans were doing, but they still had to honor the threat the strike package represented, nonetheless.

The real work would be done by the six aircraft in his group, which were currently being led toward Spokane by one of the Air Force's KC-135 tankers. All of the FA-18 aircraft were taking turns getting gas from the tanker, so that they would have as much as possible to fly the mission. CAG was flying in the #205 aircraft of the Blue Blasters of Strike Fighter Squadron 34. In its 75th year of service, VFA-34 had a long and distinguished history dating back to World War II. Its most recent combat experience had not gone so well; the squadron had lost two of its aircraft to Chinese fire two days previously. One of their pilots, LTJG 'Oscar' Berkman, had been killed; the other, LT 'Calvin' Hobbs, was trapped behind enemy lines. CAG and his wingman, LCDR Fred 'Hugh' Mungo in *Blaster 206*, were flying in memory of Oscar.

The other four aircraft of the flight, the four 'Kestrels' of VFA-137, were flying in memory of the aircraft their squadron had lost on the first day of the war. *Falcon 303* had been shot down and its pilot, LT Michael 'Murph' Murphy, killed. CDR Steve 'Cool Breeze' Jackson, the commanding officer of the squadron, had evaded the Chinese fire on the first night of the war. He was returning with a vengeance, a feeling shared by the other three squadron pilots who were with him.

Reaching the Washington border, the Hornets detached and began descending over Walla Walla as they headed west to begin their combat run-in.

"Eagle 601, Blaster 205," CAG radioed.

"Blaster 205, this is Eagle 601, *go ahead,*" the E-2 airborne control officer (ACO) replied. The E-2 was the carrier version of the Air Force AWACS aircraft. Like its bigger cousin, the twin-engine turboprop aircraft provided early warning of incoming aircraft and directed friendly fighters to intercept them.

"Eagle 601, *say status of the eye,*" CAG radioed, asking for the status of the former Russian A-50 AWACS aircraft.

"Blaster 205, Eagle 601, *the eye is open; I say again, the eye is open,*" replied the E-2 ACO, confirming the A-50 was airborne and operating over Seattle.

"*Roger, Blaster copies,*" acknowledged the CAG. "*Blaster and flight are proceeding on mission.*"

"*Roger,*" replied the E-2 ACO, "*good luck and good hunting.*"

"*Thanks, Eagle. Blaster, out,*" said CAG, signing off.

Onboard the A-50 AWACS, Over Seattle, WA, 0615 PDT

The AWACS intercept officer wasn't fooled. Sure, he saw the aircraft to the south, hanging around just outside the exclusion zone. As obvious as they were, they couldn't be the real threat. He figured it was far more likely the threat was the group of aircraft that had taken off from Fallon, joined with another, larger, aircraft, and were proceeding toward

Spokane. Sure enough, they detached from the other aircraft, which was probably a tanker, and began proceeding toward the Seattle area, descending along the way so the Chinese missile systems wouldn't be able to see them. The AWACS would still be able to see them, though, as they went low through the mountain valleys.

He didn't know where they were going, but he doubted he wanted them to get there. He would watch them and have some of his friends waiting.

Onboard *Blaster 205*, Cascade Mountains, WA, 0630 PDT

CAG watched as the four Super Hornets pulled forward into the lead. Like the offensive line of a football team, their job was to open up a hole in the enemy defenses and create a sanctuary in which he and his wingman could operate. All of the aircraft had continued to descend and were now flying at 200 feet above the ground and 420 knots. CAG normally loved flying low level, but was concentrating too hard on the mission to get any enjoyment out of it today.

As they reached the Cascade Mountains and began flying along the I-90 corridor, CAG could see the U.S. Army forces gathering behind the front lines to the east of North Bend. It was surprising how quickly they had been able to assemble this many troops, CAG thought, but when it's your own country you're defending, you do whatever it takes. Including driving your own car to the battle if you have to.

The formation of aircraft reached the front lines, and CAG could see the forces fighting below him. Although the Chinese didn't have much warning the Kestrels were coming, they were still able to shoot at them as they went by, and tracers filled the air. It was worse for the two Blasters. Three miles in trail of the Kestrels, the enemy had a little more warning they were coming. As the Blasters overflew the front line, tracers again filled the sky and a handheld surface-to-air missile rose from the Chinese side, but it did not lock on to either of the aircraft. As the formation cleared the fighting on the ground, the Kestrels began launching their HARMs.

The AGM-88 Hi-Speed Anti-Radiation Missile (HARM) was developed to counteract the proliferation of radar-guided SAMs. Prior to launch, the missile was given instructions for where to go, when to start looking and what type of missile system to look for. Finding a radar associated with that missile system, the HARM would follow its beam back to the transmitter, blowing up 100' above it and showering it with 25,000 tungsten cubes. Any radar hit by the blast of a HARM would be rendered completely non-operational, shredded beyond repair.

While the HQ-19 missile system in North Bend had been destroyed, CAG knew the Chinese had brought other missile systems with them. American reconnaissance aircraft had indications that a variety of them were operating in the vicinity of downtown Seattle. In addition to the Chinese Army's missiles, the Chinese destroyer that had pulled into Tacoma was also known to have a surface-to-air capability. If the Chinese chose to try to shoot down the American FA-18s, it would be a target rich environment for the HARMs.

The Kestrels launched a HARM every 15 seconds for the last two minutes they were in the mountains. As they broke out of the mountains and pulled up, the missiles raced ahead of them to their preprogrammed destinations in Seattle and Tacoma, looking for radars to attack. The Americans hoped the SAM radars would be radiating so the HARMs could lock on and destroy them. If the Chinese wanted to keep the radars off so they didn't get hit with a HARM, that was okay too, because then the Chinese couldn't launch at the American aircraft. It was a 'win' either way.

As the American fighters pulled up, the warning indicators on the Kestrels began to illuminate as the Chinese missile systems tried to lock them up. Two of the radars, a Tomb Stone tracking radar from the HQ-9 system located at McChord air base and a Grill Pan radar from an HQ-18 system attracted the attention of HARMs and were destroyed. Additionally, the PLAN destroyer *Changsha* activated the Tomb Stone radar of its naval HQ-9 system and also attracted a HARM. The blast of the missile cleaned off all of the radars and rigging on the front half of the ship, as well as four crewmen who were unlucky enough to be top-side at the time.

As the aircraft climbed, they saw what they had been briefed to expect, four J-20 stealth aircraft coming from the direction of Seattle-Tacoma Airport. The J-20 was a fifth-generation fighter designed and manufactured by the Chinese Chengdu Aircraft Industry Group, based in good part on technology stolen from the United States' own F-22 and F-35 projects. The aircraft first flew in January, 2011, and had been in full production for over a year. Although hard to see on radar, nothing that mankind had yet created was invisible to the human eye, nor would the aircraft's stealth features protect its pilots from the Americans' guns. Even better, thought the Americans, the Chinese forces on the ground couldn't fire SAMs at them while they were dog fighting the Chinese fighters.

CAG and *Blaster 206* stayed low, roaring over houses and towns at better than 500 knots. Their mission wasn't to play with the fighters one-on-one; they were looking for the AWACS. Reaching the water, they pulled up, their APG-73 radars searching for the A-50. The massive plane had a correspondingly large radar signature, and it was easy to spot by the Blasters. Both aircraft locked it up and prepared to fire their air-to-air missiles.

Onboard the A-50 AWACS, Over Seattle, WA, 0645 PDT

The AWACS intercept officer *had* been fooled. He had seen the HARM missiles being fired by the Hornets and guessed the aircraft were coming to attack something either in Seattle or Tacoma. The profile indicated a ground attack, not that they were coming for him.

He had brought in the fighters to dispatch the Americans, but the Americans had already been climbing as if they expected the fighters and welcomed battle with them. This was wrong, as it indicated they were doing something other than what he was prepared to defend against. He lost the other two aircraft in the ground clutter, but quickly picked them up again as they began climbing, *coming right for him!* He immediately began screaming at the fighters to come and help him, trying to get them to disengage with the decoys and come eliminate the two Americans who were coming to destroy him.

One of the J-20s broke off and was immediately destroyed by *Falcon 300*, flown by the Kestrels' Commanding Officer, CDR Steve 'Cool Breeze' Jackson. One of his other pilots, LT Carl 'Guns' Simpson in *Falcon 310*, also succeeded in shooting down a J-20. Guns, chosen for this mission because he had the highest gunnery scores of anyone in his squadron, had been unable to lock up the J-20 he was fighting with a missile. He had calmly switched to guns and hit the cockpit with a spray of cannon fire. The Chinese fighter had gone out of control and flown into the ground, its pilot already dead.

Onboard *Blaster 205*, Over Seattle, WA, 0645 PDT

The plan worked, and both *Blaster 205* and *Blaster 206* had shots at the AWACS. "Fox 3," CAG called over the radio, indicating his air-to-air missile launch. The call was echoed seconds later as his wingman fired his own advanced medium-range air-to-air missile (AMRAAM), and then two more times as they each fired another missile at the lumbering AWACS.

"*Watch out, CAG,*" shouted Lieutenant Commander Dave 'Swimmer' Malloney over the radio. "*You've got a bogey coming around toward your six!*" Swimmer, the pilot of *Falcon 301*, had been fighting the J-20 when the enemy fighter had left to help the AWACS.

Leaving the AMRAAMs to find their way to the AWACS, CAG broke off to defend himself. *Falcon 301* had given him enough warning that the J-20 wasn't able get a shot at him, and they began a turning fight, both looking to get an advantage over the other. The J-20 had a better turn rate than the Hornet, and CAG was starting to lose position. Just before the enemy was able to get a shot, CAG's wingman intercepted the J-20 and fired a burst of cannon fire down the side of the aircraft. It hit the J-20's fuel tank, and the aircraft exploded.

Only one J-20 remained, and it was trapped between *Falcon 302* and *Falcon 310*. It evaded *302*, but flew right into the gunsight of *310*, and 'Guns' Simpson had his second kill of the day.

The J-20s taken care of, CAG looked for the AWACS. Hit by at least two of the Blasters' AMRAAMs, he found it going down with its left wing in flames. Wanting to be sure, he fired one of his heat-seeking Sidewinders. The missile guided on the greatest heat source, the burning engine on the left wing. The wing, weakened by two prior hits, failed, and the outer half separated from the airplane; the A-50 spiraled out of control and crashed into the bay off Seattle's coast.

With the demise of the last Chinese aircraft, there was nothing to prevent the Chinese SAM systems from shooting at the American aircraft, and the Americans' threat warning systems quickly indicated a variety of active missile systems. *"Blasters and Falcons, this is Liberty,"* CAG transmitted, using the code word that identified him as CAG, *"Let's hit the deck and get the hell out of here."*

All of the pilots executed heart-stopping descents as they frantically tried to get below the radars' horizons, dispensing chaff and flares to confuse any missiles that might be coming their way. The aviators could see bright fires erupt in several places around the city as missile after missile was launched. With the loss of the AWACS, though, the Chinese lost the person who had been running the air defense; it took a few seconds for the next person in the chain of command to realize he was in charge and then additional time to authorize the SAM commanders to fire. The Americans used this time to run back toward the safety of the Cascades.

One commander, a HQ-18 battery commander in Seattle, was faster than the rest and launched three missiles at the fleeing aircraft. *Falcon 301,* a little slower than the other F-18s due to some minor battle damage, was hit by two of these missiles and knocked from the sky. Flying at 200 feet when the aircraft was hit, Swimmer didn't have time to eject prior to the aircraft's impact with the ground, and he blew up with his aircraft.

The other aircraft made it back to the safety of the mountains. Aside from a few bullet holes *Falcon 300* picked up going back across the line of battle, the rest of the aircraft would all make it back safely to Fallon, having somewhat evened the score with the Chinese. They wanted more.

Bangor Naval Base, WA, 0645 PDT

Colonel Bart Williamson now had nearly a regiment's worth of men and women of the 7th Infantry Division at the naval base in Bangor, with more trickling in all the time. The 4,000 or so troops he had were not well-armed, though, as they only had hunting rifles and shotguns. They had beaten off the attack yesterday, but just barely. If they hadn't caught the helicopters by surprise, they would never have prevailed. Over the last day, they had taken the wounded off to the nearby hospitals and had buried the dead; it was never good for morale to have dead bodies lying around.

He expected the Chinese to be back. Without the nuclear weapons to hold the Americans hostage, the Chinese were going to get their butts kicked. Not by his under-armed forces, but he knew the Army would be sending everything it could to take Seattle back. If his troops could just hold Bangor, everything would be all right. If his troops could just hold.

He had used the time since the last attack to fortify his position. He didn't know how many helicopters the Chinese had left, but it couldn't be many. The next attack would probably be on the ground, with possibly some air support. As long as they didn't send tanks, he thought his men and women could hold for another day or two.

Armored fighting vehicles would be bad enough, but he had enough men that the Chinese *probably* couldn't overwhelm him with numbers. As long as they didn't bring tanks up to support the assault.

"Colonel *Williamson, sir.*" shouted his communications sergeant. "We just got a call from the State Patrol. We've got tanks and other armor inbound! At least 25 of them! The State Patrol is going to try and stop them, but their commander doesn't think they'll be able to hold out very long against them."

With a sinking heart, he knew they were screwed. He wondered if this is how the Americans at Lexington and Concord had felt. A militia armed with their personal hunting rifles was about to go up against a well-armed, modern army. Somehow, he didn't think the Americans were going to fare as well, this time.

Highway 16, One Mile East of Gorst, WA, 0645 PDT

"Lieutenant, we just got word from the scouts," the trooper said, running up. "We have armor inbound. At least 25 tanks and about that many more armored fighting vehicles. There's also a big bunch of those Chinese black vans following them."

Lieutenant Geoffrey Mason looked around the roadblock his men had worked throughout the night to prepare. It wasn't everything he wanted, but it would have to do. "Did they say how many vans were coming?"

"No sir, they didn't say how many, they just said there were 'a lot' of vans," the trooper replied.

"Call them back and get a number, if possible," Mason ordered. "We need to know what we're dealing with." The trooper ran off to comply.

Lieutenant Mason had just finished his dinner the night before when his long-time friend, Bart Williamson, had called.

"Geoffrey, I need your help," he had said, "and if I don't get it, we may just lose this war." Mason had listened intently as Williamson described the nature of his three-fold problem: an indefensible objective, not enough effective weapons and a lack of intelligence. Throw in the fact that nuclear warheads were involved, and Williamson not only had his complete attention, but his offer of support as well.

Mason would have helped anyway. He had been a classmate of Williamson's at West Point, and they had been commissioned as lieutenants together. They had also served in several of the same crappy places, and they had become good friends before Geoffrey had chosen to get out of the army. They had renewed their friendship when Williamson had been stationed in Tacoma; Mason would have done whatever he could for him.

He couldn't defend the nuclear weapons depot any better than Williamson, though, nor did he have a stockpile of weapons with which to engage the Chinese armor. He could, however, at least help with intelligence and maybe, just maybe, his men could also provide some assistance with the depot's defense. The Assistant Commander for the Bremerton District of the Washington State Patrol, Lieutenant Mason had instructed his operations group to do what they could to help with the defense of Bangor.

Intelligence was easy. Unlike cell phones in some parts of the area, their car radios worked, and he had set up a daisy chain network to let Williamson know what Chinese forces were headed his way and when they would be there. Right now, Williamson would also be getting the bad news about the approaching Chinese armor. Hopefully, they could get a better idea of the exact nature of the Chinese force and send that up, too.

Mason wasn't done there. He intended to do what he could to stop the Chinese advance. His men, most of them veterans of various branches of the military, had whole-heartedly agreed and had called all of their friends who had military training. Overnight, he had gathered 150 State Patrolmen, National Guardsmen and various other men and women who refused to let the Chinese have their way. If they could, they would stop the Chinese armored column right here. Mason had also spoken with a Trooper Bob Davidson from District One, who had ambushed a Chinese column the day before. His SWAT team had also volunteered to come up and participate in the roadblock.

Mason looked at the ambush Davidson had helped set up. He approved. State Patrol District Eight had always owned the highways in the Bremerton area, Mason thought. Today would be no different.

White House Situation Room, Washington, D.C., 1005 EDT (0650 PDT)

The Chairman of the Joint Chiefs of Staff concluded, "Yes, Mr. President, we are good to go. If you give the word, we are ready to execute Operation TITANITE for the defense of Taiwan. You asked for a bold and daring plan, and we have put together the boldest and most audacious plan we could.

In one swoop, this has the potential to win or lose the war. All of the services are contributing and are giving their maximum effort."

"Those who don't study the mistakes of history," the president said, "are doomed to repeat them. It's time for history to repeat itself. Launch Operation TITANITE."

"Yes, *sir!*" said the Chairman enthusiastically. You have to bet big to win big, and he was making the gamble of his life. The plan had a *lot* of moving pieces, and it was going to take everyone's best efforts to bring it off successfully. And a lot of luck. An industrial-sized helping of luck. Before he could start giving the orders to initiate the attack, a staffer broke into the room and ran over to the Chief of Staff of the Army. He spoke excitedly to him in a hushed voice.

Finally, the Chief of Staff knew enough to proceed and waved the staffer down. Turning to the rest of the group, he said, "We have a problem in Seattle. It appears the Chinese are making another attempt to get the nuclear warheads at Bangor. This time they brought tanks."

Grouse Ridge Quarry, East of North Bend, WA, 0655 PDT

The 101st was formed up and ready to go to battle. Calvin had led the formation of helicopters down out of the mountains and to the quarry where they had assembled for the attack. By staying along the ridge line, Calvin didn't think they had been seen by the Chinese; if they had, they hadn't taken any fire, which almost seemed too good to be true.

He was glad he had come with the 101st. Shortly after they landed, five FA-18s had gone screaming over, and at least one of them had the Blue Blaster logo of his squadron on its tail.

"Get some, boys!" he yelled to the aircraft. It was great to see them still in the fight and to know their mission was possible because of what he and the platoon had done over the last 24 hours. Seeing the Blasters survive combat almost made all of the unmitigated terror worthwhile.

He had just said goodbye to Colonel Daly when his phone (well, Master Chief's phone, but he was now holding onto it full-time) rang. It was the CNO. Again.

Looking at Master Chief, he said, "It's the CNO. Suppose he's calling us to thank us for all of our efforts and let us know the Army's got it from here?"

"I doubt it, sir. He wouldn't be a senior officer if he wasn't calling to task us with something stupid."

Calvin answered the call and within a minute was chasing after Colonel Daly. "Wait, Colonel Daly, sir!"

The colonel stopped and turned around, looking a little annoyed. "Yes, what is it?" he asked.

"Sorry to bother you, sir," Calvin said, "but I need to borrow whatever anti-tank capability you have, and I need it *ASAP!*"

Now the colonel's annoyance was full-blown. "Son, I'm about to go into battle with a force of unknown composition, and you want to take my anti-armor capability from me?" he asked. "It's not going to happen."

"Sir, I've got a tank force trying to get onto the base at Bangor and take our nuclear weapons," Calvin explained. "Last time, the Chinese used our nuclear weapons to keep us from attacking both here and in Taiwan. If they get them, we're screwed. I need whatever anti-tank folks you have so I can go take care of it."

"Well, that's important," the colonel waffled, "but I need some, too. How big a tank force is it? Do you even know?"

Calvin was beyond exasperation; now he was pissed. The Chinese are going to get our nukes again, and this guy wants to draw straws for the capability he needed? Screw that. He pulled out the phone.

"Who are you calling?" the colonel asked.

"The President of the United States," Calvin answered. "I've had him on speed dial since yesterday."

"Bullshit!" Colonel Daly said as the phone connected. Calvin said a couple of things to the person on the other end of the line and handed the phone to Colonel Daly.

Fifteen seconds later Master Chief and Calvin were on their way to the Boeing Hangar with four teams of M67 90mm recoilless rifles. The need dire, they took two Black Hawk helicopters into town, flying down the streets and over forests 10 feet off the ground, climbing when necessary to avoid power lines. Master Chief's SOAR buddies flew as quickly as they could, while still trying not to either hit anything or fly high enough that any of the remaining surface-to-air missile systems could see them. For an aviator used to flying a lot higher, it was a harrowing ride for Calvin. He closed his eyes at one point when he was *sure* they were going to hit an advertising sign (he didn't want to go out as a topping on a Billy Bob's Big Beefy Burger) and was so tired he immediately fell asleep.

Master Chief woke him up 10 minutes later on their arrival. The 10 minutes' worth of sleep hadn't helped much. Master Chief and Calvin woke up the other members of the unit in the hangar. They had been able to get a couple of hours of sleep, just enough to make them good and groggy. After convincing their coxswain to drive them to Bangor (another $100,000, and a promise he wouldn't get shot at this time), Calvin held a quick briefing.

"Okay, guys, here's the deal," Calvin said. "We're tired, we're beat up and we're really tired." He didn't notice the repetition. "The bottom line is the Chinese are trying to get our nukes again, and this time, they brought tanks. The only anti-tank squads in the area with ammo, aside from the four RPG rounds we have, are these guys, right here." He indicated the 101st Infantry recoilless riflemen. "We have to get them to Bangor and protect them long enough to kill the tanks leading the assault."

"Then we can leave them there?" BTO asked.

"No, then we all withdraw from the area, with them included, and we come back here. I told their colonel I would return them to the battle east of here as soon as we were done with them. I'm sure he'd appreciate their return."

"And the piece of ass the president tore off him, too," Master Chief said in a stage whisper that everyone heard. Having seen the president give a reaming before, most of the men chuckled. It was a good way reduce the stress of immediately going back into combat.

"Yeah, he'd probably like that back, too." Calvin shrugged. "But hey, I warned him."

The men were well-versed in manning up the LCAC and were quickly on their way.

Highway 16, One Mile East of Gorst, WA, 0700 PDT

"*Red One, Red Five*," the lead tank called.

"*Go ahead, Red Five*," the column's leader, Captain Zhu Jing, replied from the tank designated Red

One.

"We have a problem up ahead," Red Five said. *"It looks like a traffic accident. There are flares on the road and police vehicles ahead. I can see one of the Americans' log-carrying trucks, as well as a smashed up car that is upside down in the roadway."*

"Can you see any people around the accident?" Captain Zhu asked.

"Yes," Red Five replied. *"There are several people walking around the cars and it looks like they are assessing the damage to the vehicles. No traffic is being allowed through. There are two automobiles stopped in front of us waiting to get by."*

Captain Zhu was a suspicious man by nature. It had kept him alive on many occasions, and something didn't seem quite right. He had heard that a column had been ambushed by an American paramilitary organization the day before. That attack had been a roadblock ambush with log trucks, too. This didn't seem quite the same, but it was better to be on the safe side. He had 20 tanks, 25 infantry fighting vehicles (IFVs), four anti-aircraft guns and 400 soldiers in the column. With that much firepower, he wasn't *too* worried about being attacked, but it was better to be too paranoid than not enough.

He opened his hatch and took a look around. If he was going to set up an ambush, this would be the perfect place. The road was heavily forested with embankments on both sides. While the forest on the right was a thin strip that divided the highway from Sinclair Inlet, the forest to the left was about a kilometer thick. There was also a concrete barrier between the northbound and southbound lanes, but it was less than a meter in height. His armored vehicles could get over it if needed, but the vans containing the soldiers wouldn't be able to negotiate it. They would have to go back and around it or have Red Five push the concrete blocks out of the way with the bulldozer blade attached to its front.

"*Red One to all Red units,*" Captain Zhu called. "*This may be a trap. Something doesn't feel right. Everyone button up.*" He climbed back into the tank and shut the hatch. "*Red Five, find out from the people when the road will be open. If it is going to take too long, push open a gap in the concrete blocks.*" He wished the vans had radios so he could communicate with them.

"*Red Five copies; I will go find out.*" The tank pulled up behind the waiting cars, and the tank commander got out to talk to the Americans.

Highway 16, One Mile East of Gorst, WA, 0705 PDT

The Chinese soldier climbed down from the tank and walked over to where Mason was standing, pretending to look at the upside-down car he had towed in.

"When will this road be open?" the soldier asked when he was within 10 feet.

"Well," Mason said, "I guess that depends on you. If you head back to the south, we'll have everything packed up and the road open in no time. If you decide you want to pass through, it will take a lot longer, because we'll have to move the wreckage of your tanks."

The trooper near Mason turned so the soldier could see the trooper was pointing a pistol at him.

Mason heard the radio in his car squawk. "SWAT's in place." Mason smiled at the Chinese soldier. "So," he asked, "what's it going to be?"

The soldier looked back toward the armored column. Was it his imagination, or was the grass moving toward the armored vehicles? The grass *wasn't* moving; there were people *crawling through it towards the tanks!*

He turned and began running toward his tank. "We're under atta—" he managed, before the trooper shot him in the back. He went down.

Chaos broke out along the length of the column.

As Mason ran toward the safety of the forest, Molotov cocktails began raining on the armor from both sides of the highway. Davidson had explained to Mason that tanks are like sharks. They are more efficient and powerful when they are moving, which is why everything they had done was to get them stopped and buttoned up. That way, the tank crews couldn't see his men sneaking up on them.

At the front of the column, several tanks and IFVs were immediately incapacitated as burning fuel ran into their air intakes. Fires sprang up all over from both the firebombs that hit armor, as well as those that missed. Several tanks weren't hit on the first barrage and began moving; the grass shivered again, and three pairs of men rose and ran forward to jam railroad ties into the sprocket wheels of the tanks, momentarily immobilizing them.

At the back of the column, Trooper Davidson led his SWAT team and a detachment of National Guard out of the forest by Anderson Hill Road; the Guardsmen augmented his team's 10 machine guns with their tripod-mounted .50 caliber machine gun. They spread across the highway 50 meters behind the last of the vans and readied their weapons.

"Light 'em up!" Davidson yelled, and the afternoon stillness was broken by the sounds of machine guns firing and the metallic twangs of bullets hitting the vans.

Chinese soldiers dove out of the vans to return fire at Davidson's detachment; focused on the machine guns, they didn't see the second volley of Molotov cocktails from the forest. The smell of cooking flesh and the sounds of screams filled the air.

Cannon fire added to the mayhem as the Chinese armor began chewing up the forest on both sides of the highway. Camouflaged in the forest, the Americans were hard to see, so the Chinese simply began firing. At everything. Every cannon and machine gun began firing at once, shredding the forest and some of the troopers who hadn't retreated to cover after throwing their firebombs.

Most of the Chinese fired to the left, the source of the Molotov cocktails. Seeing their opportunity, troopers ran forward with fire-bombs from the right, climbing onto the tanks that had been immobilized with railroad ties. The easiest way to clear infantry from a tank, though, is to have another tank shoot them off, and several of the closest tanks fired their 7.62mm machine guns at them. Although the bullets didn't penetrate the tanks, they tore the Americans apart, throwing them from the tanks.

The tanks and IFVs shredded the forest around them, aided by the anti-aircraft guns; their quad 25mm cannons made a tearing sound as they joined the rest of the armor in chewing up the forest. Recognizing the anti-aircraft guns as the danger they were, one of the troopers stepped out from cover to throw his last firebomb at the closest one. It hit and exploded, consuming the vehicle. The trooper didn't have long to admire his handiwork, as a 100mm round from one of the IFVs exploded next to him, blowing off one of his legs.

Faced with a volume of fire unlike anything they had ever experienced, the troopers began retreating up the hill as the Chinese armor started rolling, some of them climbing over the concrete divider in order to get closer to their tormentors. The retreat became a rout as the Chinese soldiers in the IFVs unloaded and assaulted up the hill, firing their weapons and launching grenades at the retreating troopers.

At the rear of the column, Trooper Davidson saw the Americans' time was running out. Chinese soldiers continued to spill from the black vans, and the volume of incoming fire grew exponentially. Two of his soldiers were already down, and as he watched, the .50 caliber gunner was hit. The loader took over the grips of the gun and resumed firing, walking the rounds back and forth across the Chinese soldiers. A third trooper went down, and Davidson realized it was time to go.

"Retreat!" Davidson yelled. He turned and ran to where he had parked his patrol car at a roundabout on Bay Street, and the rest of the troopers and the remaining National Guardsman followed; they jumped into their cars, sped off and were quickly lost in traffic.

Ten minutes later, the Chinese column continued its journey north. They left behind ten tanks, two IFVs, a PGZ-95 anti-aircraft gun and over 100 of their soldiers.

HMCS *Victoria*, Possession Sound, Two Miles off Everett, WA, 0730 PDT

"Down scope!" CDR Rodney Jewell said.

The *Victoria* had arrived off the coast of Everett, Washington, and CDR Jewell, the commanding officer of the *Victoria*, was scoping out Naval Station Everett. He was able to look into the piers and see the ships, including the PLAN *Kunming* tied up there. Just like snipers, submarine crews were silent hunters who were, by their very nature, the epitome of patience. The *Kunming* did not appear to be going anywhere at the moment, but if it did, the *Victoria* was ready.

The Americans, Bangor Naval Base, WA, 0740 PDT

Colonel Williamson's men and women were being driven from the field. They were willing, but they were woefully under-armed for the fight. If they had their normal gear, they would have made short work of the force before them; as it was, they had to keep falling back before the tanks and infantry fighting vehicles (IFVs). It wasn't that there were so many of them; their overwhelming firepower and near invulnerability to his troops' weapons made them unstoppable. Based on the reports, the Chinese only had about 10 tanks, total, split about half and half between their top-of-the-line Type 99 main battle tank and their nearly-as-impressive Type 98. They also had about 20 of their IFVs, although they had more troops than the 140 that could have been carried inside them. The extra troops must have come up in the black vans reported with the column. The three remaining PGZ-95 anti-aircraft guns were probably the worst, though. Once they got the quad-barreled guns going, they chewed through anything. Especially his troops.

The only thing his troops had going for them was numbers. At the start of the battle, they outnumbered the Chinese force in combat troops about 4,000 to 300. Those odds were coming down as the armored vehicles took their toll, but they still substantially outnumbered the Chinese. The Americans had encircled their enemy, which the Chinese hadn't been ready for, and a group of about 100 troops had attacked the enemy armor from behind. Although they hadn't been able to take out any of the tanks, they had killed two of the PGZ-95s and had even gotten one of the IFV's, before they'd been overwhelmed and killed. The slaughter was staggering, but their sacrifice had been worthwhile for a couple of reasons. The rate of fire was a lot less without the PGZ-95s; not having two of them made the battlefield much more survivable. The other thing the attack had done was to show the Chinese they were vulnerable from behind. Now, about 1/3 of the Chinese soldiers and vehicles were watching the rear, which meant they weren't shooting at the people in front of them, also reducing the level of fire.

Now, if the Americans only had something worthwhile to shoot back at the Chinese.

He saw it no longer mattered. The Chinese had reached the weapons storage facility. They set up a defensive perimeter and began collecting the American nuclear warheads.

The Chinese, Bangor Naval Base, WA, 0740 PDT

When he was a little boy, Captain Zhu Jing had seen a pirated copy of one of the Star Wars movies. In that movie, the Imperial forces had invaded a planet and crushed the resistance of a bunch of panda bear-looking beings. He still remembered the scene where the Imperial machines walked through the woods, shooting all the little vermin as the beasts ran screaming from them. Life was imitating art today, he decided as he drove through the woods shooting down all the Americans he saw. They might as well have been using the slingshots the little bears had for all the good it did them. As he came to the edge of the woods, he saw his target, the storage facility for the nuclear weapons. Unlike Star Wars, there would be no savior for today's bears. He fired his 125mm main gun and watched the round explode in a group of Americans firing a machine gun at him. Their machine gun might have scratched his paint…but probably not. Now they were all dead.

They reached the storage area, and he began issuing orders over the radio to set up a perimeter so that the troops outside could be protected while they acquired the weapons. It was too bad he had lost two of the PGZ-95s. They were great for holding off men armed with nothing but rifles. No matter, he still had plenty of firepower with the tanks, the last PGZ-95 and the IFVs. He formed the vehicles into a circle around one of the weapon depots, with all of the guns facing out. Too easy, he thought, as his men went to make their withdrawals.

The Americans, Bangor Naval Base, WA, 0810 PDT

Colonel Williamson's heart sank as he saw the crate with the nuclear warhead being loaded into the back of the infantry fighting vehicle. They were going to get away with it, and there was nothing he could do. His men and women kept trying to sneak forward to get shots at the Chinese soldiers as they loaded the weapons. They might get one shot before they were killed by Chinese fire. Sometimes, they didn't even get that. He had ceased sending them forward, as it was nothing short of murder. Still, his troops knew their families stood to die in a nuclear fire if the Chinese set off one of the warheads, and many of his men and women continued to try to sneak forward to do their duty anyway. They slid forward on their bellies, with only their heads exposed to the enemy fire. There weren't going to be many wounded after this battle; most of his troops would be dead.

He had ceased being their commander a while ago. There was nothing he could do besides send his men and women to die, and he just couldn't do it anymore. He couldn't. He was out of ideas and torn with grief at every life he saw his troops give for their country. Finally, he couldn't take it anymore. Grabbing his rifle, he went forward to make his own sacrifice. His men and women were; he could do no less. Reaching the edge of the woods, one of his female troopers grabbed him.

"Sir, get back!" she said. "They can see you here—" Her voice cut off suddenly as she was shot in the face, the force of the bullet flipping her over backwards. She couldn't have been more than 18; younger than his daughter. Filled with impotent rage, he stood up and fired his entire magazine at the closest tank. If he'd been rational, he'd have known how pointless it was. But he was no longer rational. He wanted to die, and he wanted to go out shooting. Might as well shoot at the source of his misery. He fired until his rifle clicked empty and then stood waiting to die, looking down the barrel of the rifle at the tank.

It blew up.

Something hit the tank's ammunition storage, and the vehicle blew up with several secondary explosions, the force of the blasts blowing the entire turret off the tank. A stunned moment of silence ensued as everyone looked around in astonishment, trying to determine the source of the blast, and then every weapon the Chinese had seemed to fire at once. Not knowing what had happened, the enemy soldiers decided it was better to shoot and maybe hit something, then wait and get hit by the next round.

In the stunned moment of silence, someone tackled Williamson. As every weapon in the world seemed to fire in his direction, all he could hear was a voice in his ear saying something about "Stupid officers not knowing when to duck."

After 10 seconds of furious gunfire, there was a lull, and another voice said, "Hey, Master Chief, could you get off the colonel now so I can talk to him?"

The weight on his back lifted, and he saw a group of men nearby he couldn't remember seeing before. The one who seemed to be their leader, a Corporal Sanders, motioned him deeper into the woods.

"Who are you guys?" Colonel Williamson asked.

"I'm Lieutenant Hobbs," the newcomer said. Seeing that Williamson was focused on his name tag, the man sighed. "Don't worry about the uniform, it's not mine; it's the best I could do on short notice. I'm the leader of a special forces platoon here to stop the

Chinese from getting the nuclear weapons. It looks like we were almost too late."

Calvin could see Colonel Williamson was still not over his reprieve from death, and that his mind wasn't firing on all cylinders. He tried again. "Sir, I brought some anti-tank forces here to help, but I can't do this alone. I need your help. That's why I had the corporal blow that tank as a distraction. I didn't want to give away our presence, but I need your help now! *Sir!*"

The final "sir" seemed to do the trick, and Williamson shook his head to clear the cobwebs. When he looked at Calvin again, his eyes seemed clearer and more focused. There was a short pause, just long enough for Calvin to wonder if the colonel had indeed lost his mind, but the senior officer was just gathering his thoughts.

"Okay," the colonel finally ground out, "thanks for coming. What kind of support do you have?"

"I started out yesterday morning with a platoon of special forces soldiers," Calvin said. "I've had some attrition, but just picked up four M67 recoilless rifle teams. The rest of my troops are down to being riflemen due to some supply problems," he grinned wryly at his attempt at humor, "but we do have some M203 grenades, and I've still got a couple of RPG shots left." He looked out toward the field. "It looks like they've got more armor than I've got rockets, though."

"It's my intention to use the recoilless rifles to take the tanks out first, and then work on the IFVs," Calvin continued with a shrug, "but I need your troops to continue to draw off some of the fire from the M67 crews. They're the only thing I've got that can really hurt those tanks from this distance, so I don't want to lose them. I'm going to have them shoot, then move, then shoot again." He paused. "Unless you have a better plan, that is."

"No, lieutenant, I don't have anything that can hurt the tanks, and that plan's as good as anything I've got." A funny look came over the colonel's face. "The M67s have to be from the 506th; they're the only ones that still have them, right? I was in one of the other 101st Infantry regiments in Afghanistan when they reissued them to the 506th. But a Master Chief and a lieutenant...What unit did you say you are from?"

"We're Navy SEALs," Calvin said, not wanting to admit to being an aviator and then have to explain how he came to be commanding army troops. It was enough to let the colonel think he was a SEAL; he didn't have time for anything else. The colonel just nodded. It made as much sense as anything else had in the last couple of days. He was just glad to have the help.

Having agreed on the plan, Calvin sent the troops to spread out around the Chinese. The riflemen and grenadiers weren't of much use against the tanks, so he told them to hang back and let the regular army folks draw the fire; he knew he'd need all of them later. Similarly, the RPGs weren't worth wasting. The distance was about 200 meters, making them long shots to go against the tanks' frontal armor. Not a good bet and not worth wasting them. Once they started moving, maybe they could get a shot into the side or back of a tank, or an IFV, which would work even better.

As the Chinese soldiers continued removing the nuclear warheads, the Americans developed a routine. One side of the ring would start firing, hoping to focus the Chinese fire, and then a M67 would take a shot from somewhere else. It was a dangerous game, and one not even guaranteed to get a kill. The frontal armor on a tank was built to take hits (so the shots often bounced off), and shots hitting the side were glancing blows (so they often bounced off). The

IFVs would have been easier to destroy, but they were lower value targets; they had smaller guns and less armor. If the soldiers could kill the tanks, they could pick off the IFVs at their relative leisure.

The recoilless rifles were hard for the tanks and troops to see until they fired, though, and the gunners had some success. Before long, six tanks were burning, along with the last PGZ-95. When the recoilless rifle teams saw the amount of fire it put out, they'd killed it first. Unfortunately, the Americans were now down to three M67 teams. A tank round had hit one of Calvin's crews, killing his men and, even worse, destroying the weapon.

The Chinese, Bangor Naval Base, WA, 0830 PDT

Captain Zhu Jing didn't like how things had changed. The Americans had gotten an anti-armor capability from somewhere, and it had changed the battle. It wouldn't make enough difference in the end for, as he watched, the seventh IFV was loaded with a weapon. They had what they came for, and it was time to leave. That was a good thing, as he was almost out of ammunition for the main gun; the only problem with a 125mm gun was the size of the shell. Much larger than its predecessors, the Type 99 tank could only carry 22 rounds for its main gun...and he only had two shells remaining.

This was going to be tricky, for leaving meant getting even closer to the Americans' guns, as well as possibly giving them shots at his more vulnerable sides and rear. His tank had already been hit twice, but they had bounced off his frontal armor, failing to penetrate. He didn't want to try his luck for a third time, especially on the sides or rear. Still, he was a sitting duck in the field and almost out of ammunition; it was time to go.

With a radio signal, the armored vehicles leapt into motion. Captain Zhu drove his tank straight ahead, with the other two operational tanks charging around and forward to form a wedge formation with him, one on each side and about halfway behind him. The IFVs surged forward in their wakes, with the weapon-laden ones in the middle. The unladen ones were on the outside; they were expendable if he could complete the mission.

He was going to have to leave a lot of his troops behind, but they were expendable too. If the men made it back to their vans, good, but he wasn't waiting for them.

He saw one of the American's recoilless rifle teams in front of him, aiming at his tank, and he fired his machine gun at them. It missed, but it appeared to distract them; the American's shot went wide, too. His driver aimed for the team and drove over them; at least one of the men went under his treads.

He made it past the Americans and onto the main road, although he lost both of the other tanks to rocket attacks. Looking back, he saw he still had at least half of his IFVs. Now he just needed to get them back to the base.

The Americans, Bangor Naval Base, WA, 0830 PDT

Calvin swore as the round aimed at the lead tank went wide. That had to be the luckiest bastard in the world. He had already seen one round bounce off the front of that tank. He turned away, disgusted, as the tank ran over his crew. Its right tread went over the gunner; he knew that both the gunner and the recoilless rifle would be total losses.

The lead tank was going to make it out. It had forced a way out of their containment ring, but as he watched, the two tanks that were accompanying it took hits from the other two recoilless rifles he still had left. Both were knocked out, burning. That left only IFVs for the RPGs, and all three of them scored hits as the vehicles came within 50 yards of the launchers.

As their armor roared to life and leapt ahead, most of the Chinese soldiers were left to run behind them in the dust. Seeing their first opportunity all day, the rest of the 7th Infantry rose as one, yelling battle cries, and charged. Finally, their massed rifles made a difference, and the only problem they had was shooting too high and hitting their comrades on the other side of the Chinese forces. The vehicles escaped, but the ring closed back down on the troops. It was a slaughter on both sides as quarter was neither asked for, nor given. The American numbers and their ferocity carried the day, and the remaining 37 Chinese troops threw down their rifles and put up their hands. Only one or two more were shot after surrendering before the colonel could rein them in.

Seeing the Chinese escaping, the recoilless rifle teams had gone to their maximum rate of fire. The gun could maintain a sustained rate of one round per minute. It could also fire one round about every six seconds at its maximum rate of fire, but it could only fire five rounds this way because of the excess heat generated inside the gun. One of the remaining gunners fired five rounds then stopped; the other fired seven. On the sixth, the barrel deformed due to the extreme heat and, when the gunner fired the seventh, the round wedged in the barrel. The round's exhaust wasn't balanced by its exit from the gun and the rifle was torn from the gunner's hands. The trooper suffered a broken wrist and a concussion; the rifle was destroyed. Master Chief and Calvin counted; seven IFVs and the tank had gotten away.

"If you have anyone that can drive an IFV, send them down the road toward Tacoma," Calvin said to Colonel Williamson. Turning to his platoon, Calvin yelled, "*Rangers, back to the boat.*"

The chase was on.

The Chinese, South of Bangor Naval Base, WA, 0845 PDT

All they had to do was make it back to Joint Base Lewis-McChord, thought Captain Zhu as he drove south down Highway 3. Forty kilometers to Tacoma, another 24 to the base, and they were home free. Although he would have to watch for additional American roadblocks, it didn't look like there was any pursuit. He didn't plan to get complacent, but it looked like he would get to be the hero, after all.

The Americans, Tacoma Narrows, WA, 0915 PDT

"So, Master Chief, ever heard of the old western saying, 'Head them off at the pass?'" Calvin asked.

"Yeah, I have," Master Chief said, "but on flat land, there isn't enough elevation to make a pass."

They had driven the LCAC as fast as it could go down the bays to the Tacoma Narrows. At 60 knots, the LCAC had a speed more than double that of the armored force, so the Americans *should* have beaten them to the Narrows. By going around the Chinese force on the waterways, Calvin hoped to make them complacent; they wouldn't know they were being followed, and it might buy them a little extra time. The Chinese would have to go over a bridge to get back to Tacoma, and that was the Americans' chance to stop them.

Calvin had come up with a plan that, while crazy, gave them their best chance for success. It also cost the U.S. government another $100,000 in danger pay to their Chinese coxswain. Calvin hoped that Wu was keeping a record somewhere, because Calvin had lost track. He *had* gotten a 15 minute catnap, though, and was feeling a lot better.

"Well, sometimes you have to use what you have available," Calvin said. "This is what we've got."

They were waiting on the down slope of the entrance ramp onto Highway 16 from 24th Street, just prior to the bridge over the Tacoma Narrows. 24th Street was an overpass across Highway 16, just past where the southbound traffic had to slow for a toll plaza prior to the bridge. Calvin intended to use all of this to the Americans' advantage. They had been waiting for 10 minutes, and Calvin was starting to get worried; the Chinese should have been there by now. They had run the LCAC full out to get there, but they had a longer distance to travel; it should have been nearly even. Just as he was about to give up on them, BTO started waving madly from the overpass where he, Tiny, Top and Reggie were waiting. The wave meant that the Chinese were in sight, and the tank was still out in the lead. Calvin wasn't surprised the tank was leading; it was better positioned to take care of any problems there. Shortly after the wave, BTO gave him the "go" sign. The tank was crossing under their position.

Calvin signaled the coxswain, and the LCAC roared forward at its best acceleration. As they started forward, he could see the tank coming out from underneath the overpass, nearly even with them. BTO had called it right; the timing was perfect.

The Chinese, Tacoma Narrows, WA, 0920 PDT

Thirty-five minutes into the drive, both Captain Zhu and his loader were riding halfway out of the turret, enjoying the beautiful morning. Captain Zhu had relaxed and was already enjoying the accolades he was going to get for saving the entire mission. The Americans had wiped out a whole helicopter assault force the day before, but he had been successful where they had failed. Yes, he had lost some tanks, and some IFVs, a few anti-aircraft guns and a bunch of men (assuming they didn't make it back), but they were all expendable. He was returning with the nukes. The invasion was going to be a success, and it was all because of him. There was no doubt he was going to get the Hero's Medal for this; the only question was whether it would be First Class or Second Class award. He figured it would be the First Class medal, which would be awarded at a ceremony to educate the entire People's Liberation Army on the example he had set for it. He smiled, envisioning the ceremony in his mind.

As he passed the toll plaza he laughed. He wasn't going to stop and offer them tribute so that he could drive on their road. They should give him tribute to keep him from killing them like the vermin they were. He was so lost in thought he never saw the person on the approach side of the 24th Street overpass waving, nor the three men waiting on the back side of it. As he came out from under the overpass, he heard a loud noise, like the roar of several jet engines. Looking to the right, he saw a strange vehicle hovering above the ground, roaring down the on-ramp onto the highway, on a collision course with his tank.

He had just opened his mouth to call out a warning when the .50 caliber bullet passed through his head.

The Americans, Tacoma Narrows, WA, 0920 PDT

The only indication of Tiny's perfect shot was a small smile he would never allow anyone else to see. Hitting a person that was going 30 miles an hour and was less than half visible in the open hatch of a tank turret was a pretty nice shot. He knew there weren't many people in the world that could have done it.

Top was one of them. As Tiny switched his aim to the gunner sticking out of the other hatch, the soldier slumped forward on the turret and slid down and off the tank, bouncing onto the highway. Top had been a sniper when he was younger, a fact Tiny had been unaware of until a couple of minutes prior. Apparently, his skills weren't too rusty.

Calvin saw both the tank commander and gunner get shot and was amazed at the shooting skills of Tiny and Top. He would have been happy to hit the tank as it drove down the road, much less a person sticking out of it.

Tiny and Top had been good to their word; they said they could make the shots, and they had. Now it was just up to his group.

The tank driver didn't realize his commander and gunner were no longer onboard; he continued driving straight toward the bridge

and Tacoma. It had been a long, scary day, and he was looking forward to a drink when they got back. They were going to be heroes
for completing what the navy couldn't.

As the tank reached the on-ramp, the LCAC pulled up alongside.

"Boarders away," Calvin yelled, and the twins and Master Chief
leaped out onto the tank. Master Chief slid through the gunner's
hatch, looked at the driver and yelled "Gundan!" ("Get out!") while
pointing his pistol at him. The tank slowed as the driver started out
the hatch; the twins pulled him the rest of the way up and out. He
went over the side, bounced once and went into the water as the
tank crossed onto the bridge.

Good Twin slid into the driver's seat, as it was his turn to drive,
and the tank kept rolling. Master Chief went back out through the
hatch so Bad Twin could get into the gunner's seat. No longer needed, he jumped back over to the LCAC, and Shuteye stepped over and
took the commander's chair. As he got settled, Bad Twin rotated the
turret so it was facing backward, and Good Twin brought the tank
to a stop, turning it to block the road. The IFVs behind it were
forced to stop as well. Shuteye keyed the microphone and said over
the Chinese tactical network, "This is General Shuteye in the main
battle tank. In my mercy, I will allow you to surrender and not be
destroyed if you exit your vehicles and go to the end of the bridge. If
you do not get out now, you *will* be destroyed." He gave the signal to
Bad Twin, and he fired the main gun, just missing the closest IFV.
"You are, of course, aware that you are carrying nuclear weapons,"
said Shuteye. "If we have to shoot you, I don't think the results will
be good for any of us."

Nearly as one, the hatches of the IFVs opened, and their crewmen got out and began walking back to the end of the bridge. The

Americans once again had control of their nuclear weapons. Calvin yelled to Master Chief as the LCAC shut down, "See? We beat them to the pass!"

Master Chief nodded a couple of times, but then a puzzled look came over his face. "Did I really hear you tell the colonel you were a SEAL?"

Joint Base Lewis-McChord, Tacoma, WA, 0945 PDT

It was obvious to Colonel Zhang Wei that something happened to the force he had sent to the Bangor Naval Base. They were powerful enough that nothing in the area should have been able to stop them, yet they were overdue. Although he did not want to admit defeat, it was time to let Beijing know they had failed. There were other things at stake beside the battle for Seattle. He called the president.

When the president came onto the line, Zhang reported his inability to capture any of the Americans' nuclear weapons, and it appeared the Americans had broken through his forces to the east. He was surprised at how calmly the president responded.

"Is that so?" the president asked. "So what do you intend to do about it?"

"Mr. President," Colonel Zhang replied, "Seattle is lost. Without the nuclear weapons to hold the Americans at bay, they can attack us at will. We can make the fight bloody by making them fight us in the downtown area, but they will rapidly have more troops in the area than we will be able to stop. By pulling back into the cities, we will also lose the mobility advantage we currently have with our armor, and they will quickly be destroyed. It is time to salvage what we can by boarding our ships now, before the Americans get here, and sailing for China."

"*That is unacceptable!*" the president roared. "I knew you were unworthy of this task, but allowed myself to be talked into using you as the leader of our forces. We need more time to capture Taiwan, and you have to give it to us! You must redeploy your forces to hold the Americans! *You! Must! Hold!*"

"But, sir, without the nuclear weapons, we don't have anything to make the Americans pause," Colonel Zhang explained. "Their forces are swelling rapidly along all of their axes of attack, while our men are being killed by some unknown group or groups. I don't have the men required to make another attempt to capture more American weapons from the base at Bangor and still hold the Americans at bay. Regardless of what I do, we are going to be overwhelmed!"

"It is good thing I planned for this, then," the president replied. "You did not need to know before, but we have a backup plan. One of our own nuclear weapons was brought to America and is currently on American soil. Call the American president and tell him they missed getting one back, and their forces are currently fighting near it. If they don't withdraw immediately, they will risk setting it off."

Colonel Zhang breathed a sigh of relief; he could redeem himself. "Yes sir, I will do so. Am I permitted to know where it is?"

"Looking at your record so far with safeguarding nuclear weapons, I don't believe you can be trusted with that information," the president said. "I believe I will let the people who are currently watching over it continue to do so."

"I understand, Mr. President," Colonel Zhang said. "I will not let you down again."

"See that you do not," the president instructed. "You must hold. We are at a critical time. The next 24 hours will determine whether we win or lose."

"I will hold, Mr. President," Colonel Zhang promised. "I will give our forces in Taiwan the time they need!"

White House Situation Room, Washington, D.C., 1250 EDT (0950 PDT)

"**M**r. President, there is a call for you from someone claiming to be the leader of the Chinese forces in the Seattle area," a staffer said running into the room with a phone handset. "He says he needs to speak to you urgently."

The president took the phone. "This is the president."

"Good morning Mr. President," the voice on the other end of the line said, "this is Colonel Zhang Wei, the leader of the ground forces of the People's Republic of China in Seattle. I am calling with a most urgent message for you. I am aware you have a group behind our lines who has recovered some of the nuclear weapons you so carelessly misplaced. I am calling to let you know they missed one. Unfortunately, that weapon was moved forward to the front lines. If the fighting continues, it is very likely the weapon will be damaged, irradiating the area at a minimum, and potentially setting it off. If your forces do not withdraw immediately from the Seattle area, I cannot be responsible for the safety of your men or your cities."

"If that weapon blows up or spills nuclear material on our soil, I can guarantee there is no way you will ever make it off U.S. soil alive!" the president yelled. "You will end up in a jail somewhere and will never be seen again!"

"You may threaten me all you would like," Colonel Zhang said. "Unfortunately, it is not that simple. Due to the success of your attack, I have lost the ability to contact my forces. If you do not call your troops back, I can virtually guarantee something will happen to the weapon, and you will have no one to blame but yourself. I will personally inform the media in the area, assuming we survive the nuclear explosion, that I warned you about it, and you chose to disregard my warning."

"Where is the weapon?" the president asked. "Tell me where it is, and we'll secure it."

"I don't know," Colonel Zhang answered. "It was taken forward, but I lost contact with the men who had custody of it. My advice to you is to pull back your troops. Now." With that, he hung up.

The president looked at the Chief of Naval Operations. "Is it possible your men missed any of the weapons on their missions?"

The CNO considered a few seconds before replying. "No sir, I don't think that's possible. Of course, we don't have anything but the most preliminary of reports, but I don't see how it would have been possible to miss any of the warheads, had they been with the ones we recovered." He paused a second before continuing. "It is, however, possible that when the Chinese first acquired the weapons, they split them up prior to our recovery efforts. If so, they wouldn't have been around for our guys to see. I can't know whether they did that or not. It's possible...I doubt it happened, but it's possible."

The CNO thought for a moment and then said, "It's also possible they brought some of their own nuclear weapons to the area onboard one of their ships. They have four military ships that came over, as well as another six or eight freighters. Any one of them could have been carrying a nuclear weapon or two. They've had plenty of time to transport it anywhere they want." He paused again. "There is no way to know whether there are any other nuclear weapons in the area or not."

"Do you want us to call off our attack into Seattle?" the Army Chief of Staff asked. "We were having great success in the east after the 101st hit the lines from behind. The Chinese were broken and reeling."

"That is certainly what *they* want us to do," the president replied. "It may be this is made up, just to try to get us to call off our attack. It certainly is convenient a nuke turns up in the place they need it, right when they need it. It's even more convenient they can't call the people who have it, either. It's all very fishy."

"Still, Mr. President," the Air Force Chief of Staff interjected, "we can't risk it, can we? If we caused nuclear material to spill on our own soil, we'd never be able to live that down with the American people."

"I think he's bluffing," the president decided, "and I'm in favor of continuing the attack. We appear to have them on the run."

"He may not be bluffing," the National Security Advisor interrupted as he walked into the room. "We just intercepted a call between Colonel Zhang and the Chinese president. During the conversation, the president told the colonel they sent one of their own bombs ashore. They may very well have a bomb after all."

"Did the president say where it was?" the CNO asked.

"No, he did not," the NSA said. "In fact, Colonel Zhang asked the same thing and was told it was better if he didn't know where it was being held, based on his previous track record of losing the ones they had. Colonel Zhang also admitted to the president he didn't have any of our nukes left, so our team *did* get them all back." He paused. "Of course, that doesn't tell us where the Chinese nuke is, or what they might do with it if we continue to attack. The people who have this one are not the same ones who had the earlier bombs. In fact, we have no idea who is holding this one, or where. Even worse, we don't know their intentions. The bomb is a complete wild card."

"That changes things somewhat," the president mused. "In fact, based on that information, I think we will call a halt in place for the moment. I don't want to do anything that is going to get our people irradiated or, God forbid, nuked. If we hold for the moment, they will probably keep the weapon wherever it is, giving our troops a chance to find it. We have them broken and can restart the attack whenever we want to. They can't have many people available to bring up and reinforce their lines." He looked at the CNO. "Give your team a call and see if they have any ideas where it might be. If so, let's see if they can stage a third recovery operation and pick up the Chinese one, too. I'd like to have it to show the international community."

"Yes sir," the CNO agreed. "I'll contact them. I don't know how much they have left to give; they've been pretty much at it non-stop for over 24 hours now. But if they can do it, I'm sure they will."

"Until we have some word," the president instructed, "let's stop all of our attacks for the moment."

The color drained simultaneously from all of the service chiefs' faces. "I'm sorry," said the Army Chief of Staff. "It's too late to stop the attack on Taiwan. It's already underway."

Kaohsiung, Taiwan, 0100 China Standard Time (1000 PDT)

Nicknamed Operation TITANITE, the assault was named after Operation CHROMITE, the Korean War Battle of Inchon, on which it was loosely modeled. The Battle of Inchon was an amphibious invasion and battle that resulted in a decisive victory for the United Nations' forces. During the attack, the United Nations staged an amphibious assault far from Pusan, the last enclave the allied forces were desperately defending. The assault behind the enemy lines at Inchon opened up a new front that cut into the enemy's supply lines. It was a risky assault over extremely unfavorable terrain, but it was a gamble that paid off and reversed the fortunes of the United Nations' forces, who were very much in danger of losing the war.

Similar to the opening stages of the Korean War, the war in Taiwan had resulted in the defending forces withdrawing to a small enclave. In Korea it had been to the Pusan Perimeter at the end of the Korean Peninsula; in Taiwan it was to the Taipei Encirclement at the northern end of the island, where the Taiwanese had been able to throw up a defensive perimeter that held the Chinese, just barely, outside the twin cities of Taipei and New Taipei.

Throughout the day prior, the U.S. had done everything possible to make the Chinese think they were going to reinforce the Taiwanese positions in Taipei. They had run airstrikes against the Chinese positions on the north of the island to try to beat them back. They had aggressively probed the seaborne defenses to the east and north of the area as if they intended to get seaborne reinforcements into the port facilities. Finally, and more importantly, they had even gone in front of the media saying they would do just that.

On the 6:00 evening news the night before, the president had gone on camera to tell the American people the United States had to come to its ally's defense in Taiwan before it was too late. Just like Seattle had fallen to a 'vicious sneak attack,' so too had most of the island of Taiwan; it was up to the United States to reinforce the Taiwanese positions in Taipei because there was no one else that could *and that's just what we're going to do*.' All of the stations showed surveys which indicated overwhelming support for the reinforcement and defense of Taiwan. The Chinese saw this as an obvious indication the Americans would try to reinforce the Taipei area, either by air or sea, or both.

The Chinese, therefore, put all of their efforts into breaching the Taipei Encirclement and defending the northern end of the island from outside reinforcement. The Chinese pulled most of their forces on the island to the north to race against time and wipe the Republic of China's forces off the map before reinforcements could get there. If they could just finish the Taiwanese off, they thought, then the Americans would no longer have anyone left to help and would go away. They would leave angry, certainly, but they would depart and leave Taiwan to the People's Republic of China. The PRC forces *had* to prevent the reinforcement of the Taipei Encirclement, so they flew combat air patrols to the north of the island and moved their ships to the north to try to prevent a seaborne reinforcement of Taipei.

But that wasn't where the Americans were headed. Instead of reinforcing Taipei, they swung around the southern part of the island and landed at Kaohsiung.

Located in southwestern Taiwan, Kaohsiung is the largest municipality and the second most populous. The airport that serves the city is the second largest in Taiwan. The city's port occupies the largest harbor in Taiwan, and the city is a major road and railway hub for the island. Taking Kaohsiung would give the Americans a mobility advantage, open up a second front on the island and would put tremendous pressure on the PRC's supply lines. If they could capture the airfield and open it up for military operations, they would have a good start on beating back the Chinese assault.

It would not be easy; in fact, it would take all of the United States' military services working together in a joint attack, something that, traditionally, they did not always do well. Under the leadership of the president and a strong Chairman of the Joint Chiefs of Staff, however, the services had come together with a bold and daring plan.

All of the ships forward deployed to Japan put to sea. The aircraft carrier USS *George Washington*, along with Carrier Air Wing Five embarked, left port and was joined by two cruisers and seven destroyers. It was the most powerful battle group that had been put together in many years. The mission of this group was to provide an impenetrable air shield under which the United States' forces could act. With nine AEGIS ships providing air cover, they were successful.

The marines came ashore at the Port of Kaohsiung. Operating under the air cover provided by the USS *George Washington's* battle group, two Marine Expeditionary Units conducted the largest amphibious operation since Korea, shrugging aside the light resistance offered by the few remaining Chinese soldiers, and captured the port complex.

The Army/Air Force team captured the rest of the city. With eight battalions at the forefront of the assault on the island, the 82nd

Airborne led the way into Taiwan. In order to get all these troops to Taiwan, the U.S. Air Force had to use 80 of its C-17 Globemaster aircraft, over 1/3 of its entire fleet of 220. It was a logistical nightmare to get them where they needed to be from countries around the globe, but the Air Force pulled it off and had 74 of the aircraft delivering troops 'on time, on target.' Four more aircraft were there, but up to 20 minutes late due to last-minute mechanical issues, one aircraft had to abort its launch due to an engine malfunction, and one aircraft landed its soldiers 15 miles off target due to a man-made navigational error. For an operation this large, with this little notice to put it together, it was a tremendous feat.

Two battalions of the 504th Parachute Infantry Regiment were responsible for seizing the airfield. Taking a page from the Chinese, the assault was conducted in a manner eerily similar to the one the Chinese used in taking Naval Air Station Whidbey Island at the start of the war. The transport aircraft came in pretending to be 747 passenger carriers from Canada and Chile, only to deviate at the last minute and start dropping paratroops. In addition to the assault and capture of the airfield, two battalions of the 325th Airborne Infantry Regiment secured the north side of Kaohsiung, two battalions of the 505th Parachute Infantry Regiment secured the east side of Kaohsiung, and two battalions of the 508th Parachute Infantry Regiment secured the south side of Kaohsiung. The United States had entered the war in Taiwan in a big way.

Boeing Airplane Programs Manufacturing Site, Renton, WA, 1005 PDT

The platoon had brought the tank and the IFVs, as well as their precious cargo, back to the hangar. Two aircraft had to be moved outside in order to make enough room for the armored vehicles. Calvin had been so tired he had immediately fallen asleep once they transferred yet another group of prisoners and nuclear weapons to the Ranger platoon's XO. He was tired enough he had slept through the ringing of his cell phone, the first time it rang. Top had heard it, even though he would swear later that he hadn't, but had let him sleep. There was nothing more important to Top than letting the man who held his unit's fate in his hands get a little sleep. The second time it rang, though, it woke Calvin up and he answered it. He spoke softly, so Top couldn't hear what he said, but it appeared there was an awful lot of swearing involved. Top went over to the cooler and got a soda for the officer. Judging by the look on the lieutenant's face they would all need a caffeine infusion soon.

Hanging up on whoever had called him, the lieutenant woke up Master Chief and Deadeye and came over to the table where Top and Jet were sitting on watch. A large pile of empty soda cans already covered much of it.

"Okay," Master Chief asked, "what's the brain trust in D.C. have for us now? The war in Taiwan going badly, and they need us to go capture the island for them?"

"Nope, something much easier than that," Calvin replied. "They just need us to find a needle in a haystack."

"How big is the needle, and how small the haystack?" Master Chief inquired. "Let me guess. The needle is itty bitty, and the haystack is Alaska, right?"

Calvin gave him a sad smile. "Unfortunately, you're not too far off. The needle is a nuclear weapon, and the haystack is the Seattle area of operations."

Top looked up, "Don't tell me we missed one. I *know* we got all of the ones at the university's gym, and I know none of the IFVs escaped. I counted all of them, back when I was still awake enough to count."

"No," said Calvin, "it's even worse. Or better, I'm not sure which. Apparently, the Chinese brought one of their own weapons here. The Beijing leadership didn't trust their guy in charge, so they sent another one that was off-loaded somewhere, sometime, and is in the area. The intel folks intercepted a phone call between the Chinese president and the head army guy here. The president gave him a hard time about us recovering all of the weapons he stole and then told him they had a 'Plan B.' Unfortunately, the president wouldn't tell him where they were holding it, because the president didn't trust him to guard it."

"Okay, let me see if I've got this right," Master Chief said. "We've done everything asked of us, and have done it so well the folks in D.C. now think we're miracle workers and can find something no one even knew existed until just a few minutes ago? Is that about it? Let me guess. It also has to be done immediately because the attack on Taiwan is being held up until we find it, right?"

"Well, that's mostly right," Calvin confirmed. "The only thing you missed was the attack has already gone into Taiwan. They probably *would* have stopped it, but the troops were already jumping out of the airplanes when they found out. They did, however, stop the attacks here in Seattle until we could figure this out, so if you were looking forward to seeing more of the 101st coming to relieve us any time soon, you're going to be sadly disappointed."

"I'm too tired to be disappointed anymore," Master Chief growled, shaking his head. He looked at Deadeye, "Okay, former intel person, figure this out, would ya'?"

"I've got nothing but a headache," Corporal Taylor said.

The men were too tired to joke about women and headaches. Instead, Top wearily reached into one of the many pockets in his uniform and pulled out a little baggy. Reaching in, he pulled out an 800 milligram motrin. "Here you go," he said. "You're not a real Ranger until you get your first supply of Ranger Candy."

"Thanks," she said. Realizing this was a golden chance to make a name for herself in the unit, she focused on the problem. "Well, I don't know where it is, but I can tell you how we would have gone about looking for it."

"If you've got anything that might help, go ahead," Calvin said. "You may not have as much experience as a Ranger as these guys, but we could surely use your previous intel skills right now."

"Okay," Deadeye said, "most times, people and countries follow patterns. If you can figure out the pattern, you can make a guess at what they will do next." She looked at Calvin and asked, "Aviators do the same thing, right sir? You try to figure out how something is being defended and then use those tendencies against them, right?"

"Yeah, that's right," Calvin agreed. "Unfortunately, we don't have much of a pattern here."

"Well, I don't know that I'd say that, sir," Deadeye said. "We've got some other data points from when they started the attack. We just need to look at those and see if they make any sense."

Top recapped the start of the war. "When they first attacked, they used our citizens as shields. They took big groups of them in three places, and they hid our nukes in the same place as one of the groups. They continued to hold the citizens in that group, but let the others go from the other two places that didn't have nukes, right?"

Deadeye nodded. "So far, so good. Keep going."

Top shrugged, frustrated. "That's all I've got. Our people were used as hostages. People continued to be held where the nuclear weapons were, but were let go where they weren't. What am I missing?"

Deadeye smiled. "The key to this is there were two people involved," she said. "The colonel who was in charge here captured the nuclear warheads from Bangor and took them to one of the places hostages were being held. This had to have been a key part of their planning all along and something their entire plan was based on. Right?"

Everyone nodded. "Go on," Top urged.

Deadeye nodded, serious. She ticked off the points. "Okay, one, the plan was to hold American citizens hostage and use nukes to scare us and keep us from doing anything. Two, all of the Chinese knew that was the plan. Three, the leadership in Beijing didn't trust the ground commander here. Add it all up, and what have you got?"

Calvin shook his head, "All I've got is a need for one of Top's Ranger Candies. Lack of sleep and brain teasers do *not* go together well." Top pulled the bag back out and handed Calvin a motrin.

"Okay sir, I'll spell it out," Deadeye said. "The plan was to hold us hostage by using the nuclear warheads on groups of civilians. Everyone involved in the planning knew that. But what if you didn't trust the on-scene commander to get or keep the nukes, but believed in the original plan as it was written?"

"You'd put a nuclear weapon of your own in with one of the other groups!" Jet shouted, making the leap of logic. "It must be at either the convention center or Safeco Field."

"That's what I think, too," Deadeye agreed. She continued to look at Jet. "Which one do you think?"

"Well, the convention center is downtown and taking it there would have involved getting it past a lot of people, and you would probably want as few as possible to see it," Jet theorized. "It's supposed to be a secret, right? If you took it to Safeco, though, you could probably get it right to the stadium without too many people noticing, especially if you did it at night."

"I agree with that assessment," Deadeye said. "Do we know what ships were close to those two places? That might help, too."

"I don't know," Calvin said, "but I do know someone that could find out for us. I definitely think you're onto something. Let me call our friends in D.C. and make them work for us for a change."

Pulling out the phone, he called the CNO. "Hi sir," he said when the CNO answered. "I think we've solved your problem."

"You have?" the CNO asked. "How?"

"Before I answer your question," Calvin deferred, "answer a question for me. What ships pulled into Seattle prior to the attack?"

"Hang on a second," the CNO answered. "I have that information here somewhere." He paused, and Calvin could hear papers shuffling in the background. "Okay, here it is. Ships in Seattle...there was a freighter and a container ship that pulled into the southern part of the port, a cruise ship pulled into central Seattle, and a bulk freighter and a car carrier docked in the northern part of the port. The LHD and the oiler went to Naval Base Kitsap, and destroyers went into Naval Base Everett and Tacoma. Oh, yeah, there was also a car carrier that went into Tacoma."

"Yes, sir, that confirms our thinking," Calvin said. "We believe the nuke is at Safeco Field."

"Based on the ships in the harbor, you think their nuke is at Safeco Field?" the CNO asked. "How the *hell* did you come up with that?"

"That's easy sir," Calvin said. "When the Chinese arrived, they held big groups of our civilians hostage and used them for nuclear blackmail. Everyone involved in the planning knew that, including the big wigs in Beijing. But what if one of those same big wigs didn't trust the on-scene commander to get or keep the nukes, but believed in the original plan as it was written?" He paused, but didn't get an answer from the CNO, so he continued. "If you didn't trust the on-scene commander, but believed in the plan, you'd put one of your own nuclear weapons into one of the other groups; you just wouldn't tell the on-scene commander."

"Well, that makes sense," agreed the CNO. "But how did you decide it was Safeco?"

"The other place was a convention center in downtown Seattle," explained Calvin. "You have to remember that *this* weapon was supposed to be secret, so the Chinese leadership wouldn't want it to be seen. If that's the case, you probably wouldn't want it being paraded through the streets of downtown Seattle. Safeco Field is a little further outside of town and is also very close to the port facility, where-

248 | CHRIS KENNEDY

as the convention center is not. Finally, the ship that was closest to the convention center was the cruise ship. It would have been hard to get a nuke on and off of it without being seen, whereas it would have been relatively easy to get it off one of the ships in the southern part of Seattle, especially the container ship. As you're unloading the containers, someone just drives off with the one that holds the nuke and takes it to Safeco. You could even take it to a loading dock, I'm guessing, and no one would ever be any the wiser." Calvin smiled, having figured out most of the last part all by himself.

Everyone around the table was nodding in agreement with Calvin's reasoning. After a pause for consideration, the CNO voiced his agreement. "I think you may be right," he said. "Certainly, everything you said makes sense." He paused again. "I've just got one more question. How'd you like to take the platoon and go pick it up for me?"

Calvin sighed. "Somehow, sir, I figured you were going to ask that."

Safeco Field, Seattle, WA, 1050 PDT

"Looks like you were right, sir," Master Chief said as he drove past Safeco Field on 1st Avenue. Judging by the number of Chinese troops standing on guard and patrolling around the outside of the stadium, it was obvious there was something important inside it. Unlike the other soldiers they had seen, these were at the highest state of readiness; guns were carried at port arms, where they could quickly be brought into firing position. These men were guarding something. Something big.

"Yeah, unfortunately," Calvin said, "and whatever is in there, they want to keep it there."

The command team of Calvin, Master Chief, Top and Deadeye finished their drive around the field, passing down the north side of the field along Royal Brougham Way. All of the main entrances at home plate, left field, right field, and center field had pairs of soldiers both inside and outside the locked gates. There also appeared to be two pairs of roving patrols on the outside. There would probably be roving patrols inside, too.

They went back to the Filson's store at Massachusetts St. and 4th Avenue; the platoon had appropriated it a few minutes earlier, telling all of the store employees and customers it was time for them to leave. Most of the customers got the hint when a large group of armed men came into the store. One manager objected and took a little more convincing, but even he left when told there would probably be a lot of gunfire in the vicinity he really didn't want to be a part of. Paris showed him what a bullet wound looked like; he was out of the store within 5 seconds, looking queasy.

The command team entered the store and quickly built a model of the stadium located a couple of blocks away. "This isn't going to be easy," Master Chief said, "but we ought to be okay if everyone knows and sticks to the plan." He looked around and saw he had everyone's attention. "All of the entrances have pairs of soldiers both inside and outside them, and all appear to be chained." People started shaking their heads; this was going to suck. While it would be easy to kill the soldiers outside the gates, it would be far more difficult to kill all of the soldiers on the inside simultaneously; there was a good chance they would miss someone who would then raise the alarm. Or set off the bomb.

"That's why we're not going in that way," Master Chief continued. Calvin had been watching their faces and saw several look up in surprise. Master Chief pointed to the east side of the field. "Train tracks run along this side of the field, and it is harder to patrol. Also, the field bends around a little bit, and the guards at the center field gate aren't able to see the east side of the field. I'm sure they're not worried about it because there aren't any gates on that side. There are, however, roll down access doors for bringing in supplies. I'm going to pick the lock on one of those doors, and we are going to enter that way. That should get us into the back of one of the concession stands. From there, we're going to exit onto the main concourse and work our way around until we can see the field, leaving defensive positions as we go."

"Once we see the field," Master Chief added, "we'll make a decision on how to proceed. The weapon is either going to be on the field or up in an office, although it will *probably* be at field level because it weighs several hundred pounds. If it is on the field, we'll try to get it back out the same way it came in, which is probably an access door they drive the field's vehicles through. Basically, it will be a smash and grab at that point. We will hit them hard and use whatever transportation we can find there to take the weapon out. We will then evade and return back here, jump into our cars and head back to the hangar."

Master Chief looked around. "The goal is to be as stealthy as we can for as long as we can. Once our cover is blown, we hit them with shock and awe, and then we run. Fast. Any questions?"

There weren't any, so the platoon filed out the southern door of the store and went across the train tracks to the Seattle Transportation Building. A storage building for train cars, it ran in a north-south direction to within about 100 feet of Safeco Field. The building was also a blind spot for the guards at the Safeco Field gates; they were unable to see the approaching Americans from where they were. That wasn't true for the roving patrols. Master Chief stuck his head around the corner and saw one of the patrols walking past the door he had selected as their point of entry. He waited until the patrol was out of sight, then the platoon sprinted the last 100 feet to the walls of the stadium.

Lock picking wasn't a skill Master Chief had practiced recently, and he knew he didn't have much time before one of the roving patrols came by. He examined the lock; it was a simple pin-and-tumbler type, which *should* be relatively easy to open using the pick and wrench he had improvised. The process of picking the lock was simple in theory, but more difficult in practice, especially since he hadn't done it in a while. Picking a lock required a great deal of patience, which conflicted with his need to go quickly.

Master Chief inserted the wrench into the lower portion of the keyhole and determined which way the cylinder had to be turned by putting pressure on the wrench. Turning it counterclockwise resulted in a stop that was firm. Turning it clockwise, the stop had a little more give to it; that was the correct way to open the lock.

Putting a little tension on the wrench to hold there, he stuck the pick into the upper part of the keyhole and began to feel the pins. He found the pin that was the hardest to move and pushed it up until it set, then pushed the upper pin out of the cylinder; when he let go, the lower pin fell back down, but the torque on the cylinder resulted in a misalignment where it couldn't fall all the way down. After setting the first pin, he continued to hold the pressure and set the remaining pins in the lock. Once he set all of the pins, he continued to turn the wrench, and the lock opened. He looked back at Calvin. "Piece of cake, sir; just like stealing a...I mean, just like *riding* a bike."

Calvin shook his head. "We can talk about how you acquired your skills another time," he said. "Let's go!"

Master Chief rolled the door up, and everyone hurried into the storage area. He gently lowered the door again, just before the next patrol came around the corner. There was nothing to see, and they kept walking.

Daylight seeped through the cracks of the doors, and there was enough light to see by once their eyes adjusted. Master Chief led them to the door at the front of the storage room and saw it was locked from his side. He slowly unlocked the door with just the smallest 'click.'

He pulled the door open a crack. Although it was dark on the other side, he could tell the door led to a concession area; he could see the various cooking and food preparation areas. All of the service windows had their roll-down doors shut.

Master Chief walked through the dim light to the door to the concourse that went all the way around the first floor of the stadium. Quietly, he opened the door a crack and peeked out. He didn't see anyone in the direction the door opened; he opened it a little further and stuck his head out to look in the other direction.

The concourse was empty.

Well, not totally empty. He could hear voices coming from the left. He listened for a few seconds and determined they were coming from the troops guarding the right field gate. Those soldiers *probably* wouldn't come in their direction, as long as they were quiet. Opening the door all the way, he signaled the troops and they proceeded out into the cavernous concourse. Master Chief looked at the seating signs. They had come out behind Section 107; moving quickly, he went to the passageway between Sections 106 and 107, waving the men forward. The men advanced while Private First Class Adam Severn and Sergeant Daniel Nguyen stayed behind to guard their emergency escape route.

Master Chief crept down the tunnel leading to the field and looked onto the playing surface. In the center of the field sat two Chinese ZBD-08 infantry fighting vehicles, with deep tracks in the grass from where they had been driven into the stadium. In addition to the vehicles, around 100 men were camped out in right field.

They've only got us outnumbered five-to-one this time, he thought with a smile; it's our best odds of the day! Although outnumbered, they had surprise and concentration of forces on their side if he used his troops effectively; the problem would be getting to the vehicles without the Chinese sounding the alarm. Once inside the vehicles, the platoon would have sufficient firepower to overwhelm the Chinese. As he looked out to center field, he could see the gate the Chinese used to bring the vehicles into the stadium was still open; they could take them out that way, too...if they could get to them first.

Although the Chinese had made it harder for them to get into the stadium by chaining off all the entrances, it was also going to make it harder for the Chinese soldiers who were outside the stadium to get back in. Master Chief came up with a plan and sent four of his men to attack the right field gate, as well as three additional soldiers to hold off the Chinese troops at the center field gate. He also sent the sniper team with the group going to the center field gate. Once the gate was taken, they would cover the field; Tiny's powerful .50 caliber sniper rifle would be able to reach out and touch anyone, anywhere within the stadium.

The rest of the troops would be with him for the shock and awe phase of the assault. Judging by the numbers of troops he had seen on guard and on patrol in the stadium, Master Chief estimated that about 1/3 of the Chinese soldiers were down with their tents on the field. Although there was no way of telling which tents were occupied and which ones weren't, he wasn't worried about it; they still had three anti-personnel rockets for their RPGs, and this was as good a time as they were ever going to get to use them. Having given the teams headed to the right field and center field gates time to get into position, Master Chief signaled the twins, who were once again going to lead off the platoon's attack.

Playing Surface, Safeco Field, Seattle, WA, 1130 PDT

Bad Twin fired an incendiary anti-personnel round from the tunnel between Sections 106 and 107. The rocket burst over the tents in right field, slightly right of the group's center, scattering its 900 steel balls and 2,500 incendiary pellets on detonation. Fires broke out as the tents ignited, and ammunition inside them detonated from the heat.

Good Twin fired another anti-personnel round at the same time from his position in the tunnel between Sections 105 and 106. The rocket landed just to the left of the center of the group of tents, with its warhead bouncing back up to detonate in an airburst that sent 800 anti-personnel steel balls ripping through the tents in search of victims.

In what was probably overkill, the remaining 101st Airborne M67 Gunner, Corporal John Duncan, fired an anti-personnel round of his own from the tunnel between Sections 104 and 105 into the tents. During the course of the battle at Bangor, the M67 teams had fired off nearly all of their anti-tank rounds, but had been so busy shooting at the armored vehicles they hadn't used any of their anti-personnel rounds. The M590 round was perfect for clearing an area of enemy personnel, as it was a cartridge filled solely with flechettes, pointed steel projectiles with vaned tails for stable flight. When fired, the sides of the canister split, sending out its payload of 2400 steel-wire flechettes. Although they only weighed half a gram, the little pieces of wire dispersed into an eight degree cone that shredded everything in their path. The sides of the soldiers' tents did nothing to impede them, and they swept through the area like the wind, blowing the life out of the soldiers in the tents.

Only four of the 37 soldiers in the group of tents were combat effective after the triple blast. Stunned by the detonations, they came out of their tents trying to comprehend what was happening. All were cut down by the members of the platoon as they charged down from the stands.

As the first of the anti-personnel rockets exploded, the other two teams fired M203 grenades into the gate areas from around the nearest corners. The grenades were precious, as the platoon only had a few remaining, but if they could get the nuclear weapon, hopefully the main body of the army would be in town soon with some needed supplies. The groups of guards at the center field and right field gates were taken completely by surprise, and the two soldiers who survived the grenade blasts were quickly finished off.

The platoon had killed or rendered ineffective over half of the company in its initial assault, but the other half responded rapidly. Most of them were on the other side of the main concourse, having lunch as they prepared to come on duty. They discarded their meals and picked up their weapons, running toward the field to see what was happening. Their company commander, Captain Ma Gang, was in the press box, which he had made into his headquarters. This gave him an excellent view of the field, as well as access to the stadium's public address system.

Watching the attack unfold in front of him, he quickly began calling off instructions to his men. He could *not* allow the nuclear weapon to be taken, and he directed his soldiers to kill the men running onto the field, while telling the groups at the gates to come around from behind them.

The nine members of the assault force made it to the vehicles as bullets from the other side of the stands started to rain down around them and ricochet off of the IFVs. The twins threw down their RPG tubes, and one climbed into each of the vehicles; within seconds both of their motors roared to life. Pausing outside the vehicles, the M67 team stopped to load another anti-personnel round into the weapon, and Corporal Duncan fired it into the main group of Chinese shooting at them from the tunnel between Sections 142 and 143. All of them went down.

Seeing the M67 for the threat that it was, Captain Ma began screaming at his troops to take it out, and the majority of the fire focused on the team. The crew had just finished loading the next round when Corporal Jose Gonzalez, the M67 team's loader, was hit in the shoulder and went down. Corporal Duncan braved the incoming fire to stand and launch the next round, clearing out the Chinese soldiers who were in the tunnel between Sections 141 and 142.

"Into the vehicles!" Calvin yelled, and the soldiers clustered around the vehicles began climbing into them, Corporal Duncan dragging Corporal Gonzalez into the closest IFV. Sergeant Hylton and Corporal Taylor provided covering fire while the rest of the group got into the backs of the vehicles. As they ran to get in, Paris was hit in the leg and went down.

"Damn it! Not again!" he yelled as he tried to crawl to the back of the vehicle. Deadeye came back and helped drag him into the vehicle, with bullets hitting the field all around her.

The fight at the center field gate was well in hand. Sergeant Chang had heard the Chinese commander over the public address system and knew that troops had been ordered to come around the concourse and hit the platoon from behind. Realizing that both Chinese-speaking Americans were in his group, he sent Private Li around the concourse to the right field gate to warn the others on that side. That left him with only Corporal 'Colonel' Sanders, who had one of the Chinese light automatic weapons.

Placing Sanders behind cover with a good view of the concourse, he went to the other side of the passageway. It wasn't long before they heard the slapping footsteps of running men, and 10 men came running down the concourse. Both Shuteye and Colonel pulled the pins on the grenades they had ready and tossed them at the group of incoming soldiers. Colonel's grenade hit a pole and bounced into an alcove, where most of the blast was muffled. Shuteye's landed in the middle of the group and exploded, killing or wounding the majority of the group.

While the Chinese soldiers dove for cover, looking in Shuteye's direction, the Colonel opened up on them from the other side of the concourse, firing an entire magazine into the group on full automatic. He looked for movement while he changed out the magazine but didn't see any. Levering a round into the chamber, he nodded to

Shuteye, who cautiously advanced toward the remnants of the Chinese squad. Their caution was unnecessary; the Chinese were dead.

Things on the other side of the stadium were not going as well for the platoon. Jet arrived to find the team heavily engaged with a squad of Chinese soldiers who they had run into at nearly hand-to-hand range. Each side recoiled from the other, with the Americans slightly more prepared than the Chinese for the contact. Sergeant Nguyen and PFC Severn had each fired off most of a clip, killing nearly half the squad before the Chinese soldiers began returning fire, hitting Corporal Beck in the chest. Jet could see him lying in the concourse. It looked like his chest was still rising and falling slowly, but the size of the puddle of blood he was lying in indicated he wouldn't last long.

After the initial contact, a stalemate had ensued. The remaining three Americans had slightly better cover, which allowed them to hold off the numerically Chinese superior forces. Both sides were trapped, though, and neither could disengage without exposing themselves to fire from the other side.

Jet knew that they needed to rejoin the main body of the platoon, which ought to be almost ready to leave. He had stopped around a corner from the fighting when he heard the rifles firing. Although he hadn't been seen yet by the Chinese forces, he could see Private First Class Woodard.

"Psst," he said to get Woody's attention. When Woody looked, Jet gave him the signal for "how many men?" Woody stuck his head out around the corner, dodging back quickly as several Chinese soldiers fired at the movement. He looked back at Jet and held up five fingers and shrugged, indicating that it might be a man or two more or less. He then held up three fingers and pointed to the left side of the concourse and then two fingers and pointed to the right side. Jet nodded; more soldiers on the left than the right.

Wanting to end the confrontation quickly, Jet pulled out his last two grenades and prepared to throw them. Woody shook his head and held out his hands as if to catch one. Jet lobbed one to him, keeping it low so that the Chinese wouldn't see it. Woody then pantomimed for Jet to throw to the left side, which was an easier throw for him, while Woody would throw to the right. They both pulled the pins on their grenades, arming them. Woody held up fingers, one...two...three... and they both threw their grenades down the hall. Jet had to look around the corner to see where to throw the grenade, so it took him a half second longer to throw it and also exposed him to enemy fire for a longer period. As he completed the throw, he was hit in the upper arm and spun back around the corner.

Two explosions filled the corridor with smoke and shrapnel, and Woody rolled out into the concourse firing down the hall at the two soldiers exposed by the blasts. As the soldiers went down, PFC Severn and Sergeant Nguyen rose and charged down the corridor. The one remaining soldier was stunned by the twin grenade blasts; slowed, he wasn't able to get his rifle up quickly enough to defend himself and was shot by Sergeant Nguyen from point blank range. He looked back at Woody, who was kneeling next to Corporal Beck. Woody shook his head; they had won, but Becks was dead.

Center Field Playground, Safeco Field, Seattle, WA, 1135 PDT

The voice continued yelling over the public address system in Chinese. Although they couldn't understand it, the tone sounded like he was giving orders. "I'm gettin' awful tired of that man's squawkin'," commented Tiny to his spotter. "Please find him for me, so I can shut him up for good."

Leaving Tiny to continue to pick off the targets in the tunnels, BTO shifted his gaze to the press boxes in the upper level. It wasn't long before he found a man in one of the windows, talking into a microphone with one hand while gesturing frantically with the other.

"Got 'em," BTO said. "Look straight up from the IFV on the right. He's in the window right above it. Wind calm; send it when you see him!"

Tiny shifted the rifle, looking through the scope. "Yup," was all Tiny said to acknowledge he had seen the man. There was a pause as Tiny relaxed into the shot and gently stroked the trigger. The gun fired, and a star appeared in the glass in front of the officer.

The stadium's designers had put reinforced glass into the windows as a safety precaution, but they had never considered trying to stop a .50 caliber round, and the glass was not up to the challenge. The giant round penetrated the glass, only slowing slightly as it passed through. The glass did have one effect, as the impact of the bullet on the glass caused it to deform and begin to mushroom. The round that struck the Chinese captain was no longer pointed; its tip was much bigger and flatter, making the impact as it hit him significantly more destructive. The captain was blown backward missing most of his head.

"Thanks," was all Tiny said as the public address system went silent.

BTO scanned the field looking for targets. As he watched, the turrets traversed on the infantry fighting vehicles, and the 30mm cannons of both began sweeping the tunnels on the opposite side. With the IFVs providing cover, it was time for the sniper team to leave, and they jumped over a railing and began running down to the field, along with the other two teams.

Seeing the teams in motion, the twins began firing the IFVs' main guns in concert with the cannons. The big guns were effective for keeping any remaining Chinese soldiers' heads down, and Chinese fire was reduced to only an occasional shot or two. It was going to be a while before the Mariners played another home game, though.

As the teams reached the IFVs, Calvin and Master Chief realized they had a problem. With only 21 remaining platoon members, they had thought everyone could ride out of the stadium in the IFVs. They had forgotten that the squad bay of one of the vehicles was filled with the large wooden box holding the nuclear warhead.

Master Chief quickly devised an alternate plan. Half of the platoon loaded into the IFVs for transport back to the hangar, while eight men and Corporal Taylor went back with Top on foot to retrieve their cars from the department store. Calvin wanted to go with that group, but Master Chief convinced him to go with the IFVs so he could call Washington as soon as possible.

The two vehicles continued firing their guns while they drove for the exit. The gate to the exterior of the stadium was chained, but not impervious to the 100mm round that hit it. The rest of the gate was demolished as the lead armored vehicle crashed through it. They were free, but not out of the woods. With the IFVs in the lead, the platoon drove down Royal Brougham Street and turned south toward the Filson's where they had left their cars. As they rounded the corner, they found a group of six soldiers who had been locked out of the stadium. The Chinese soldiers started gesturing at the IFVs as they rounded the corner, thinking that reinforcements had come to their aid. Unfortunately for them, aid was not to be had, and Shuteye's head popped out of the commander's hatch to tell them to put down their rifles and surrender.

One of the soldiers made the mistake of trying to draw his rifle; a burst of 30mm shells cut him down, as well as four of his comrades. As the smoke cleared, the remaining Chinese soldier was allowed to surrender and was marched back to the department store with the platoon. They made it back to the store without any further complications.

* * * *

CHAPTER FIVE

Afternoon/Evening, August 21

Joint Base Lewis-McChord, Tacoma, WA, 1205 PDT

Colonel Zhang Wei still hadn't heard from the force he sent to the Bangor Naval Base. As long as they had been gone, he had to assume they were lost. Even worse, one of his subordinate commanders had just informed him the Americans had taken the president's nuclear weapon, along with the loss of yet another of his companies. If the president had only confided in him, he would have sent a company of tanks or IFVs or even some of his precious remaining troops to help guard it...anything to keep the Americans from getting their hands on his final nuclear weapon.

It was now incontrovertible; they had lost Seattle. He didn't have enough troops to send another expedition to Bangor while still holding off the Americans. If any of his defenses pulled out, the remaining men would be swarmed under before the first group could return with one of their weapons. They had gambled and lost.

The Chinese still held the northern part of Seattle and Whidbey Island, but had lost the eastern I-90 corridor. His commander in the east reported the men there were in full retreat, although it sounded more like a rout. The Americans had paused when he told their president about the additional nuclear weapon, but with its retrieval, the Americans were now attacking again in full force. His troops had been able to regroup slightly during the lull and had initially held their own against the renewed American attack, but then they had been hit from behind again. The middle of the line had broken and, just like a break in a dam, the Americans had poured through faster and faster, sweeping away the Chinese forces. It wouldn't be long until the Americans reached the city of Seattle. He had instructed his troops to blow the bridge onto Mercer Island; that would at least make them take the long way around through Renton.

Without the nukes, they were finished. He didn't have much time.

It was time to save what he could. He ordered a general withdrawal.

The troops in Bremerton were a lost cause. With the *Long* sunk, they had no way to get the amphibious tanks back. All they could hope for was that the oiler *Qiandaohu* could get underway. If it could make it into the Pacific with the destroyers, they could make it back to China as a group. He ordered all of the warships to collect everyone they could and make for the Pacific.

Everyone else was ordered to return to the civilian ships that had brought them, and for those ships to get underway at 1400, regardless of who was able to make it aboard by then. Those ships had the ability to transport a lot of equipment and personnel; it was far more capacity than they needed. The *M.V. Xin Beijing*, the *M.V. Hanjin Kingston*, the *M.V. Erawan*, the *M.V. Xin Qing Dao*, and the cruise ship *Henna* would all be leaving from Seattle half full, at best. He intended to be aboard the destroyer *Changsha* when it sailed from Tacoma. If the rest of his forces in the area could make it onto the *M.V. Xin Fei Zhou* car carrier in the Port of Tacoma, they might make it out of America, too; otherwise, they were to blow up their equipment to keep it from falling into the Americans' hands.

He could only hope the war in Taiwan was going better.

Boeing Airplane Programs Manufacturing Site, Renton, WA, 1245 PDT

After talking to the CNO for a few minutes, Calvin called Master Chief and Top over for a strategy session. "Congratulations," he told them. "It appears we've won. The CNO says it looks like the Chinese are running like rats leaving a sinking ship. They are loading all of their ships, and the brass thinks they're going to flee."

"Great!" Master Chief said. "Our job here is done."

"Well, almost," Calvin responded. "The CNO asked if there was anything we could do about the destroyer that's here in Tacoma. The Navy and Coast Guard are sending a bunch of warships to intercept the merchant vessels that are leaving, but they thought it would be easier if we could do something about the *Changsha* before it got underway, rather than fighting it at sea where it could use all of its weapons." He looked at Master Chief. "Got any good SEAL ideas for sinking a ship?"

"Well, if I had my scuba gear and a bunch of explosives, it would be really easy to swim up and put an explosive charge on its side. I don't have either one of those, though. How much time do we have before they leave? Any idea?"

"No, the brass doesn't know," Calvin said, "but they think the Chinese will be leaving really soon."

"Well, sir, I may not be a navy guy or well-versed in the art of sinking ships," Top said, looking around the hangar, "but I know where we can find an awful lot of firepower we can bring to bear on the problem."

"Hey, sir," Corporal John Duncan interjected. He hadn't been returned to his unit yet, despite Calvin's earlier promise. "I know we're new to the platoon, and we don't have a lot of ammo left, but we'd love to come blow up a ship."

"Yeah," his gunner, Corporal Juan Gonzales, agreed. "It sounds like fun." Like Paris earlier, the wound he had received at Safeco Field was minor. He had been sewn up and was ready to continue the fight.

"I like them," Master Chief said. "Can we keep them?"

"It's possible," Calvin answered. "I suspect their commanding officer would probably do just about anything I asked of him, now that he knows I have the president on speed dial." He looked at Top and then the armored vehicles. "Do we have anyone who can shoot these things? I'm guessing the twins can handle the tank, once they decide whose turn it is to drive, but can anyone run the IFVs?"

"Give me a couple of minutes with the twins as instructors," Top replied, "and I'm sure we can work it out."

Top went over to talk to the twins, but came back a minute later with the twins in tow. "Sir, there's something you should know." He looked at the twins.

"Umm, sir, before we, like, go fight a ship with these things," one of them said, "we thought you ought to know that, like, the tank is out of ammo for its main gun."

The other one nodded his head. "The shot I took on the bridge over the IFVs was the last round it had in it. When I tried to load the next round, I was like, dude, there aren't any rounds left. Bogus! So, we, like, looked at the IFVs when we got back, and most of them were just about out of ammunition for their main guns, too. It was a pretty long battle, and those things don't carry as much ammo as you would think." He paused, looking embarrassed. "The shells are pretty big and just take up a lot of room, dude. I mean, sir."

"So basically, the tank is nothing now but a big bluff?" Calvin asked.

"Pretty much," the twins chorused.

"You probably want us to be in, like, one of the IFVs we just captured," the first one suggested. "They've still got a bitchin' load of rounds for us to fire, if needed."

"Okay," said Calvin. "I still want the tank there for looks, but I want at least one of you in an IFV with a full load of rounds. The gun on it may not be as big as the tank gun, but it'll do a lot of damage. If you can teach someone to drive the tank, then I want each of you in one of the new IFVs."

Navy Pier, Port of Tacoma, Tacoma, WA, 1345 p.m. PDT

They had waited long enough, thought Colonel Zhang Wei, as he paced across the bridge of the PLAN *Changsha*. We need to leave before the Americans get here. He had just opened his mouth to tell the ship's commanding officer to get underway when a column of armored vehicles drove onto the pier. There was a Type 99 tank in the lead, followed by at least nine of the ZBD-08 infantry fighting vehicles. As the hatch of the tank in the lead popped open, he realized that these were the missing vehicles he had sent to Bangor. If they had returned with some nuclear warheads, maybe they could still salvage something from this operation. His hopes soared.

Stepping outside onto the bridge wing, he yelled down to the tank commander, "Do you have the weapons?"

"I'm sorry," the tank commander yelled back, "but I don't recognize you. Who am I talking to?"

"I am Colonel Zhang Wei," he replied, "the head of the ground forces in Seattle. Who the hell are you? Do you have the weapons or not?"

"Yes," the tank commander said, "we have the nuclear weapons. In fact we have all of the weapons, including the one you brought from China. Who am I? I am Sergeant Jim Chang of the 1st Special Forces Platoon, and I'm here to accept your surrender." As he said it, the tank's turret turned to point at the ship and the gun elevated to point at the colonel. All of the IFVs' turrets turned to point at the ship too. Colonel Zhang was suddenly looking down the barrels of one 125mm gun, nine 100mm guns, nine 30mm cannons and more machine guns than he wanted to count. Sergeant Chang continued, "I am instructed to tell you that you can either come down onto the pier and surrender, or we will fill your ship so full of holes that it will sink right where it is currently tied up. What is it going to be?"

Although he was tempted to try to run for it, he knew the ship's guns would not depress far enough to be able to shoot at the armored vehicles. Anybody trying to untie the ship would be massacred, and the ship destroyed. It was over.

He put his hands up and walked off the ship.

Navy Pier, Port of Tacoma, Tacoma, WA, 1345 PDT

Calvin smiled as the Chinese colonel walked off the ship, followed by most of the ship's personnel. The bluff had worked. He imagined there would still be some people aboard to tend to the ship's engines, at least until they could get shore power re-attached. There was going to be a lot of prisoners to take care of...around 300 or so, if the Chinese ship was manned to about the same level as a similarly-sized U.S. vessel. He would have to call someone for help. His bone-weary 20 people wouldn't be able to control the Chinese sailors for long.

Calvin looked at the ship they had just secured. He wondered when a major warship had last been captured by ground forces. He couldn't remember ever reading about it happening, so it must have been a long time ago. The *Changsha* was a good-looking ship, although it was missing most of its top-side gear on its front half. It must have been hit by a HARM missile when the FA-18s had attacked Seattle. That was the only thing he could think of that would have given it that nice "sand-blasted" effect.

Cool.

HMCS *Victoria*, Possession Sound, Two Miles off Everett, WA, 1410 PDT

I t was the moment the *Victoria* had waited for; the *Kunming* was moving. If the Chinese had decided to leave port, they must be fleeing the country. As soon as they hit open water, Commander Jewell expected them to go to full speed to try to get to the Pacific Ocean as quickly as possible. The *Victoria* was waiting at the southern tip of Gedney Island in the middle of the Puget Sound. As the *Kunming* left port in Everett, Washington, it would have to go either to the north or south of Whidbey Island, located to the west of where he lay in wait. While both ways would take the *Kunming* to the Pacific Ocean, the shortest and easiest route was the southern route around Whidbey; he expected the *Kunming* would be going that way.

The *Kunming* eased out of the naval station, and it quickly began to pick up speed as it continued to head west. CDR Jewell smiled as he saw the *Kunming* was going to take the southern route as he had expected.

"Engines ahead 1/3. Come right to 190 degrees," he said to the helmsman.

Both the *Victoria* and the *Kunming* were headed toward a narrow strait of water between the mainland and Whidbey Island. The *Kunming* was going faster and was going to get there first, which was exactly what CDR Jewell wanted. The destroyer was going far too fast to be listening to its sonar, even if it could hear anything in the relatively shallow water of the sound. Keeping the periscope up, though, was an unnecessary risk.

"Down, scope!" he said.

With the submarine starting to pick up speed, the periscope on the surface would have raised a wake as it traveled through the water, which would have been easy for the lookouts on the destroyer to see. He didn't need the periscope, anyway. He had the entire scene engraved in his mind and, at a range of only 3,500 yards, he really couldn't miss.

As the *Kunming* reached Mukilteo point, he decided to end the facade. The motto of the *Victoria* was 'Expect No Warning;' it was time to put that slogan into action. They had a lock on the *Kunming* ever since it left port, and the targeting data had been loaded into two Mark-48 torpedoes. One torpedo could easily have done the job, but CDR Jewell was not going to take any chances in the narrow waters. If they didn't kill the destroyer in the first exchange, the *Kunming* could easily spin around and attack the submarine. In the shallow water, the advantages would all go to the destroyer.

Depending on the tactical need, the torpedo could be set to run at one of several speeds. The *Victoria's* were set to run at their fastest setting. With an unsuspecting target, CDR Jewell wanted to get the torpedo to the target before the ship went through the narrows. The torpedo had plenty of range; it could run 23 miles at its 55-knot setting, and it only needed to go two.

"Fire Tubes One and Two," he ordered.

The boat shuddered as compressed air kicked the torpedoes from their tubes, and CDR Jewell received a report from the sonar operator shortly after that the torpedoes were running normally. The

272 | CHRIS KENNEDY

torpedoes continued to track the *Kunming*, overhauling it by over 30 knots.

The torpedoes had covered over half the distance to the *Kunming* before it became aware of their presence. The *Victoria* could hear the *Kunming* go to its highest power setting, and it began to conduct a series of radical maneuvers while dropping noise makers, hoping to confuse the torpedoes. The ship might have had a better chance if its crew had more time or maneuvering room, but the torpedoes were already upon them and they were out of options. The torpedoes completed their journeys and detonated under the *Kunming*.

Unlike the contact torpedoes of World War Two, the two Mark-48 torpedoes were set to blow up underneath their target, and the 650 pounds of high explosive in the warheads combined with their unused fuel to make spectacular detonations in the shallow water. The force of the explosions was effective in buckling some of the hull of the *Kunming*, but that was not the most destructive part. By exploding underneath the ship, the warhead vaporized an enormous amount of water, creating a huge bubble of air under the center of the ship. As ships are not made to support all of their weight by their ends, when the first torpedo detonated, the center of the *Kunming* sank into the void from which the water had been evacuated, breaking its back. The second torpedo shredded these two pieces further, hastening the rate at which the *Kunming* sank.

The commanding officer of the *Victoria* brought his boat to the surface to rescue any of the survivors they could find. As quickly as the *Kunming* sank, though, there weren't going to be many.

Kaohsiung, Taiwan, 1100 China Standard Time (2000 PDT)

The will of the Chinese forces was broken. Seemingly unbeatable a day earlier, the remainder of their force was now trapped, isolated and pinned up against the mountains running down the eastern part of the country. With the seaport and airport open for business at Kaohsiung, the Chinese forces' days were numbered. The United States held the southern portion of the island in an iron grip, and more forces were entering the country from a variety of allied nations every day.

It was impossible for the Chinese to get any assistance to their troops on the island. The Chinese could no longer move by sea. With two U.S. submarines, 10 Japanese submarines and four South Korean submarines in the East and South China Seas, the Chinese ports were effectively blockaded. Anything that tried to leave port would not last long against them, much less against the air power that was being amassed on the island. With the Japanese task force augmenting the American oversized carrier battle group, it was also foolish to try to fly across the intervening 100 miles. The allies had one simple motto; "If it flies, it dies."

Cut off, low on supplies and with their morale in a shambles, the Chinese forces exercised the only other option available to them. They surrendered.

* * * * *

CHAPTER SIX

Epilogue

Bangor Naval Base, WA, August 27, 0945 PDT

Calvin watched with a sad smile while several bulldozers started leveling the trees next to the nuclear weapons facility. Most government contracts take a long time to be finalized. This one had not.

He had never been as proud of his countrymen as he was the day the platoon had arrived to see the remnants of the 7th Infantry Division attacking the Chinese tanks and armored infantry fighting vehicles with nothing more than hunting rifles. Completely outmatched in range and firepower, much less armor, the Americans fought on, trying to prevent the Chinese from capturing the nuclear warheads stored nearby. Most would only get to take a shot or two before being killed, but they persevered and gave their lives to avert a nuclear holocaust for their families. They attacked the Chinese armor for their loved ones and for the love of the men and women next to them.

On August 20, records showed that 287 Americans gave their lives at Bangor Naval Base, and another 426 were wounded, when 2,895 infantrymen held off a force of attack helicopters, armed solely with rifles. This sacrifice was duplicated the next day when 4,318 soldiers, including all of the surviving veterans of the fight the day before, stood their ground against an overwhelming armored force, losing 1,895 dead and 1,224 wounded. Nearly 3/4 of their force were casualties, but when the Chinese tried to run, they had stood as one and charged, preventing the escape of most of the opposing force.

Calvin had already commissioned the statue that was going to dominate the nation's newest national cemetery. The platoon had arrived on the scene just in time to see Colonel Bart Williamson, the officer in charge that day, stand and empty an entire magazine at one of the tanks across the field from him. While Calvin knew it was the last desperate act of a despondent commander, his willingness to give his life for his country was no greater and no less than the willingness of his troops to do the same. The statue that would be at the center of the memorial was a man standing, firing a rifle at a distant tank, with two other soldiers lying nearby, also firing rifles at the tank. The two soldiers were a man and a woman, to show that all gave equally in the service of their country.

The bill to donate the land had gone through the Senate and House of Representatives in one day, a Congressional record, after he had called his senator and proposed it. Calvin had a little clout as a national hero and that had probably helped. A lot. He had never called a senator before...but then again, he had never talked to the president until a couple of weeks previously, either. It had also helped, he was sure, that no money was required of Congress; Calvin had promised his senator he had the funds to pay for it all, courtesy of the multi-million dollar offer he had received for the rights to the platoon's story. He just needed the land for the memorial and cemetery.

He had thought a lot about how the plaque would read. He wasn't sure about the exact verbiage yet, but he liked his latest version:

On August 20-21, five thousand soldiers of the 7th Infantry Division met the enemy at this place while defending the nuclear warheads held nearby. Despite being tremendously overmatched, they stood their ground against tanks, armored vehicles and attack helicopters, armed only with light rifles, refusing to yield. 2,182 soldiers gave their lives and another 1,650 were wounded during the two-day battle. Their sacrifice kept the Chinese from capturing the nuclear warheads and helped quickly end the war. This memorial is for the 2,182.

# # # # #

1st Joint Special Operations Platoon

Commanding Officer	Lieutenant Shawn 'Calvin' Hobbs
Executive Officer	Master Chief Petty Officer Ryan O'Leary
Platoon First Sergeant	First Sergeant Aaron 'Top' Smith

First Squad

Squad Leader	Staff Sgt Patrick 'The Wall' Dantone
Fire Team 'A' Leader	Sergeant Jim 'Shuteye' Chang
Rifleman	Private John 'Jet' Li
Grenadier	Private First Class Steven 'Bait' Shad
SAW Gunner	Private First Class Adam 'Nine' Severn
Fire Team 'B' Leader	Sergeant Daniel 'Dreamer' Nguyen
Rifleman/Missileer	Corporal Matthew 'Dale' Evans
Grenadier	PFC Justin 'Spaz' Richardson
SAW Gunner	Corporal Jimmy 'Colonel' Sanders
Rifleman	Corporal Suzi 'Deadeye' Taylor

Second Squad

Squad Leader	Staff Sergeant Dave 'Ski' Kowalski
Fire Team 'A' Leader	Sergeant Jacob 'Paris' Hylton
Rifleman	Corporal Tyler 'Becks' Beck
Grenadier	Private First Class Nick 'Radio' Borneo
SAW Gunner	PFC Christian 'Woody' Woodard
Fire Team 'B' Leader	Sergeant Jose 'Boom Boom' Morales
Rifleman/Missileer	Corporal Ken 'Fergie' Ferguson
Grenadier	Private Calhoun 'Spencer' Spence
SAW Gunner	PFC Trevor 'Mad Dog' Hall

<u>Weapons Squad</u>

M240 Gunner	Sergeant Logan 'Lawyer' Hale
M240 Loader	Corporal Berron 'Reggie' Wayne
M240 Gunner	Corporal Cornelius 'Boot' Hill
M240 Loader	Private First Class Hector 'Macho' Carrasquillo
RAWS Gunner	Corporal Austin 'Good Twin' Gordon
RAWS Loader	Private First Class Jamal 'Bad Twin' Gordon
Sniper	Private First Class Steve 'Tiny' Johnson
Spotter	Private First Class Mike 'BTO' Bachmann
M67 Gunner	Corporal John 'FNG' Duncan
M67 Loader	Corporal Juan 'FNG' Gonzales

#####

The following is an

Excerpt from Book 1 of The Theogony:

Janissaries

_____

Chris Kennedy

Available now from Chris Kennedy Publishing

eBook, Paperback and Audio

Excerpt from "Janissaries"

Snoqualmie National Forest, WA, August 28, 1430 PDT

"I may never finish all this paperwork," said Calvin, "even if you give me a hand." Lieutenant Shawn Hobbs, or 'Calvin' as he was known to the other aviators in his F-18 squadron, was catching up on all of the administrative things that hadn't been done during the several days of the Sino-American War. He had started out with a huge pile of post mission reports to put together, tons of awards to write up and too many next of kin letters to send.

He looked at the other two occupants of the small cabin for support. He didn't find it in Master Chief Ryan O'Leary. "I'm not helping you do it," replied his second-in-command during the war. "That's what they make officers for." Although he generally liked his former commanding officer, Ryan generally didn't like authority. Ryan believed that the reason officers existed was to take care of the administrative things, which freed him to focus on the little things...like fighting and winning the nation's wars.

Two weeks previously, China, after patiently waiting decades for the peaceful return of Taiwan, had finally decided on a more aggressive approach. Until then, the threat of a United States' counterattack had kept them from invading the island nation, but the Chinese had finally come up with a way to keep the Americans out of a war in Asia.

They invaded Seattle.

Not only did they invade Seattle (and Tacoma, as well), they also attacked and captured nearby Bangor Naval Base, with its arsenal of nuclear warheads for America's submarine-launched ballistic missiles. With some of these warheads in hand, they hoped to keep the

United States from not only counterattacking them in Seattle, but in Taiwan, as well, for fear that one of these warheads would 'accidentally' go off.

Lieutenant Hobbs, along with Master Chief O'Leary, a former SEAL living in the area, had led a group of Rangers on a number of dangerous missions behind enemy lines during the brief conflict. These missions included recapturing the stolen nuclear weapons, which enabled the U.S. military to not only go on the offensive in the northwest, but also to stage a daring raid on Taiwan that turned the tide of the war.

Unfortunately for Calvin, as the platoon's only officer, he was the one responsible for filling out all of the post-war paperwork. Buried under an avalanche of it, he had requested a couple of weeks of temporary duty in the Seattle area after the war to get it all completed. Hoping for at least a little grudging assistance from Ryan, Calvin and his girlfriend, Sara Sommers, had come out to Ryan's cabin in the woods.

"All of this paperwork might be my responsibility," said Calvin, "but I've got a lot more of it than I can do. Take a look at this one, for example. This is the award for some idiot that saved a colonel from getting his dumb butt shot off when he tried to attack a tank with just a rifle. Who'd do a stupid thing like that?" He paused, looking at the award. Ryan looked up, recognizing that the award was for him. "A Distinguished Service Cross?" Calvin asked, his voice a little louder. "No way! I'm throwing this one away." He crumpled up the piece of paper and threw it at the garbage can, missing badly.

"Really?" asked Ryan, "A Distinguished Service Cross? The only thing higher than that is the Medal of Honor. Shoot, sir, I was just doing my job. That was hardly worthy of a Distinguished Service Cross."

"Well, I say it as worthy," said Calvin, "and that's all that matters. I still have a little bit of influence at the moment, and I plan to use it before my 15 minutes of fame are over. I'm writing up everyone I can think of for everything that I can remember. I just need your help in remembering all of the things our troops did that need to be recognized."

"The navy said he could only stay here in Seattle until he got his paperwork done," added Sara Sommers. She had met Calvin during the war and hadn't let him out of her sight since the war ended. "Don't help him too much. I don't want him to get finished too quickly."

"I see," said Ryan. "If you're only staying in Washington until you finish, you're not in much of a hurry to get it all completed, are you?"

"Let's just say that I'm trying to do a thorough job of it," replied Calvin. "Besides, when I get back to the squadron, we're still going out on our scheduled six month cruise." He paused and looked at Sara. "I'm not sure that I want to do that anymore."

All three of them were quiet for a moment, full of thought.

Without warning, Calvin's head snapped around to look at one of the far corners of the room. "We're not alone," he said.

"What do you mean?" asked Ryan. "I don't see anyone."

"No, I'm telling you, I heard something," argued Calvin. "For the last week, I've felt like someone's been watching me, and I know that I just heard something over in the corner."

Suddenly, in the corner were three...beings. They were generally humanoid but didn't appear to be human, as they were too short, and their heads were too big.

"Hello," said one, stepping forward. "Although I guess the proper thing in your society is for us to say, 'take us to your leader.'"

"What?" asked Ryan, unable to come to terms with the sudden appearance of the humanoids. "Who are you?"

"My name is Arges," the same one said. "We need your help."

* * * * *

ABOUT THE AUTHOR

A bestselling Science Fiction/Fantasy author, speaker, and publisher, Chris Kennedy is a former naval aviator and elementary school principal. Chris' stories include the "Theogony" and "Codex Regius" science fiction trilogies and stories in the "Four Horsemen" military scifi series. Get his free book, "Shattered Crucible," at his website, http://chriskennedypublishing.com.

Chris is the author of the award-winning #1 bestseller, "Self-Publishing for Profit: How to Get Your Book Out of Your Head and Into the Stores." Called "fantastic" and "a great speaker," he has coached hundreds of beginning authors and budding novelists on how to self-publish their stories at a variety of conferences, conventions, and writing guild presentations, and he is publishing fifteen authors under various imprints of his Chris Kennedy Publishing small press.

Chris lives in Virginia Beach, Virginia, and is the holder of a doctorate in educational leadership and master's degrees in both business and public administration.

* * * * *

Titles by Chris Kennedy

"Red Tide: The Chinese Invasion of Seattle"

"Occupied Seattle"

"Janissaries: Book One of The Theogony"

"When the Gods Aren't Gods: Book Two of The Theogony"

"Terra Stands Alone: Book Three of The Theogony"

"The Search for Gram: Book One of the Codex Regius"

"Beyond the Shroud of the Universe: Book Two of the Codex Regius"

"The Dark Star War: Book Three of the Codex Regius"

"Asbaran Solutions: Book Two of The Revelations Cycle"

"The Golden Horde: Book Four of The Revelations Cycle"

"Can't Look Back: Book One of the War for Dominance"

"Self-Publishing for Profit"

"Leadership from the Darkside"

* * * * *

Connect with Chris Kennedy Online

Website: http://chriskennedypublishing.com/

Facebook: https://www.facebook.com/chriskennedypublishing.biz

* * * * *

Made in the USA
Las Vegas, NV
01 April 2022

46710704R00164